CRUISING THROUGH MIDLIFE

CRUISING THROUGH MIDLIFE 1

ADDISON MOORE

Copyright © 2022 by Addison Moore
Edited by Paige Maroney Smith
Cover by Gaffey Media
This novel is a work of fiction. Any resemblance to peoples either living or deceased is purely coincidental. Names, places, and characters are figments of the author's imagination. The author holds all rights to this work. It is illegal to reproduce this novel without written expressed consent from the author herself.
All Rights Reserved.
This eBook is for your personal enjoyment only. This eBook may not be re-sold or given away to other people. If you would like to share this eBook with another person, please purchase any additional copies for each reader. If you're reading this book and did not purchase it, or it was not purchased for your use only, then please return it and purchase your own copy. Thank you for respecting the hard work of this author.

Copyright © 2022 by Addison Moore

BOOK DESCRIPTION

An impending divorce. An ornery homicide detective. The cruise of a lifetime. And ghosts.
Midlife on the high seas is proving to be a real killer.

A Paranormal Women's Fiction Novel: Cruise Ship COZY MYSTERY

If I thought the first half of my life was a bumpy ride, I'd better buckle up because I'm about to go over the hill and off the rails.

*A laugh out loud Paranormal Women's Fiction Novel by *New York Times* Bestseller Addison Moore* A cruise ship cozy mystery!

My name is Trixie Troublefield, and I see ghosts. It's sort of a new thing, and it's more than a problem.

While I was busy running around doing some last-minute packing for my tropical anniversary cruise, my husband was busy bedding three other women—at the same time. So I did what any other sane person would do—I grabbed my suitcase and took to the high seas, alone.

Here's the thing. I've never been on a plane or a cruise ship.

I've never left the state of Maine. I've never been on my own. I've never seen ghosts before either, but that seems to be on the universe's agenda for me, too.

I've got eighteen nights to recalibrate, rethink my life, recharge, and eat all the food I can get my hands on. And I might look into a poltergeist pest control service while I'm at it.

Of course I'll start a travel blog and log all of my adventures for the world to see. Why not rub all the fun I'm having in my cheating ex-husband's face? I'll call it *Suddenly Single! What a Trip*.

But no sooner do I step on board of that stately cruise ship than I stumble upon a body.

Midlife on the high seas is proving to be a real killer.

From the **NEW YORK TIMES** and **USA TODAY** bestselling author, Addison Moore— **Cosmopolitan Magazine** calls Addison's books, "...easy, frothy fun!"

CHAPTER 1

My first thought is that they had fallen.
Honestly, I thought they had *fallen*.
I thought my husband and the woman we hired to watch our home while we were away on our twenty-fifth anniversary cruise, a pretty young thing of twenty-five, had fallen onto our bed, naked, and he was merely trying to help her up.

Again.
And again.
And again.
And again.

My next thought is something a little more on target. Something is up.

Something was *up*, all right.

Parts are bouncing. The mattress is squeaking—I'm ashamed to say it's squeaking like it's never squeaked before. As if that wasn't bad enough, the headboard is pounding out a Morse code against the bedroom wall that my brain clearly translates as *get out and take the fool for all he's worth*. Or maybe it's saying *it's time to put the electric knife to the test and Jackson Pollock this place with the blood of a cheating Irish man*. Not that Stanton is Irish per se, at least not in the sexy accent fresh off the boat way. He's third-generation American with a familial history of utilizing beer as a nighttime sleep aid.

But Stanton isn't sleeping now. And if booze had any role in this coital equation, I couldn't care less. There aren't enough beer bottles to excuse this behavior—or for me to drown it from my memory.

Stanton flips the woman around and takes her midair with the deftness of a professional aerialist, and suddenly it feels as if I'm being treated to a pornographic version of Cirque du Sol-*Lay*.

And to think I thought Stanton and I had built a decent life together—married twenty-five years with two kids, a boy and a girl.

A rush of adrenaline hits me. I can't stand here all day watching my marriage crash through hell in a hand basket—not when Stanton and his hussy with a tramp stamp are rocking the hand basket so violently with their incessant rutting.

Two primal options vie for my attention: fight or flight.

I choose to fight. Murder isn't exactly off the table either.

I'm about to take a baseball bat to the two of them when in walks a naked woman holding a bottle of champagne.

A howl of a scream evicts from me and reverberates off the walls like a hurricane.

The girl screams back. All activity on the mattress comes to a halt. And out of the bathroom door to my right walks yet a third nude nudie—a blonde with a turned-up nose who looks quasi-familiar.

"Oh my word." The words leave my lips along with an entire profanity-laced tirade.

"*Trixie*," Stanton the Stamina King riots from the bed. "What the hell are you doing here?"

"*Me?*" I screech so loud I hardly recognize my voice as it echoes around the cavernous room. "*I* live here. The better question is, what are *they* doing here?" A hard groan escapes me. "Never mind. It's obvious what they're doing here—they're doing *you!*" I glance around the room in a rage and spot the oversized matching suitcases already packed and ready to go for our silver anniversary cruise, so I head on over and grab the one that belongs to me.

"What do you think you're doing now?" Stanton asks as he quickly herds his naked harem into his closet—and considering his closet is the size of a small city, they could have been living there for years for all I know.

"I'm leaving." I quickly hustle my rolling suitcase and myself to the door, but Stanton beats me there and barricades the exit. He's as naked as the day he was born, albeit hairier and scarier in places. And once he catches me glowering at his body, he snatches a straw hat off the rack next to him—my gardening hat —and lands it precariously over his privates.

"Well, that's a good look," I tell him. "Maybe the four of you can do a little 'Farmer in the Dell' role-playing once I leave. I hope one of them takes on the role of a gopher who rips your turnips and cucumber off when you least expect it."

I lost an entire vegetable garden that way one year and it taught me a valuable lesson, much like Stanton and his hussies are teaching me now.

Stanton Troublefield is handsome by nature. His once chiseled features are what initially attracted me to him. He is also a very smart man. Although it appears after twenty-five years those brain cells have dissipated. He's tall, barrel-chested, and has the face of a deity—if that deity was a hundred pounds overweight and had a chin that dipped down to his belly. His blond hair has gone gray and his soft brown eyes have hardened over the years. Currently, his face is full of gray stubble, his hair is rumpled, and his ears are hiked in the way they get when he gets unnaturally aroused, and I mean that in the nonsexual sense, although given the circumstances, maybe it works both ways.

"Out of my way." I slap him silly until he's forced to step aside and I bump and thump my way down the stairs as I leave our palatial six thousand foot home that happens to be equipped with enough wrought iron and marble to make any mausoleum jealous.

I told him it was too pretentious, that we needed to raise the kids in a humble home, and at half this size it still would have been ample room for the four of us. But no—Stanton Troublefield, plastic surgeon to the imaginary stars, had an image to uphold. And today I got a firsthand glimpse of what image really lies in the broken mirror of our marriage.

"Trixie, wait," he says, running down the stairs while pulling on the silk green paisley Veragamo robe I bought him last Christmas. It seemed ridiculously extravagant at the time, but knowing that Stanton only appreciates ridiculously extravagant gifts, I knew it would be the only one he would appreciate. "You can't go like this. We're not supposed to leave until three. What are you doing home so early? I thought you had appointments until two-thirty?"

"My hair lady canceled and my nail lady had a slot open up early." I fan out my fingers in front of his face so he can get a good look at my shiny new French manicure. "And really? That's why you were hosting some sort of perverted bon voyage party upstairs? Because you thought I'd be *gone* for the afternoon? What if Abbey or Parker showed up out of the blue?"

He inches back as if I struck him. "I don't see why you have to drag the kids into this. You know as well as I do they're both hundreds of miles away in college."

"Parker is hundreds of miles away," I correct him. "Abbey is a short drive down the highway. Never mind. I don't see any point in trying to talk some sense into you. All of your good sense went out the window once those floozies showed up." I pull out my phone and call a rideshare service to pick me up, stat.

"What the hell are you doing?" he squawks. "I still need to

shower and shave. Call them back and tell them to show up in an hour."

"You don't have to shower and shave for two weeks, for all I care," I riot at him. "You are not coming with me," I shout as I stampede past him, rolling over his bare feet with my suitcase on the way out.

"Ouch, *geez*," he shouts, following me out into the frozen January air.

January in Maine is never kind, but this January it feels particularly sinister with its knife-sharp winds and temps so low you could freeze both lungs solid if you happen to sneeze. Of course, I'm used to it—we both are. We've grown up in Brambleberry Bay—high school sweethearts, college sweethearts, the whole nine oxygen-depriving yards. And even though Brambleberry Bay is a seaside town, neither of us has ever been on a cruise before, let alone a boat.

For the most part, Stanton is a workaholic and doesn't believe in vacations in general. He always said he planned to retire early and that we would make up for lost time when he got to the finish line. But our kids pooled their knowledge of how to use our credit cards and booked us an eighteen-night cruise that leaves out of Los Angeles tomorrow morning.

Honestly, if they had consulted me on the matter, I would have booked one out of Portland, or even New York would have been close enough. We could have swapped out Hawaii for the Caribbean, but my daughter thought it was probably a good idea to get her father as far away as possible from his office. And now it will be just me headed that way. All alone in the South Pacific. All alone on that big giant boat. I've never so much as seen a movie on my own, let alone been on a plane by myself.

A part of me thinks I should cancel and go to my mother's.

A chill runs up my spine at the thought. I know most people get sappy when thinking about their mothers, but I don't have most people's mothers. There's no way I could ever move back in with her. I wouldn't last ten minutes. I wouldn't want to.

"Trixie"—he barks— "you're not traveling all the way to Hawaii without me. This is my anniversary cruise, too, dammit."

"Well, maybe you should have thought of that before you asked those hussies to hop on pop. And guess what, you lunatic? We're not having any more anniversaries because our marriage is *over!*"

"You can't be serious." His chest pulsates with a dull laugh. His hair is wild and wiry, stretching inches off his scalp, and his face looks piqued the way it does after a good run—a testament to the cardio he just pulled off, no doubt. "Divorces are expensive. The last thing I want to do is line some attorney's pocket with my hard-earned money. All you ever do is spend my money, so of course, you don't care."

"I don't spend *your* money—I spend *our* money. And for the record, I'm not even a big spender—not that it's neither here nor there. But had you allowed me to get a job, I would have had my *own* money to spend!" I gag on my words. "Allowed?" I shake my head. "I can't believe I listened to every word you said. I obeyed you like an idiot because I wanted to be an obedient wife, never causing any waves. Well, guess what? I'm about to cause a few waves—on the high seas! Have fun filling this house with cheap hookers because I'll be on a tropical beach sipping mai tais while chatting on the phone with my shiny new divorce lawyer!"

"*Trixie,*" he growls. "Enough of this talk. Now give me a minute to get dressed. We're going on this cruise together, and I'm sure we'll work it all out. I wasn't in my right mind. I was—"

"Caught red-handed," I finish for him as a black SUV pulls up to the front of the house. "Go on and get back to your live-action porno. I've got a plane to catch. I'm taking this vacation by myself. I'm going to catch up on my reading, paint—and I'm going to have a fling, too. I'm going to sleep with every man on that ship, from the cabin steward, to the bartender, to the captain.

I'm going to work my way up in rank, and I'm going to laugh in your face while doing it, too." I take a bold step in his direction and look into those brown eyes that I used to think loved me. "Goodbye, Stanton Troublefield. This is the last time we will be in the same space together without an attorney present for a very long time. Don't come after me, don't call me, and don't try to twist this around as if it's all my fault the way you do when anything goes haywire in our lives."

A beefy man with a goatee steps out of the SUV and pops my suitcase into his trunk before opening the passenger door for me.

"*Trixie*," Stanton barks again in a way that lets me know he's drawing a hard line in the sand. "Don't you dare get in that car. If you do, things will never be the same and it will be all your fault."

"Things will never be the same, Stanton. And it's all *your* fault," I say, climbing into the gargantuan SUV that smells of new leather.

"What are you going to do without me, Trixie?" he shouts. "Think about it! I can afford the best of the best. You'll get nothing. You'll end up under a bridge without my money in your pocket. You can kiss your ritzy lifestyle goodbye. You'll never make it in the world without me. Get back here right now, Trix. I mean it."

"Drive," I tell the man as I slam the car door shut. "Bangor Airport, please," I say as we pull away from the house I've lived in for the last two decades. We leave the neighborhood and soon we're out of Brambleberry Bay altogether, and a part of me wonders if I'll ever come back.

Bangor.

The word mills around in my mind a moment too long and the irony isn't lost on me.

Stanton can bang whoever he wants now.

I'm going to Hawaii.

CHAPTER 2

Twenty-five years of marriage up in smoke.

And for what? A cheap thrill with a couple of dozen floozies? How long has this been going on? And was this his first foray into fornicating in our marriage bed with others? How the heck was I not clued into this behavior sooner?

A thought comes to me.

Wait a minute…that blonde with the turned-up nose that popped out of the bathroom wearing nothing but a grin— isn't that his new secretary down at the office? I hardly recognized her what with all the nipples and the hairless body parts from her eyebrows down.

And what's with that, anyway? That's one trend I'm not hopping on board with. My husband can have all the hairless hussies he likes. I'm keeping my fur coat and my dignity.

I hope that ship has a decent doctor because I should probably get checked for lice or mites or something worse that invades on a cellular level. And I sure as hell hope that ship's doctor is cute, too. Not that I'm really going to sleep my way up the food chain once I get on board. That was just something I threw out there to crawl under his skin.

Stanton has always had a jealous streak a mile wide. He once fired the pool man because he caught him leering at me. The poor man happened to be leering at me because I was asking him a question. Stanton always thought the men in the room were paying far too much attention to me. That might explain why we hardly went anywhere.

The driver drops me off at the airport, dumps my bag onto the curb in front of my airline, and zips off without so much as a *good luck*. I turn to look at the mammoth structure before me as travelers zoom past me clutching their luggage and everything feels so very real, so very alone.

I've never flown anywhere all by my lonesome. The last time I was on a plane was a year ago when Stanton and I flew to England to help our son Parker get settled at Hollingsworth University where he's currently a grad student. And every time I've flown before that I've always had someone else with me, usually Stanton. We mostly went to Florida to visit his parents, something that Stanton had the nerve to classify as a vacation. I will never quantify those jaunts to the seventh circle of Hell as a vacation. Florida was paradise, it was the company we kept who portrayed themselves as warlords of the underworld—which might explain a thing or two about Stanton.

But now I was truly alone.

My kids have basically flown the coop, and Stanton certainly doesn't need or deserve me. And even the scant art projects I've done over the years have dried up. I like to dabble in all sorts of mediums, but painting is where my heart is. I wanted to teach, but Stanton said it would be too demanding and take time away from our own children, so I volunteered during art classes at the elementary level first, then I followed my kids right through high school. Over the years I've done my fair share of wall murals for friends and friends of friends. Turning their daughter's bedroom into fairy-tale landscapes or aquatic scenes. They offered to pay me handsomely, but I always declined. We would go back and forth until I'd settle to let them take me out to lunch. Stanton made so much more than most of my friends in Brambleberry Bay, but now even my friends' children are all grown up, and there are no more rooms to paint. Most of those friends have moved on and so has my husband.

It's time for me to do the same.

I waltz into the buzzing beehive that serves as a distribution center for humans and pestilences alike.

"Okay, I can do this," I mutter as I try to move ahead, but for some reason, my toes seem to have screwed themselves into the floor. "Wonderful."

A couple pushes past me, glaring at me as if I'm what is wrong with the world today. And if I keep talking to myself, they might have a point.

Someone knocks into me from behind, and just like that, I've got one foot in front of the other and I don't stop moving until I hit the line to check my baggage. The attendant gives me a ticket in exchange for a piece of luggage that hardly meets the weight requirement. What in the heck did I pack in there, anyway? I made it a point to pack light. I guess I was wrong about that just like I was wrong about the fact my husband was faithful.

"Flight thirteen at gate thirteen," the woman behind the counter says as she hands me my ticket. "Just follow the arrows. You'll be fine." She winks as if she knows every doubt in my mind.

I follow the arrows dutifully, determined not to get lost in this big, scary airport, let alone the world, and when I reach gate thirteen, I double-check with the agents at the desk to make sure I'm in the right place, and lucky for me, I am.

Not that I'm lucky in general—an hour ago that very fact was brought to my attention in the most vulgar way.

Flight thirteen *and* gate thirteen, really?

Never mind. I may not live under a horseshoe, but I'm not

superstitious either. I glance back down at my ticket and scan my eyes over it until they snag over my seat number—13 C.

Thirteen, wow. I am on a superstitious roll.

I shove the ticket in my purse. It's probably best not to dote on the odds of seeing that number three times right before I board a flying coffin that has the gravity-defying task of teleporting me to the other side of the country.

Since I've got some time before my flight, I think I'll run to the restroom before hunkering down with a book. Thankfully, I had already packed that, along with the charger for my e-reader, and shoved it in my purse this morning, in addition to my cell phone charger. That way, if my luggage decides to say aloha before I do, I'll still have a way to communicate with Abbey and Parker.

A dull smile rides on my lips at the thought of my children as I schlep myself to the restroom. It's bright, has lots of tiny blue tiles, no backlogged line of women all clambering to find their way into a stall, and smells slightly of bleach, which for some reason comforts me on a hygienic level.

A stocky woman in a tank top dries her armpits with the hand drier near the back. She looks about my age, has brassy blonde hair that comes to a fried finish near her shoulders, and an all-around frazzled look about her as if she's been traveling for seventy-two years nonstop.

I head that way and wash my hands before dousing my face with water. I take a moment to examine myself. My blonde shoulder-length hair is peppered with gray. My green eyes look dull and listless, and my face looks pasty from a long winter and a longer afternoon. I stand at an average height of five foot five and have kept on the slender side of the scale mostly in part because of Stanton's insistence that my foray into cheeseburgers and French fries might be bad for business.

"Are you coming or going?" the woman next to me shouts as she pinches her dismal gray tank top in an effort to cool off.

"I'm going." I nod as I opt to shake my hands dry. "Los Angeles." I hike on my toes when I say it. "I've never been."

"Long flight." She wrinkles her nose as if it were a bad thing before pulling some change out of her pocket and depositing it into the one-armed bandit next to her and out comes a tiny pink square which she quickly shakes out. "But you'll love it. The weather is in the seventies. My sister lives out there. I just spoke to her last week. And all that sunshine will blind you with bliss. I wouldn't do all the touristy things, though. And for goodness' sake, don't hop onto one of those cheesy tours. They'll take all your money, drive you through a toilet bowl, and you'll be expected to like it."

"Actually, I'm going on a cruise," I hear those words leave my lips, and before I know it, I've spilled every last detail of the last two hours—my new connection to the number thirteen included.

"Holy wow." Her eyebrows connect in the middle as she expresses her horror. "Well, you'd better take this." She plops the pink square the sanity dispensary just spit out and lands it in my hand.

"What is it?" I twitch it with my fingers in an effort to identify the thing.

"It's a diaper," she all but mouths.

"Oh, I'm not traveling with children. Mine are both actually in college at the moment." And clearly, I'm not going to win any awards for communication since I thought I already ran that bit past her.

"Not for the kids." She laughs. "For you. Here, let me." She takes it from me a moment and expands it with her fingers enough for me to see the tiny pink glob can morph into a cute pair of plastic panties to accommodate just about any woman's derrière.

Lovely.

"Last month, I had to fly out to Houston on business," she continues. "Just a few hours on a plane, no big deal, right? Wrong.

We got stranded on the tarmac for six hours straight while they deiced the plane, and some other nonsense they tried to feed us. We weren't allowed to get up out of our seats or they threatened to shoot us." She gives a solemn nod, and by goodness, I believe her. "That meant no bathroom either. A few of the men around me peed in their coffee cups, but we ladies were out of luck. Let me tell you, it turned into some demonic Zen exercise that I never want to repeat. In hindsight, I should have wet the seat. I ended up with a bladder infection and antibiotics up the wazoo. I vowed never again." She quickly drops a few more coins into the depository and comes away with another pink square. "I'm going to put this sucker on. My flight boards in ten. Good luck to you. And don't worry about all that thirteen stuff. It's not like the universe is out to get you or anything." She ducks into a stall. "You'll probably meet the love of your life on that cruise. Good things are waiting up ahead. Just you wait and see." She emerges in record time and blows me a kiss. "Happy travels." She trots off then backtracks, her face frozen in a grimace. "But just in case things keep going in an unfortunate trajectory for you, I'd put on the diaper and maybe find yourself some mace."

"Mace?" My eyes double in size as she takes off.

Good grief, she's probably right. The world is filled with weirdos. The odds are much higher of me finding a psychopath I'll need a restraining order to shake, rather than the love of my life.

But I draw the line at wearing a diaper. What are the odds of the plane being grounded for thirteen hours? I'll probably never even hear that number ever again, let alone have my fate tied to it like some sort of backward kismet.

Ding. A small bell goes off overhead. "Flight thirteen will begin boarding in approximately thirteen minutes. All passengers please make your way to gate thirteen," a disembodied female voice chirps and a breath hitches in my throat.

"Thirteen minutes?" I mutter in a panic.

I put on the diaper without giving it a second thought—or thirteen. And I pick up another one just in case and shove it into my purse.

If I thought Stanton had tried my sanity, I have a feeling the universe is about to say hold my beer.

The flight to LA is a harrowing one filled with enough turbulence, belligerent passengers, and a serious lack of free snacks as we touch down on west side soil. But thankfully, I didn't have to resort to using my diaper.

We land and I'm miraculously reunited with my luggage. It's as if a weight is lifted off me. I pull out my itinerary and call an Uber to take me to the hotel I reserved across the street. Of course, I reserved it for Stanton and me, so I chose a more economical location a little farther out from the airport than I feel comfortable with, but then I thought I'd have my big, strong husband to protect me. Little did I know he'd be eyeing the loose girls standing in the corner, sizing them up in an effort to decipher whatever service they might specialize in.

A kind concierge helps to check me in and hauls my bag to my room for me and I'm only out ten bucks. The room is cool, smells slightly of cigarettes, and has a '70s vibe to it. Honestly, I can't tell if the décor was left over from that era or reconstructed to look that way. Either way, it's hideous.

I hoist the suitcase onto the bed, all five hundred pounds, and wonder if I'll find Stanton somehow miraculously stowed away in there. I unzip it on both sides and gasp when I open it.

"Oh crap." The words gravel from me.

It's not Stanton, but the contents are just as damming. These are *his* things. I grabbed the *wrong* suitcase.

"*AARRGGHH!*" I let out the wild cry of a yeti before collapsing onto the bed.

Tears start to fall as I reach for my purse and take my phone off airplane mode. There's a text from both Abbey and Parker in our family group chat, wishing Stanton and me the cruise of a lifetime. And there are two biting texts from Stanton himself.

I can't believe you did this to me.

Not to be outdone by, **You'll regret this.**

I already regret so much—like not listening to my gut when that blonde tart started working for him a year ago. And coincidentally not prodding him when he needed to work very, very late from then on. At least now I know it wasn't *Gray's Anatomy* he was boning up on—it was hers. And most likely a few other girls, too.

I put my phone back into my purse and my fingers brush over the itinerary for the cruise along with the pamphlet from the cruise line.

Emerald Queen of the Seas, a proud ship from the Royal Lineage Cruise Lines Collection.

They make it sound like a line of fine china. An image of me wobbling out to sea in a teacup from my mother's Royal Albert collection runs through my mind. I can see myself now, struggling to hold onto the edge of the cup while taking on water.

Wonderful.

I glance over the itinerary.

Emerald Queen of the Seas, Royal Lineage Cruise Lines
Itinerary
18 night Hawaiian cruise (back on the 19th day)
Day one Los Angeles departure 4:00
5 nights at sea
Night 6 and 7 Honolulu (Oahu)
Night 8 and 9 Lahaina (Maui) (Tender)
Night 10 and 11 Hilo (Big Island)
Night 12 Kona (Big Island) (Tender)
Night 13 Nawiliwili Harbor (Kauai)
Night 14, 15, 16, 17 time at sea!
Day 18 Los Angeles
Aloha!

Eighteen glorious nights, and the ship boards tomorrow starting at eleven. We'll spend four days on the water, two in Oahu, two on Maui, and two on the Big Island, one night in two different ports. Two on Kauai then it's back to sea and back to Los Angeles. That doesn't sound so bad. I think I can do this. I know I can.

If anything can take my mind off the nightmare my life has devolved into, it's Hawaii and endless miles of crystal blue ocean. And if that doesn't work, I'll pull out the paints and markers I packed to—

"Oh no." I moan. All my art supplies are in my suitcase back in Brambleberry Bay, along with all the cute dresses, sandals, and bathing suits I squirreled away for this trip.

What the hell—easy come, easy go, just like my marriage.

I pull out the pamphlet with a gleaming picture of one of the biggest cruise ships in the world on it. Innumerous water attractions poke from the top of the mammoth structure in tubes of every shape and color.

Good luck getting me into one of those deathtraps.

I quickly scan the inside of the pamphlet. The ship boasts of two surf simulators, twenty-three swimming pools, nine outdoor hot tubs, six indoors—two cantilevered, whatever that means—over forty dining venues, a fourteen hundred seat theater, and over eleven thousand works of art.

"Huh," I muse at the thought and my heart warms at the idea of feasting my eyes on every last piece. If one thing can soothe my soul, it's oil and acrylic over canvas, the delicacy of watercolor, and a decent sculpture of a very naked man.

A sigh expels from me as I read on. Two zip lines, miniature golf, an ice-skating rink that converts to both bumper cars and laser tag, an entire garden level, an aerial gondola, a wind tunnel, skeet shooting, bungee cord diving, escape room, twenty-four-hour fitness facility (have fun with that one), rock climbing, arcade, casino, discos, clubs, Broadway productions, karaoke, comedy shows, galley tours, bingo, and too much more to list.

I scan over the papers attached that I printed out. The cruise is all-inclusive, the room will be cleaned twice daily, prepaid gratuities, early dinner seating at six-thirty, and a midnight buffet every night.

"Just give me the food." I moan as I set my alarm for the morning.

All I want to do is eat my troubles away. I might come away from this trip the size of a ship, and oddly, I'm okay with that. Because no matter what I look like, what I do, or whatever unlucky predicament I find myself in, I'll be enough for me. I'll still love me even if my husband won't.

Turns out, I never needed him to begin with.

I twirl my wedding ring with my thumb and my heart wrenches as I relive the last twenty-five years on a loop—and the memories sting like a mother.

∽

IN THE MORNING, the sun shines through the split in the curtains and I wake with a start, half-afraid I'll miss my ride to paradise. I quickly rake my hair with the complimentary comb, brush my teeth with the complimentary toothbrush—both of which I promptly shove into my purse—put on a fresh pink sanity barrier between me and my sanity at the moment—I refuse to entertain the fact I've shoved myself into an adult diaper for the second time in a twenty-four-hour period. I take Stanton's suitcase with me as I head to the boarding terminal at the port.

For a hot second, I toyed with the thought of leaving the suitcase behind, but I take it with me for two reasons. One, I plan on filling it with my own things after a glorious and much-needed shopping spree. And two, all night long I fantasized about throwing Stanton overboard at midnight. And since he's not with me, his things will do quite nicely. One by one I plan on sending his designer duds to the bottom of the ocean, the exact location he's thrust our marriage—ironically with every thrust of his own.

The air in Los Angeles is far warmer than Maine could ever hope to be in May despite the fact January is still virginal at this point. The sky hangs heavy and blue, and there's a humid breeze that holds a thickness to it that I can actually taste. I shoved my thick snow jacket into the suitcase, but my heavy sweater and jeans aren't exactly the most ideal travel clothes either. I had planned on changing yesterday after getting my nails done, but I didn't want to be the fourth woman to strip in my bedroom.

The cruise terminal is a dome-like structure teeming with far too many people with far too much luggage and far too little patience.

Have I mentioned the bad acoustics? Think airport without all the glossy pathways and eateries.

A cluster of bodies surround the reception desk, and a slew of interconnected seats spread out all around me, each of them occupied with travelers who look as if they need a vacation from their vacation.

A couple of older women are bickering while playing tug-of-war with a long svelte blue bottle with a label slapped on the side. My guess is it's good hard liquor. The taller of the two is a well-coiffed redhead, dressed in cranberry slacks and a matching blazer. The other woman has shaggy gray hair and is wearing a hot pink muumuu with bright yellow and green flowers causing visual chaos all over it.

Behind them stands a frazzled mother with three kids under five. The little boy looks as if he just learned to stand and he's holding a balloon in the shape of mouse ears. I bet they took a trip to Disneyland, trying to squeeze in all that Southern California has to offer before stepping aboard the *Emerald Queen*.

That poor mother looks zonked, with hair falling out of her ponytail and the dark, puffy circles under her eyes. Here's hoping she gets a moment to herself in the next eighteen days—let alone eighteen years. I know how expensive those balloons can be and yet how much peace they can bring to a mother. I wouldn't have blamed her for dragging along an entire bouquet of balloons to pacify her brood. And maybe a bouquet of nannies to go along with it, too.

"Potato, poo-*ta*-to," the redhead shouts at the gray-haired woman.

"Don't you cast a spell on me," riots the granny in the muumuu.

"Ha!" the redhead fires back. "How could I do that when the only witch around here is *you*?"

"All right, you asked for it." The gray-haired woman knots her hand into a fist and pulls her arm back, accidentally jarring the balloon right from the little boy's hand, and up it begins to sail.

"Oh no, no, no." I moan just as a seat before me clears out. "I got it!" Without giving it a second thought, I hop onto the seat and stretch my hand out and the ribbon the balloon is tied to floats over my fingers. I somehow manage to wrap the ribbon around my pinkie just enough, but the balloon stubbornly continues to inch its way to the ceiling. "I think I have it," I say as I step onto the arm rail of the chair in hopes to secure it.

"I got it!" the gray-haired woman shouts as she hoists the blue bottle into the air and knocks the ribbon my way. "Teamwork makes the dream work!"

I reach out another notch and my foot slips.

"She's going to fall!" someone shouts, and as I look down I see that blue glass bottle twirling in my direction and bonking me square over the forehead.

"*Oof*," I grunt as I flip through the air like a cat trying to right myself, but before I ever hit the ground, I land in a pair of strong arms.

Black suit, white dress shirt, silver tie. Blue eyes, black hair, a face that can stop a freight train of women with functioning ovaries.

It takes a minute to register that his hands are on my bottom right up until he flexes his fingers and he squishes that diaper I'm still stuck in.

We both suck in a quick breath at the very same time— me out of fright and sheer embarrassment—and him—well, most likely the very same reasons.

"Be careful," he says, landing me back on my feet and taking off for entry to the gangway.

"Oh, honey." The redhead dusts off my jacket as if it needed it. "Are you okay?"

The gray-haired woman lands the bottle in my mouth. "Take a sip of this," she says as she pours a few quick gulps into me before I can pull away.

"*Vodka*." I gag and sputter before the redhead begins to swat the gray-haired granny.

"Who are you here with, honey?" the redhead asks, holding the gray-haired woman a safe distance away, and for that I'm thankful.

"I'm traveling alone." I cringe when I say it because I'm pretty sure rule number one when traveling alone is never tell anyone you're traveling alone.

"Good," the gray-haired woman says. "So are we." She takes the papers from my hand a moment. "Early seating." She gives them back.

"You'll have dinner with us," the redhead insists. "I'm Bess Chatterley and this is Nettie."

"Nettie *Butterworth*," the gray-haired woman adds with a touch of buttery pride—and suddenly I'm craving pancakes with lots of butter and syrup.

"Nice to meet you both. Dinner sounds wonderful," I say, not sure it's wonderful at all. I glance over to the gangway and catch that tall, dark, and handsome man that just had the misfortune to feel up my diaper and catch him looking right at me.

He glowers a moment before turning and disappearing right out of the terminal as he heads for the ship.

"Don't worry." Nettie, the gray-haired granny, leans in. "Handsome Ransom will be there, too. And try not to look so interested. Rumor has it, he likes 'em hard to get."

"Oh, I'm not interested," I assure them. "He won't ever get me."

No man will because I've officially closed up shop on my love life.

A bell goes off overhead and a disembodied voice comes over the speaker. "On behalf of Royal Lineage Cruise Lines, we'd like to welcome all passengers headed from Los Angeles to Hawaii. Boarding is now beginning for the *Emerald Queen of the Seas*. Please make your way to the security checkpoint with your luggage. It's time to sail away and forget all your troubles. Aloha."

Forget all my troubles, indeed.

Aloha to my old life.

I have no clue what lies ahead, but I have a feeling I'm about to find out. Here's hoping I don't live up to my surname.

I've had enough trouble for one lifetime.

Maybe two.

CHAPTER 3

No sooner do my luggage and I part ways once again than Bess and Nettie talk my head off as we follow a mass of humanity onto the gangplank. The briny sea air hits me, and sadly it reminds me of home, but I do my best to push all thoughts of Brambleberry Bay out of my mind.

"You're going to love it here," Nettie says. "Bess and I have been living on the ship for four years now. Eighteen nights is just a blink of an eye."

"Four years?" I gasp at the thought. "You mean you never go home?"

"This is home," Bess says. "There's a small handful of us regulars. And the crew has become like family. We'll fill you in on all of it during dinner. Ask for table thirteen and they'll lead you right to us."

"Thirteen?" I muse as I catch my first full glimpse of the ship.

Massive is the best word I can find to describe the stately structure.

"Wow. It's the size of a small city," I pant at the sight of it.

"Try small country," Nettie says. "If they didn't have roadmaps every three feet, people would be wandering around for days trying to find anything. Except for Ransom Courtland Baxter. I'm pretty sure he has a compass rose in his pants the way the women have no problem tracking him down."

Those blue eyes come back to haunt me, and something tells me she's right.

We walk the last leg of the gangway and step inside what looks like the most opulent hotel I've ever seen. A marble entry with ornate tile work glitters in shades of crème and copper. An atrium-like ceiling hovers far above and a row of crystal chandeliers hangs like works of art all the way down the promenade. An entire row of shops is lined up like dutiful retail soldiers up ahead—sunglasses, clothing, makeup, and more. Street signs mark off the corridors in an effort to orient the passengers, and it feels as if we've just been dropped off in another world entirely.

The fresh scent of sea air and lemon mingles in the air and up ahead a row of crewmembers greets the passengers as they walk on by.

"You'll have to meet the captain," Bess says, pulling me in and giving my arm a pat. "He's an old friend of mine by now, even if he is my son's age."

"And he's a looker," Nettie adds, her gray hair traveling ahead of her like a tumbleweed threatening to fall right off her scalp.

"He's a hottie." Bess gives a furtive nod to punctuate her point.

Nettie shrugs. "And seeing that you already crossed Ransom off the list, I'm betting Captain Crawford will be more to your liking."

"I'm betting he won't," I say. "This is supposed to be my twenty-fifth anniversary cruise. Let's just say we're not exactly singing a duet anymore. My husband decided to go solo—if you consider one man and three women a solo act. It's a long, sordid story."

One that's been replaying itself on a loop inside my head, and I have no idea how to find the shutoff switch.

"Ooh." Nettie gets a mischievous gleam in her eyes. "Lucky for you, I enjoy long, sordid stories to go with my dinner."

"I'm afraid this one has the power to ruin your appetite." Although mine is surprisingly making a comeback.

"Are you kidding?" She snickers. "I've got a stomach of steel and an insatiable appetite for revenge. We'll exchange war stories from the frontlines later."

We come up next in line to be greeted by the crew, and I watch as a petite woman in a red dress, hair of the same hue that runs down her back in coils, shakes a crewmember's hand. Her round eyes, her droopy brows, the thin line of her pale lips—she definitely has a cartoon factor to her, and yet everything about her seems oddly familiar to me.

There's a big wall of muscles blocking my view, so I can't see the faces of the crew, or more importantly said *hot captain*. That wall of muscles seems to be tailing the woman in the red dress. Although, at the moment, there's a slender man with a wreath of gray hair with an arm loosely around her waist. I suppose she has an entourage.

To my right, over by a glorious fountain, I spot a woman with jet-black hair and a blonde looking this way as if waiting patiently until the redhead finishes up with the crew. But it's the slender man with the gray hair who heads their way. And in less than two seconds the dark-haired woman carts him off a few feet and begins chewing him out.

Huh. Maybe she's the wife and the redhead was someone he was hitting on?

Thanks to Stanton, I pretty much have a one-track mind when it comes to cheaters.

I spot the redhead pull that wall of muscles to the side, and without missing a beat, the big, beefy man swoops in and wraps his arms around her waist, whispering something to her. I can't help but think it looks intimate. Odd since she was just being held by the other man she was with.

Hey? Maybe this is one of those swingers cruises? Boy, won't

Stanton be disappointed he's missing out.

"Captain Crawford," Bess chirps as we step up to see a tall man in white captain duds. He's tan, has dark wavy hair with kind amber eyes, and a knockout smile, lots of teeth, all of them white and perfectly straight. Next to him stands a brunette and a blonde, both looking equally unimpressed with the three of us. The two of them are dressed in white button-down shirts with navy pencil skirts and a pair of navy kitten heels to finish off the look, but something tells me that's where their similarities end.

The brunette clasps onto his arm and takes a moment to glare my way. I'm not an expert, but if I didn't know better, I'd think she was peeing a circle around him in an effort to steer me away from her territory.

"Meet my new friend..." Bess' mouth squares out. "I'm so sorry. I didn't get your name."

"Beatrix," I say to both her and Nettie. "But everyone calls me Trixie." I nod at the captain and my heart thumps unnaturally. "Trixie Troublefield." With *trouble* being the operative word as of late.

"Captain Weston Crawford." He pulls his shoulders back and his chest broadens the size of a door. I can feel his eyes lapping me up, and my cheeks heat at the thought of a man like the captain here showing any interest in me.

"You mind if I get a quick picture of the two of us?" I ask, pulling out my phone and scooting in close before he can answer.

"By all means." His cheek lands next to mine, so close I can feel the warmth emanating from him, and there is certainly a warmth about him you can't deny.

I snap a few pictures and we share a quick laugh as I send one off in the group chat with my poor, unsuspecting children. I hope Stanton chokes on his breakfast when he sees it—and odds are that breakfast will be a boob. Although, come to think of it, Maine is five hours ahead of us. It's more like lunch.

"Are you traveling alone?" The captain's amber eyes sparkle as he asks the question.

"Sure am," I try to sound chipper about it, but honestly, I feel like a baby giraffe who just fell out of its mother's womb and is expected to walk from the get-go.

"I insist you have dinner with me."

"Get in line, big guy," Nettie says. "She owes me one sordid tale and she's ponying up at the dinner table."

"Ah." He looks pleasantly confused. "In that case, I'll drop by with a bottle of the best wine in the house."

Bess holds a hand out to the brunette ensconcing him on his right. "And this is Tinsley Thornton, our ever-present, ever-busy cruise director."

Tinsley looks to be in her late thirties, early forties, has an impossibly perfect body, glowing tawny skin, and a pretty face. She could easily be a model.

"Nice to meet you," I say.

"Likewise." She frowns while giving the captain the side-eye.

I get the feeling the supermodel here has the hots for the man who holds the wheel in his hand.

"And last but never least"—Nettie says, pulling me by the elbow toward the woman with the blonde shoulder-length hair—"this is Elodie. You want more booze like that liquid gold you took a sip of outside? She's your girl."

The woman averts her eyes. She has a pert little nose and heavy lids that hang over her pale blue eyes. "How many times do I have to tell you it's a secret, Nettie?" She winks my way. "Elodie Abernathy." She extends her hand and I shake it. "I manage the shops—and the men on the ship." She motions to the rows and rows of retail stores that could fill up a shopping mall—or maybe she was pointing out that beefy man that just wrapped his arms around the redhead. He's standing in front of the sunglass shop and he's looking lean and mean, and well, like he deserves a little attention for all that effort he put forth at the gym.

"All of them?" I tease.

"All of them." She nods.

And I believe her.

"Then I'll be seeing you come morning. Shopping and eating are the top priorities on my agenda, and I don't plan on wasting any time to get either done." My upcoming divorce is a priority, too, but we'll save that fun for later.

"Shopping and eating are two of my favorite things." She gives a Cheshire cat grin. "We're going to get along famously." There's a slight lilt to her voice and it sounds like a faint accent.

I glance at the brass tag pinned to her shirt and see *South Africa* printed under her name.

I bet they all have their point of origin printed on their nametags.

But before I can glance at the captain's nametag, another party has moved in and Bess, Nettie, and I quickly shuffle to the side.

"You'll see him again at dinner," Bess trills, and a thought hits me.

I can't wear these clothes another minute, let alone at my first dinner on this fancy ship.

"Oh, Elodie"—I take a half step back— "scratch what I said about the morning. I need to buy a few things before dinner—a new shirt, some yoga pants, maybe a dress." I don't bother telling her I happened to put on these clothes yesterday morning, and let's not ever bring up the glorified Saran wrap I've got both protecting and humiliating my bottom.

She makes a face. "Sorry, hon. The shops don't open until we're well out to sea. But feel free to stop by after you eat and I'll pull out the new stock I just got in. You'll love all the pieces." She wrinkles her nose as she looks at my forehead. "You've got a bit of an egg brewing. Did you knock your noggin?"

Bess grunts as she points to Nettie, "*She* knocked her noggin. And then she tried to poison her with moonshine she picked up in the back of some longshoreman's car." She makes a face my way. "Those are the men who took our luggage as we checked in. They get tipped pretty well, but what people don't know is that they make more than most brain surgeons."

Nettie nods. "It's good work if you can get it."

"Good to know," I mutter. "I might need it." And I wish I were kidding.

Nettie flicks her fingers my way. "Let's exchange numbers. This book grows bigger by the minute."

We do just that and say our goodbyes for now.

"I'll get some ice," I tell Elodie. "And I'll see you tomorrow." I sigh as she walks away with a wink.

A crowd fills in between us and the sound of classical music fills the air. It feels like a party, one of the grandest parties I've ever been to.

Both Bess and Nettie hustle off to their room, but they're holding my feet to the flames when it comes to dinner, so I let them know I won't be late. But Bess told me to head to the lido deck if I was hungry for a quick snack, and I think I'll do just that.

My stomach rumbles, and just as I'm about to make my way to the elevator, I spot that petite redhead that was in line in front of me to meet Captain Crawford, and this time she seems to have ditched both of her potential suitors and is having a rather heated conversation with the blonde that was with her party.

The blonde plucks at the redhead's elbow as if she's trying to drag her off somewhere. And since they're in the direction of the elevator, I head that way.

I just know I've seen that redhead somewhere.

Is she an actress?

A model?

One of those newfangled shopaholics who sits around taking pictures of themselves all day while demanding that retailers send them free merch?

Too bad I was born in the wrong era. I could have aced that

career.

Maybe Abbey stalks her on social media and that's how I know her?

Doubtful.

Abbey doesn't follow anyone on social media unless they're under twenty-five.

The women disappear into the thicket of people, and I'm about to do the same when I spot an older woman, late eighties at least, with a pleasant face, doughy and wrinkled, maybe a little too much pale powder and rouge. Her orange hair rises above her head in a beehive, and she's dressed to the nines in a green velvet skirt and matching coat with a peach ruffled blouse peeking out from underneath. She's pressed into the alcove of a darkened shop with a gilded sign out front that reads *The Queen's Boutique*. And no sooner does she offer an exuberant smile my way and an equally exuberant wave than she turns around and walks right through the window of that shop.

"What?" I squint that way, but the lady is gone, and the darkened shop looks just as uninhabited as it was a moment ago.

I must have hallucinated it. Or maybe she walked through the door and I saw her reflection along the window?

My hand floats to that egg sitting on my forehead, and as if the plastic panties I've donned don't already have me feeling like a freak, this horn growing out of the middle of my forehead is finishing the job.

Need food, ice, a shower, and maybe a little revenge sex, stat—not necessarily in that order. My life has definitely gone off the rails.

The Emerald Queen Boutique snags my attention once again and I spot that woman in the window staring back at me, her face glowing like the moon, then just like that, she evaporates into thin air.

Scratch that.

Both my life and my mind have gone off the rails.

CHAPTER 4

Cabin 1313.
My cabin is on deck thirteen.
Of course, it is.

First of all, I thought it was illegal for any hotel or otherwise hospitality-centered lodging to tease superstitious weak-minded people like me.

And as if that wasn't bad enough—cabin 1313, really?

It's pretty clear the universe is doubling down on giving me the finger—thirteen times over.

Unlike the rest of the hive of humanity buzzing around the *Emerald Queen* in a hurry to check out their new digs, I decide to eschew deck thirteen altogether and feed the cat growling in my belly instead. And according to the wrinkled pamphlet in my hands, the portal to all my culinary fantasies is located on the lido deck.

I head over to the elevators and stop cold as I take in the grandeur of the *Emerald Queen*. Marble floors, crystal chandeliers, a glossy black piano sits on a platform, and at the helm is a man in a tuxedo tickling the ivories. The atrium spreads out above me. To the right and left, the next two decks are exposed as glass balconies rise as far as the eye can see. The bottom of each deck is lit up with purple and green fluorescent lights, hugging the curve in the ceiling as if they were creating their own calming waves.

The elevator is comprised of mirrored tiles in a smoky gray, giving everyone who steps on board a filtered glamorous look. I guess it really is smoke and mirrors here, but I don't mind. I can't see my crow's feet or the gray hairs that are quickly conquering the flaxen locks that have greeted me all my life.

We hit deck sixteen and the elevator is quickly abandoned as we spill into a bright and light wonderland. A glittering sign reads *Welcome to the Blue Water Café.*

The floors are creamy marble, and brass and boxy modern glass light fixtures are dispersed throughout. There are enough tables and booths to accommodate all of Los Angeles, but I can't take in another detail once I spot the veritable smorgasbord laid out in front of me.

"Holy ham and cheese," I pant as I do my best to take it all in.

The entire right side of the banquet room is lined with a self-service counter of the most delectable treats I have ever seen, bread in its every incarnation, rolls, baguettes, buns, loaves in baskets brimming with the abundance of every carboholic's dream. But that's only the beginning. The rest of the wall is lined with hot dishes in cast iron pots as far as the eye can see.

There are hot and cold stations set in rows taking up the center of the room that hold everything from a made-to-order pasta station along with panini sandwiches, and an entire buffet of every kind of pizza. There's a charcuterie board that would make my daughter's head rotate on a swivel with a variety of cheeses that could be the pride of any dairy farm and enough rolled-up cold cuts to put together a few farm animals if you had to.

But the showstopper that has my feet gravitating in its direction is miles and miles of every sweet treat known to man. I head over and peruse the offerings, each neatly sliced and lined up like delicious little soldiers, and labeled in an effort to take the guesswork out of the equation. Donuts in every shape and color, a plethora of fresh baked cookies, colorful macarons, cream puffs, red velvet cake, pineapple cake, chocolate layer cake with a pink sugar sculpture jetting from the top of each slice, hazelnut praline cake, cannolis, double chocolate mousse cake, dulce de leche cake, and far too much more for me to absorb all at once.

I grab a tray and load up on white truffle mac and cheese, red miso beef short ribs, mango chicken, garlic rosemary skirt steak with chimichurri, and a side of roasted cauliflower along with gourmet mashed potatoes and gravy. Of course, I couldn't overlook the tempting desserts they're flaunting in my face—much the way Stanton inadvertently flaunted his floozies. I snap up a slice of hazelnut cake, a slice of chocolate mousse cake, and a couple of jelly-filled donuts before grabbing a tall glass of iced tea and finding myself a seat near the window.

My phone chirps in my pocket and I fish it out. It's a text from Abbey in the group chat.

Love the picture of you with the captain, Mom. Too funny! You had better be on your best behavior, Dad, or she might actually ditch you for a man in uniform! Have fun!

She punctuates it with a dozen hearts, flowers, and kissing emojis, so I send her a few right back. I don't have it in me to use actual words. It would feel like a lie. Sort of the way my marriage was a lie.

Stanton fires off a text my way. Private, of course, because he doesn't have the balls to put it in the group chat.

How dare you take off in the middle of a matrimonial crisis. You don't understand the hell I'm going through right now.

I inch back as I study the screen for a moment. A part of me wants to remind him that his hips single-handedly thrust us into this matrimonial crisis.

And the hell *he's* going through? Who is this lunatic that I shared a bed with for twenty-five years?

I opt to uphold my inadvertent vow of silence rather than tell him off just yet. Instead, I snap a picture of my food and send it to him. And just like that, I've thrust Stanton into the seventh circle of my-wife-isn't-home-to-cook-for-me Hell as well.

The food is glorious.

I savor every bite as if I've never treated my taste buds to anything other than oatmeal for the last ten years, and sadly that assessment isn't all that inaccurate.

Without missing a beat, I work my way around my plate in a frenzied fashion, moaning and groaning through every bite while my dessert plate, or platter as it were, sits patiently awaiting my attention—and boy, is it ever going to get it.

I'm about to take a break from my short ribs and sneak a bite from that double chocolate mousse cake incessantly flirting with me when I spot that redhead from the atrium deck. That red dress she's wearing looks as if it's shrunk two sizes since I saw her last and I frown because I bet if Stanton was here he'd do his best to land her horizontally.

And all these years when he's excused himself to say hello to a pretty face, I actually believed him when he said he was handing out his business card to boost business. It turns out, my husband was just as plastic as some of those women he nipped and tucked.

The redhead strides deep into the banquet hall, but she doesn't grab a tray. Instead, she glances over her shoulder in what looks to be a panic.

Odds are she got separated from her party, but that look on her face is nothing short of terror.

Huh. I watch as her coiled tresses bounce over her back as she hustles in and out of food lines, all the while watching the entry to the room. If I didn't know better, I'd say she was afraid for her life.

That face though—those big eyes, glowing pale skin. I can't

shake the fact she looks so familiar. A crowd moves between us, and just like that, she's disappeared just like that creepy older woman dressed in velvet that I saw earlier. Although I'm betting this one didn't disappear into thin air. And let's get real. The last one didn't either. It's not like the woman was a ghost. It was probably just an illusion caused by all that shiny marble and crystal blinding me.

I eschew all thoughts of ghosts, and I also refuse to give any more mental energy to either my cheating husband or his newfound obsession with nude women who are not me. Instead, I pull the dessert platter forward and dive in, taking one aggressively large bite after another.

I'm about a dozen bites in when I glance up to see a man in a suit standing in front of me no more than ten feet away. My stomach spikes with heat—most likely from the influx of entrées I've been packing in it as if I were taking part in a hot dog eating competition on the Fourth of July. But that dark hair, those searing blue eyes, that stone-cold expression arrests my abilities to think straight for a moment, let alone swallow the supersized slice of hazelnut cake I just shoved into my pie hole.

Well, if it isn't Handsome Ransom staring me down with his arms folded across his chest as if he were about to arrest me for desecrating my meal—and honestly on those grounds, he probably should.

I contemplate waving with my fork since smiling isn't a safe option at the moment, but the two of us lock eyes, and for some reason, I'm frozen, unable to look away or move or think.

Okay, so he's lethally good-looking, has a body that can rival this ship for strength, and has suddenly caused every woman at this binge-eating buffet to hit the culinary pause button as they try to scheme a way to take a bite out of him instead.

A group of elderly women cuts between us, and in a moment, he's disappeared just like the redhead before him.

Those eyes though.

I wonder what he was thinking?

I glance down at the smorgasbord spread out over my table and a part of me would like to know what the heck I was thinking. I'd like to know what Stanton was thinking, too. And on the heels of that thought—I finish out every last bite of my dessert.

It takes more than twenty minutes for me to hunt and peck as I look for my cabin. I was never good at directions or navigating my way around mazes like this. That was Stanton's department. He led and I dutifully followed, and sadly without him here, every step I take feels as if I'm doing it in the dark—while the room is spinning to boot. It's disorienting, to say the least.

Deck thirteen, room 1313—it's a wonder I don't fall and break my neck once I step inside. I waddle down the last stretch of infinite hallways with their dark green carpeting with cream-colored fleurs-de-lis stamped over it until I find my new home for the next two-plus weeks, cabin 1313.

I slide my emerald-colored plastic keycard into the slot below the handle and open it up and flick on the lights. The hint of lemon-scented cleaning products hits me as I step into the brightly lit windowless room. The emerald carpeting bleeds throughout, there's a closet to my right as you walk in, followed by a small teal sofa. On the other side of that is a bed that's tucked against two walls.

Red rose petals are strewn over the white comforter and a couple of large swans fashioned from what looks like white bath towels sit over the middle of it. They're intertwined at the beaks making a heart shape with their necks and my stomach churns at the sight designed to thrill.

In front of the bed, there's a dresser with a decent size flat screen TV, a minibar and a fridge next to that with a giant round mirror above it. There's a door to my left that almost blends in seamlessly with the wall and I peek in to see a small bathroom with a shower in the corner and the requisite blow dryer hooked to the wall with a white marble sink below it.

"It's beautiful." I gulp as I take a few careful steps inside. And it's all mine.

This is a Stanton-free zone for the next eighteen nights, and I don't plan on giving Stanton any free rent in my brain for that long either if I can help it.

A silver dome sits on top of the desk, along with a vase with a dozen long-stemmed roses, and my heart drops as I head over and pick up the notecard next to it.

Happy anniversary to the best parents a couple of lucky kids could ask for. Enjoy the cruise! Aloha and lots of love, Abbey and Parker.

Tears burn in my eyes and I quickly blink them away. Everything from the rose petals, the swans, the roses themselves, it's all so very perfect, and Stanton had to go and ruin what would have been the most romantic moment of my life.

My hand gravitates to the silver dome and I pull the lid off to reveal a platter of giant strawberries dipped in chocolate. I don't waste a single second before snapping one up and indulging in a chocolaty bite. And I don't let the fact I just enjoyed a bakery's worth of cake deter me from eating them either.

A green and white flyer catches my eye next to the flowers that reads *Sea Breeze Daily Newsletter* and I pick it up.

Welcome to the first night of your trip to paradise! Below that is an entire agenda of what's happening on the ship tonight, along with the schedule and a call for me to download the app and never be caught off guard and miss out on the F-U-N.

First up is the muster drill, which my neighbor back in Brambleberry Bay told me all about in detail—along with everything else that had anything to do with cruising, so I already know what to expect with that. And although she suggested I hide in my room and sip from the minibar instead of attending, the word *mandatory* has caught my eye, and if I'm anything, I'm a rule follower.

After six strawberries and still no sign of my luggage, the sound of a doorbell goes off overhead and it's time for the muster party to begin. After a few brief instructions, I pull a bright orange life vest out of the closet and head up to the promenade deck to my destined location D13, where hundreds of other people cram into small spaces bumping life vests as if it were the new handshake.

The brunette I met downstairs, Tinsley Thornton, the one dripping off the captain and giving me the stink eye, is the crewmember giving my group the safety spiel. She seems nice enough. I wouldn't be surprised if I misread that whole peeing a circle around him thing that happened earlier. She's pulled her dark hair into a ponytail and has a bright yellow baseball cap on with the word *muster* written across it. And after twenty uncomfortable minutes, the ship's horn goes off, signaling the end of the muster drill as the ship begins to pull away from the port.

Cheers break out, and soon bodies are swirling in every direction as music plays from some unknown speakers and the entire staff is walking around with fruity-looking drinks. Streamers are flying, and the next thing you know, the *Emerald Queen* is leaving the harbor.

I look out at the vast blue ocean that lies ahead, the tangerine horizon that holds the promise of paradise, and I fight back the tears that come.

If the next eighteen nights are about anything, they're not about what I left behind—they're about what lies ahead.

And what lies ahead is a whole lotta food and not a lot of underwear.

CHAPTER 5

I didn't exactly envision myself wearing the same clothes I've been in for two days to the first dinner on my anniversary cruise.

I sure as heck didn't foresee the fact I'd be going commando either. But I'm all out of plastic panties and was forced to put on the same clothes I've been living in as I showered and freshened up for dinner.

About a half hour after the ship started moving, my stomach did a couple of hard rolls, but thankfully the feeling passed and I'm glad to say I think I've officially gotten my sea legs.

If the atrium on the ship wowed me, and the Blue Water Café made me want to move in permanently and call it a day—the main dining room makes me feel as if I've just been transported to the most elegant venue on the planet. It's a three-story wonder comprised of sparkling black granite floors and peach velvet chairs that sit around a bevy of round tables covered with white linen, set in a series of alcoves as artsy-looking light fixtures hang from above. I step into it from the first floor and take in all the drama and glamour it can afford.

In the middle is a large banquet table with an awe-inspiring ice sculpture of the ship itself sitting on a sea of frozen water. But as taken aback by the craftsmanship that went into replicating every last detail from the hundreds of microscopic windows and balconies to the tubes from the waterslides, I can't help but think it's probably a bad omen to fashion a cruise ship from a miniature iceberg. Cruise ships and icebergs have a long and sordid history, sort of like Stanton and me.

I give Bess and Nettie's name to the bubbly blonde hostess and she quickly leads me to a round table near the center of the room not too far from the frozen ode to the *Titanic*.

It's a smaller table set for four and three of the seats are already filled. There's a menu in front of every seat along with a glass of ice water and an empty wine goblet.

Ransom stands to his feet as I step in and I can't help but swoon at the chivalry.

"Ransom"—the bubbly blonde hostess giggles his way— "I've still got your sunglasses in my room, right next to my bed where you left them." She giggles again and I can't help but frown. "If you want them back, you know where to find me. I get off at midnight."

I *bet* she gets off at midnight.

"You made it!" Nettie shakes her fist in the air with a celebratory whoop. She's donned a blue and white muumuu and her gray hair spreads over the top of her head like a storm system.

"I knew you didn't kill her," Bess says as she taps Nettie on the arm. Bess looks consummately put together and graceful in a navy dress with long sleeves, accentuated with large gold hoop earrings and a thick gold necklace that has the power to make Cleopatra jealous. "We're glad to have you, Trixie."

"Ms. Troublefield," Ransom says, pulling out the chair for me and I quickly thank him as I take a seat. His suit is dark, his blue eyes are as unknowable as the bottom of the sea, and his thick cologne just sent me back to some unknown point in my life when I still lusted for men who weren't my husband. "Glad you could join us."

He takes a seat and his lips twitch as if he were holding back a smile. It would figure that he's too stubborn to give it. Or maybe they're reserved for a bubbly blonde hostess young enough to be his daughter? I'm betting it's the latter.

"Thank you for inviting me," I say, looking at Bess and Nettie. "And please excuse me. I'm still stuck in my travel clothes, or I would have put on something a little nicer. My luggage hasn't arrived yet."

I cringe because I just spouted off a lie without meaning to. Technically, my luggage will never arrive. But I'm so frazzled, I momentarily forgot it wouldn't have my things in it.

Nettie waves me off. "They'll have it in front of your cabin by the time you get back to your room." She leans in. "All right, kid. Here's an icebreaker for you. Choose someone famous who you'd like to have on your zombie apocalypse team."

Bess grunts over at the gray-haired counterpart, "Before you scare her off, why don't you try again?"

"All right." Nettie squints over at me. "Two can play at that game."

"What game?" Bess squawks. "Oh fine, I'll do it." She blinks up at the ceiling. "Okay, I've got one. If you could have a limitless supply of something, what would it be? My answer is margaritas." She glances at Nettie. "And you can't steal that."

"Fine," Nettie grouses. "Fire hydrants. Your turn, blondie." She nods my way.

"A limitless supply..." I bite down over my lip. "Oh, I know, that double chocolate mousse cake I had upstairs." I frown briefly at Ransom again as the memory of us locking eyes flits through my mind.

Nettie moans. "That is a good one, but if you're a fan of chocolate, it has nothing on the molten lava mocha cake. It's a part of their nighttime culinary repertoire on this magic carpet ride into indigestion, and it'll make you sing in places that haven't sung since the Roosevelt administration."

"Speak for yourself." Bess scoffs. "Trixie hardly looks old enough to have seen the Nixon administration, let alone Roosevelt—unlike you. And I'm sure she's sung in places plenty of times since then—again, unlike you."

A tiny laugh strums from me. "Technically, I was born under the Nixon administration. And as for that lava cake, I'm already looking forward to it."

Nettie leans in. "The cake? Or singing in undisclosed places?"

Ransom's lips curve just enough as if he were interested in my answer as well.

"I believe you're next," I tell him.

His eyes hook to mine and a spark of heat swims through me instantly. I swallow hard and grab my menu, fighting the urge to fan myself with it.

"Coffee," he flatlines, picking up his own menu and quickly perusing it.

"Is coffee code for women?" I mutter without meaning to. All right, so I'm feeling a little cheeky, and Handsome Ransom here is impossibly comely. I'm not sure why, but I'm finding that last fact oddly annoying.

Nettie bursts with laughter.

"She's got your number, hot stuff." Nettie elbows him in the chest. "Ransom is the *Queen's* resident woman slayer. There's not a bimbo he hasn't bagged and tagged and dragged back to his lair."

"Don't listen to her." Bess shakes her head. "Ransom is a perfect gentleman. Sure, he's often seen with a beautiful woman by his side, different beautiful women each night, some nights a *few* different beautiful women, but he's single. And let's be honest, when you look like that, it would be going against nature to fight it."

Ransom tweaks his brows, still no smile. "The rumors of my roguish behavior are greatly exaggerated. But not by much."

I didn't think so.

"So please, tell me about yourselves," I say to the women before me.

Bess raises a finger. "I'm originally from Honey Hollow, Vermont. My husband was the local dentist and I taught home ec at the high school. My star student went on to open a bakery right on Main Street." She sighs hard. "And once my husband found his secretary more attractive than me, I found the high seas more attractive than him. I've been cruising ever since."

Nettie leans her head onto Bess' shoulder. "And that's where I came into the picture. We met on this very ship and we've been inseparable ever since ourselves. I'm a fellow Vermonter, Scooter Springs to be exact, where I dabbled in farming."

"Farming?" I ask, intrigued.

"Indoor farming," Bess corrects. "And believe me, you don't want any details of what went on at that funny farm." She says *funny farm* in air quotes.

Nettie shrugs. "Anyway, I made my fortune, sold the farm, and here I am—cruising for trouble."

"You can say that again." Bess snorts to herself.

Nettie tosses her hands in the air. "My unhealthy obsession with the *Love Boat* may have had something to do with it."

"That would explain why you call every bartender Isaac," Bess says.

Nettie squints over at her. "You mean Isaac isn't another name for a bartender?"

We all share a warm laugh—the sum total of Ransom's laugh is more or less a thump of his chest, but worth the show, nonetheless.

I nod to Ransom and give a pleasant smile.

"I'm from Castle Point, Maine." His brows furrow. "Graduated from law school way back when and somehow ended up with a gun in my pocket full time."

"You went to law school?" I ask with an open-mouthed smile.

"My uncle was a judge." He nods. "He highly influenced my decision. He was my primary father figure while I was young. But I saw him die on the bench. I didn't want that. His son, Everett, followed in his footsteps. He's a judge out in Ashford, Vermont, but he lives in Honey Hollow." He nods toward Bess when he says the name of her hometown. "I moved to Maine when I went to college, and it became my new home. After that, I went into the force."

"Force?" Bess huffs. "He went into the *FBI* and ended up as a detective on their Behavioral Analysis Unit. Ransom isn't exactly one to toot his own horn."

Nettie leans in. "That's because he's got an army of women lining up to do it for him."

I bite down on a laugh. "That's fascinating," I say. "The part about the FBI." The part about the women eager to toot his horn is rather obvious. "So how did you end up on the ship?" I ask him.

The table goes silent. Bess and Nettie exchange a glance before looking his way.

Okay, so it's a nonstarter, but I'm determined to get to it before I disembark.

"They had an opening." He sweeps his gaze over my features as he says it, and my cheeks burn with heat.

Bess nods. "Ransom and Quinn, his female counterpart, are the real deal."

"The rest are mall cops," Nettie says as she lifts her glass my way. "If you're naughty enough, he might just handcuff you."

A waiter comes by before my cheeks can heat for the second time tonight. He's a tall man with a friendly smile, a shock of orange hair, and sparkling green eyes. His name is Galen and his brass nametag lets me know he's from Ireland—sans an accent.

He walks us through the meal and gives us the chef's recommendations, and seeing that the meal consists of three courses, each with five choices, I opt to go with the suggestions—chilled shrimp salad as a starter—something that would have been considered a complete meal in my past life. Herb-crusted Alaskan salmon for my main dish and royal cheesecake with passion fruit for dessert.

The starters arrive as if on cue along with a basket full of warm fresh baked bread. And you can bet your dirty little soul I slathered that warm slice of heaven with three pats of butter. I would have gone for more, but for a brief second Ransom and I brushed hands as we reached for the butter.

I swear on all things holy, a fire jumped from him to me, and for a second, I felt a rush of dizziness.

And if indulging in dairy-coated carbs wasn't enough for me, the herb-crusted salmon melts in my mouth right to the last bite. No sooner are our dinner dishes taken from the table than Nettie clears her throat.

"All right, girly." She wags a crooked finger my way. "You promised me one sordid tawdry tale. Now let's hear it—the steamier, the better. I like a little raunch with my dessert."

"Fine by me, but remember, you asked for it." I quickly regale them with tales from my husband's ravenous libido and I don't believe I've ever held three people's attention in such a rapt manner as I did just now.

"You found him with three women?" Ransom's brows hike a notch, and I can't tell if he's shocked or impressed. Most likely both.

"He had them stashed just about everywhere, but that's all I had time to find." I shrug at the sad reality that has become my life.

"Forget about him," Bess tells me. "This trip is all about *you*. And we're going to make sure you live it up."

Nettie nods. "You should drink mai tais until you pass out. I'll do it with you."

"One mai tai is plenty." Bess waves off the idea of blacking out. "And you should journal."

"Good idea," Nettie says. "One of those online journals where you tell the world about the great time you're having and that way your ex can eat his heart out."

Bess scoffs. "Now that is a good idea."

"I have them sometimes." Nettie taps her temple. "You can call it *Single and Ready to Mingle*."

"*Suddenly Single*." Bess points my way. "And you should write about the trip. And it's going to be *some* trip. Just wait until you see nothing but the blue Pacific surrounding us in the morning. You'll feel more alive than you ever have before."

Ransom offers the briefest hint of a heartfelt smile. "I hope you'll have a very good trip."

"And what a trip the last forty-eight hours have been already," I muse.

"That's it!" Nettie claps her hands. "*Suddenly Single—What a Trip!*"

My mouth rounds out. "I love that." A laugh bubbles from me. "I'm going to do it. I already feel as if there's plenty to say." I'm about to babble on about my newfound blog when my attention is hijacked by the captain making his rounds at a table nearby.

"And here he is," Ransom mutters as he glances that way.

"Captain Crawford?" I ask.

Ransom's chest bucks with a silent laugh, no smile. He ticks his head to Nettie. "Why don't you fill her in on his legal name?"

Bess scoffs. "Not this again."

"What's his legal name?" I ask, suddenly far too interested as to what it might be.

"Cockburn," Nettie says without an ounce of sarcasm.

"Excuse me?" I blink over at her.

Nettie shrugs. "Let's just say, when he got married, his wife's new family highly suggested he rethink his surname or take hers. He's been using his middle name as his surname ever since."

"Cockburn?" I glance over at Ransom and my cheeks burn with heat. "Well, with a surname like that, I don't blame him."

Ransom glances back at the captain. "Why don't we get going? We'll snag the best seats in the theater."

"We haven't had dessert," I say, shocking both my stomach and myself as the words stumble from me. Today's culinary shenanigans are akin to Thanksgiving on steroids.

"Eh." Nettie shrugs. "We can cut and run if you want. After the show, I'll take you to the Blue Water Café and we'll eat our weight in lava cake."

"Sounds like a plan," I say.

No sooner do I get the words out than Ransom shuttles the three of us out the door. I couldn't help but notice the captain glaring at Ransom while he was doing it, too.

"What deck is your tomb located on?" Nettie asks as we fast approach the elevators.

"Lucky thirteen," I tell her.

"That's where we'll head first," Nettie says. "I'm sure your luggage is there by now, but the cabin steward may not have gotten to setting it inside just yet. We may as well utilize Ransom's muscles while we've got 'em. He's not just about his good looks, you know." She winks his way and he winks back.

I take them to deck thirteen, cabin 1313, and sure enough, my luggage—or Stanton's as it were—is sitting right in front of the door.

"Allow me," Ransom says as he takes Stanton's suitcase by the handle.

I let us in and lead the way. "Feel free to set it on the bed," I say as I carefully move the heart-shaped swans out of the way.

"Geez," Ransom pants under his breath as he hoists the suitcase onto the bed. "What do you have in here, a body?"

A laugh strums from me. "You won't believe what I have in here."

I unzip it, eager to show off Stanton's collection of Italian loafers, and pull back the flap and gasp.

It's indeed a body. It's a woman with red hair and a red dress, folded up like an accordion.

"Oh dear, is she dead?" a fragile voice calls from behind, and I fully expect to see Bess or Nettie, but I don't. It's the older woman with her orange hair spun in a beehive, dressed in velvet from top to bottom. She gasps as she pats her lips with her fingers. "Well, the fact she doesn't appear to be breathing isn't good, is it?" And with those words, she dissolves into nothing right before my eyes.

A breath hitches in my throat as the room fades to black, and I feel myself falling to the floor.

It's not good at all.

CHAPTER 6

"Trixie?" a deep voice commands from above. "Wake up." His voice is a touch softer this time and I can feel a pair of strong arms wrapping themselves around me.

My lids flutter and I'm relieved to see that deep voice belongs to Ransom Courtland Baxter and not Stanton the Troublemaker Troublefield.

"I'm fine." I give a quick sweep of the room, but there's no sign of the disappearing granny. "By chance, did any of you see a woman with orange hair in the room?"

"If you mean the body stuffed in your suitcase, yes." Bess hugs herself. "She's still in there."

That's not what I meant, but it's what I was afraid of. Not only do I have a corpse in my luggage, but I just had a grand hallucination to go along with it.

"Boy, you weren't kidding." Nettie shakes her head as she looks at the bed. "Your soon-to-be-ex really does have them stashed just about everywhere."

"That might be true," I say as Ransom helps me back to my feet. "And that's actually my husband's luggage, but the girl didn't come with me—at least not from Maine. I opened my suitcase last night, and believe me, she wasn't in there." I take a half step forward to get another look at her and gasp. "Is she?"

Ransom nods. "I was checking for a pulse just as you hit the floor. I'm going to call it in." He pulls out his phone and his fingers tap-dance over it with lightning speed.

I catch a glimpse of the poor woman's face and I gasp once again.

"It's her!" My hand claps over my mouth as I say it.

"You know this woman?" Ransom's eyes widen as if this might be a problem.

"No, not really." I shake my head and shudder at the same time. "She boarded the ship before us and—" A breath hitches in my throat. "Oh my word, I *do* know her. Or at least I know *of* her. That's Olivia Montauk!"

"Olivia Montauk," Ransom says under his breath as he taps it into his phone. "I just alerted Crawford to the situation." He frowns when he says the captain's name. "I'm going to have the room cordoned off. Trixie, how do you know this woman?"

"She's an artist. And I love to paint, so I'm constantly poking around in those kinds of circles. I'm nothing but a glorified home decorator, but Olivia is—or was the real deal. She's known for her cozy landscapes and her use of color to create light. Her work exploded a few years back after she did some big show. And well, everyone was in a hurry to get their hands on her work. I don't know what she's been up to lately, but she was probably still painting. I mean, I have to paint. Art is like breathing, and I'm sure she felt the same."

A woman with her jet-black hair pulled into a bun, full red lips, and a sculpted face races into the room, and this time I'm positive everyone can see her.

"Quinn"—Nettie scuttles her way— "we've got a girl in a suitcase and a killer on the loose," she shouts at the top of her lungs.

"Would you keep it down?" Bess is quick to shush her. "This isn't only bad for the girl, it's bad for the ship. The last thing we need is a panic breaking out. And then there's that whole killer on the loose thing." She holds herself tight. "We're trapped! *Help!* There's a killer on the loose!"

"Bess." Ransom steps over to her. "You're going to be okay. I have a feeling this was an isolated incident. Nettie, why don't you get her to her room?"

"You bet I will," Nettie says, securing Bess by the arm. "But we're stopping off at my room first to get a little nip of that Russian vodka."

"I'm not drinking moonshine from some longshoreman's trunk."

"His trunk was lined with briefcases full of cash," Nettie says as they head out the door. "The next time I meet up with him, I'm taking out a loan."

"You do that and you'll be the next one stuffed in a suitcase," Bess shoots back.

"Trixie"—Ransom pauses a moment to frown— "head over to the guest relations in the atrium. I'll call ahead and make arrangements for you to get another cabin. You can't take anything in this room with you."

"I don't need to," I say, securing my purse over my shoulder. "I have everything I need."

"Get a good night's sleep," he says. "I'll contact you in the morning—for the case."

"Yes, of course." I nod. "I'll be happy to help with whatever you need."

The brunette takes a moment to glower at me. "I'm sure you will."

Ransom's chest expands. "Trixie, this is Quinn Riddle. She's my partner in vessel security. Quinn, this is Trixie Troublefield. This is her cabin, and that's her husband's suitcase."

"Your husband?" Quinn looks both intrigued and relieved. "Where is he? And what is his relationship to this woman?"

"He's back in Maine," I tell her. "He cheated on me, so I left him behind and mistakenly took his luggage instead of mine. Believe me, I much prefer his luggage to him."

Her lips crimp. "I see."

The room floods with security guards along with Captain Crawford.

"Ransom." Captain Crawford steps over and leans toward the bed. "Geez, everybody out." He directs the security guards toward the door. "Ransom, Quinn, I'll contact the authorities back in Los Angeles and see what they want us to do. Trixie?" His eyes snag on me as if I just materialized in the room. "Is this your cabin?"

"Yes, it was," I tell him. "Ransom suggested I head to guest relations and get another one."

"I agree," he says, sweeping his gaze over my features. "I'll check on you in the morning."

"I appreciate that," I tell him and Ransom's cheek flinches when I say it.

They get to work, and I make my way out of the room, only to find that old woman with the beehive of orange hair, dressed in dusty musty velvet from eras long gone by—and I bet they are exactly that—because she's from an era long gone by herself.

"*You*," I hiss at her as I step in close. "Why didn't anyone else see you when you popped into my room earlier?" I whisper it so low it's a miracle if she heard me.

"How could they?" The woman scoffs. "I've been dead for fifteen years." She walks right through me, right into the room, and through Captain Crawford as she makes her way to the bed before disappearing into thin air once again.

And just like that, she takes my sanity right along with her.

CHAPTER 7

*L*ast night, a kind, young woman at the guest relations counter named Layla Beauchamp, a Georgia peach who may or may not have won every beauty pageant in three different districts while her perfectly polished toes were still hunkered down on Southern firmament, helped to locate me another cabin.

Since Ransom was the one that asked her to do it, she made sure to upgrade me to a room with a window—or a porthole as she put it. She let me know he took care of that little glitch I was having—I'm assuming with the cabin. The woman seemed extremely eager to please him in any capacity. And knowing what little I do about Ransom, she'll make a heroic effort to please him again very, very soon.

My new cabin, deck three, room 313—yes, that nefarious little number is still after me like an ominous harbinger of more bad luck to come—is basically a cookie cutter of my last cabin, but where a wall once greeted me in the back, a gloriously large, round window pours in all the glorious light it can afford. The blue skies and stunning ocean views aren't a bad deal either. And if I'm not mistaken, I think I see the shape of a heart forming in the white puffy clouds out on the horizon.

The windowsill is wide enough for me to curl up in with a cup of coffee, and I plan on doing exactly that later. But what I'd really love to do is mold my body into that windowsill and paint for hours.

That poor woman who was wedged in my luggage flashes through my mind, and I squeeze my eyes shut in an effort to rid myself of the image. I can't believe Olivia Montauk met such a horrible demise—and ended up in Stanton's suitcase of all places to boot. It's just terrible that her life was taken from her.

I shudder and do my best to push all that darkness out of my brain for now. I'm half-shocked Ransom didn't burst into my cabin last night and make me walk the plank for all the trouble I've inadvertently caused. A part of me wonders if he asked me to walk to his bedroom if I would have said no.

Speaking of my luggage, I still can't believe I left my luggage behind in Brambleberry Bay. Not only did I shop for the last three months, carefully curating every piece that I would be bringing with me on what I had deemed the vacation of a lifetime, but I bought brand-new acrylics, notebooks, a few canvas boards, and some wonderful alcohol markers and packed them as well. I knew my soul would sing once I saw the vast Pacific expanding before me, and so far from what I can see from my new porthole into paradise, it turns out I was right. Here's hoping the gift shop will have something to quell my artist needs. At this point, I'd settle for a box of crayons.

My first plan of action this morning was to head to the Queen's Boutique and buy out any and all of their clothing offerings. I don't care if I have to walk around wearing something that reads *My parents went on a cruise and all I got was this stupid T-shirt*. Or, *I'm with Dumbo*, or *I am Dumbo*.

Honestly, I'm feeling like both of those apply right about now. But it's seven-thirty in the morning, and come to find out, the shops don't open until later, so I take Nettie and Bess up on their offer to meet them on the lido deck for breakfast.

I've showered and blow-dried my hair to the point where I look as if I might have stepped into the salon for a blowout, which is something I've never done. I typically let my hair air dry, but I figure since my wardrobe is playing out its own version of *Groundhog's Day* I might as well put an effort in other areas. A gargantuan effort.

Thankfully, my bathroom has a complimentary toothbrush—of which I now have two thanks to my brief hotel stay back in LA—toothpaste, and deodorant. Luckily, I packed a brush. And, of course, I packed the bare minimum makeup in my purse as well, some lipstick, shell pink—a good *day* color but not the cranberry cream I packed in my suitcase for evenings. I'm also missing out on an assortment of other pricey cosmetics, lotions, and potions I bought just for the trip. So, I'm basically the B version of myself at the moment—and after breakfast, if fate decides to pull out all the stops and ensure I can't purchase a stitch of clothing, I'll be forced to wear my bathrobe until I can launder my sweater and jeans. Otherwise, I'm still going commando, and to tell the truth, it feels rather freeing in just about every way.

Speaking of my jeans, they are no longer my friend. After less than twenty-four hours, my button is threatening to shoot off my pants with the velocity of a bullet. The zipper isn't faring so good either.

I make it up to the lido deck and find that everyone on the ship seems to have the same idea. Blue Water Café is alive with the sound of Polynesian music filtering through the speakers, along with the heavenly scent of freshly brewed coffee, bacon, and freshly baked bread. I quickly bypass the dry cereal, oatmeal, fruit, and yogurt offerings and head straight for the good stuff.

Each culinary station is buzzing, but because there are so many of them open, I don't have to fight the crowds to gather scrambled eggs, bacon to my heart's content—something I would have considered verboten in my old life, even if my old life was less than a couple of days ago—French toast, pancakes, and last but not least, an everything bagel toasted to perfection and slathered in cream cheese and topped with an obscene amount of lox.

Stanton hated it when I ate smoked salmon. He thought fish, in general, was for the felines among us. And just for the fact he was the sole reason I indulged in so little fare from the sea, I tripled my portion. And that alone is the glory of a self-serve buffet.

I spot Bess and Nettie at a table for four near the window and quickly make my way over. Bess has a small plate of fruit in front of her and Nettie is loaded up with a few eggs benedict and enough bacon to build a salted meat fort.

How did I miss the eggs benedict?

"Wakey wakey, eggs and bakey," Nettie sings as I set my tray down.

Bess looks down at the offerings before me and chuffs. "Just three plates?"

"Is that bad form?" I ask.

"Nah." Nettie waves me off. "It just shows you're a slacker. Bess here had six the first morning she was here."

"It's true. And after spending the afternoon in the infirmary, it was my last foray into playing Russian roulette with my digestive tract." Bess toasts me with her coffee.

"Ooh, you just reminded me, I need some java," I say. "I'll be right back." I jet off and make my dream latte, full fat, extra sugar, and more than a few drops of their vanilla syrup, blood orange juice, and something fruity that winked my way and said *drink me!*

"I'm all through with not letting food seduce me," I say as I land back at the table.

"Well, you're in the right place for that." Bess honks out a laugh.

Nettie smirks. "Says the one with a grapefruit on her plate." She looks my way. "I keep telling her that's garnish she's eating."

"Oh, it is not," Bess rolls her eyes. "Is it?" She glances to the fruit buffet, and I glance back with her, only to see a handful of grapefruits, each halved with a candied cherry sitting in its navel, line the display of breakfast treats. "Okay, fine. It's garnish. But I like garnish. This garnish is going to ensure I have many more healthy years to eat more garnish, unlike that garbage you're shoveling in," she says to Nettie before looking at the virtual buffet I've selected for myself. "Not you, Trixie. You go ahead and eat whatever you want. You're still young. You have many vivacious years ahead of you. Nettie's impersonation of a garbage disposal is going to shave ten years off the backend of her life."

"She's right," Nettie says. "And you still need to put your soon-to-be ex-husband through hell. You'll need all the energy you can get."

"You can say that again." Bess is back to rolling her eyes but for a much better reason.

"Well, I'm not exactly a spring chicken myself. I'm forty-eight. And you're right, I plan on giving Stanton some heck. Lots and lots of it." I take an angry bite of my bacon. "But right now, I'm all about the food. And please excuse my attire. I'm headed straight to the shops downstairs as soon as they open."

"You should get a muumuu," Nettie says, plucking at the blue and green floral number she's donned. "What it lacks in fashion it gains in comfort."

Bess shakes her head. "You do that, and you might start filling it in. That's why I keep my trousers around—they keep me in line. Of course, in a day or so the weather will grow far more humid. That's typically when I switch to the shifts in my wardrobe."

"And that's when she breaks out the bacon." Nettie winks.

A laugh bubbles from me. "I can't believe how lucky you both are. I mean, living here? No cooking, no cleaning? The art shows, the shopping, the casino, the theater? Not to mention the exotic locales. I think you're doing this life thing right." I take a quick bite of my bagel and let the savory lox melt in my mouth. "*Mmm.*" I close my eyes and see stars for a moment. "So, what do they call people who live on a cruise ship, anyway?"

"Lucky," Bess says as she picks up her coffee and gives it a swill.

"Ha!" I toast her with my OJ. "Lucky, indeed." And that's something I'm not.

"The *Emerald Queen* is home base," Nettie adds. "It can be for you, too. The trick is to book your next cruise before this one ends. You get a better deal and there are tons of perks. We're all booked out for the rest of the year."

"Wow," I muse. "Considering the year has just begun, I'm impressed."

Bess nods. "And hot tip, don't buy meds in any of the shops unless you need them. They'll lock you in your cabin with nothing but room service as a precaution just based on your purchases alone."

"Lock me in my cabin with nothing but room service?" I make a face. "Sounds like a dream, if you ask me."

Nettie leans in. "Unless you've got another corpse in there."

"Or a ghost, or a grand delusion," I mutter under my breath as I take another sip of my orange juice. "My new cabin is great. It's on the third floor just a few steps from the main dining room and the theater. And I've got a window this time. I guess Ransom put in a good word for me." My lips twitch. "Or more to the point, the pretty young thing at the guest relations counter wanted me to put in a good word about her to Ransom."

Nettie grips the table with a dramatic pause. "Could you blame her?"

"No, I guess I couldn't." I sigh at the thought. "His roguish handsome appeal is pretty hard to argue with."

"What's this? Talking about our favorite resident, Handsome

Ransom?" a female voice chirps and we look up to see the same pretty brunette that I met upon entering the ship. Tinsley Horton? *Shorton*? Her chestnut brown hair is full and wavy. She's got on a T-shirt and tennis skirt and her shiny brass nameplate reads *Cruise Director, Colorado*.

"Tinsley Thornton." She holds out her hand and I shake it. "Wait a minute." She squints over at me. "You're not the one that found the body in her cabin, are you?"

"That would be me, Trixie Troublefield." I cringe. "But I didn't know her. I mean, I knew *of* her, but I'm not responsible for the fact she ended up in my suitcase—or in the next life." Not how I wanted to get the point across, but hey, it works.

She inches back. "I can't believe they're still letting you walk freely all over the ship. I thought for sure you'd be in the brig." There's a gleam in her eyes that lets me know she'd enjoy that to no end. Her expression falls flat. "Olivia was booked to do a showing of her artwork. It's all here on the ship and we're licensed to sell it in a few days. I guess I'll have to see what her PR team has to say about it."

"Well, like I said, I'm not the killer," I tell her. "But I *am* an artist. I've taught plenty of classes on how to paint a basic acrylic landscape. And for a long time, I used Olivia's work as inspiration. If you need any assistance with the presentation, I'd be happy to help."

Her mouth falls open. "You can paint? Olivia was set to do a few tutorials for our crafts classes. What cabin are you in? That will give me direct access to text you."

"313," I tell her. "And yes, I would love to do this. I forgot all my paints and journals back home. I can't wait to get in there and take a brush to paper. Do you think I can borrow a few supplies for myself?"

"No." Her expression darkens once again. "So, what's this I hear about you and Ransom?" She hikes a brow.

I have a feeling the reason she's holding the art supplies hostage is directly related to this question.

"Nothing is going on between Ransom and me," I tell her just as someone clears their throat from behind and a far too comely man in a suit with blue eyes that look as if they can teach the ocean all about that magical hue lands next to me. "Ladies." His lips expand in my direction before he nods to the rest of them.

Wonderful. Not only do I like to start my day with salted meats and copious carbs, but apparently, I like an extra helping of my foot in my pie hole to go along with it.

"I've gotta run." Tinsley licks her lips as she looks at the Dapper Dan among us in a suit, mind-boggling thick and luscious cologne, and don't get me started on the dewy black hair I'm ready to run my fingers and a few more creative parts through.

Wait a minute. I'm a married woman.

Aren't I?

Oh, who cares. Stanton was definitely not looking at his wedding ring before he dove into bed with half of Brambleberry Bay. More like *chucking* his wedding ring.

Tinsley takes a breath. "I'm having dinner at the captain's table tonight." She lifts her shoulder to Ransom. "See you all later."

She takes off and Bess flicks her wrist. "Don't pay her too much mind. She's got something going with the captain, and of course, everyone but you has something going on with Ransom."

My stomach squeezes tight at the thought of being left off that naughty list.

"Tinsley and I have nothing going on." Ransom frowns my way as he curls his hand around a cup of coffee. "How did you sleep?"

"I slept great." I wince. Probably not the right thing to say after finding a body in your cabin.

"Good," he says. "I need to ask you a few questions about the deceased." He glances down at the three platters of food waiting to be devoured. "After you enjoy your breakfast," he says. "You'll hear from me in about an hour." He rises to leave and Nettie moans.

"Wait," Bess says. "What's happening with the case?"

"I'm sorry." He shakes his head. "But this is an active homicide investigation. I can't disclose what I know."

"No fair, hot shot," Nettie growls. "We have our first homicide on the ship, and you won't share the dirty deets?"

His cheek flexes a moment. "No can do. But do me a favor, keep an eye on your surroundings. Just because I believe this was a one-off doesn't mean it is. Keep yourselves safe." His gaze shifts in my direction. "Especially you."

"Why especially me?" My heart lurches at the thought of what he might say next.

"The body was found in your suitcase. We can't rule out that you weren't being framed." His lips purse as he bores into me with those eyes. "Or if you're the killer."

He takes off before I can protest, and an entire gaggle of women is left sighing in his wake.

"How dare he," I seethe.

"*Ooh*," Nettie titters. "Nothing ratchets up the sexual tension like a little murder."

Bess ticks her head to the side. "You better believe it."

Both Nettie and I look at Bess, slack-jawed.

"What?" Bess harpoons her fork into her grapefruit. "That's a story for another day."

We resume with our breakfast, albeit at a slower pace, as thoughts of murder hang in the air around us.

Olivia Montauk was murdered.

And I've just corked up to the top of the suspect list.

CHAPTER 8

At nine on the button, the ringing of a doorbell goes off over the speakers and announces the fact the Queen's Mall is now open for duty-free shopping.

Bess, Nettie, and I each go our separate ways—Bess to the fitness center, Nettie to flop on a lounge chair on the promenade deck, while I speed off in hopes to buy a whole new wardrobe.

Deck five is where the Queen's Mall is located, and I take the mirrored elevator down, doing my best not to catch a glimpse of my reflection. With my luck, I won't have one and discover I'm a vampire at the rate things are going. Although, this day does seem to be moving in an upward trajectory—sans that whole lead suspect in a murder investigation thing.

But, then again, I haven't seen the old woman with the orange beehive, and personally, I think any day you go without seeing a disembodied spirit is a good one.

The elevator spits me out onto the luxurious marble and glass cacophony. The atrium is light and bright, and for the first time, I notice an entire row of palm trees planted just past the shops, giving this place that extra touch of the tropics.

Twinkle lights line Queen's Mall and bodies are already

bustling to and fro. I can't help but marvel at how this area of the ship makes me feel as if I've just stepped onto a ritzy street loaded with pricey specialty shops.

The marbled floors give way to cobbled thoroughfares and the street signs and streetlamps that line the shops make it feel as if I'm on Main Street back in Brambleberry, albeit on a much more extravagant level.

I'm about to head straight for the Queen's Boutique when I spot that dark-haired woman and the blonde I saw yesterday when I boarded the ship. They're huddled together, no more than six feet away, as they slowly meander in this direction.

I suck in a quick breath and scuttle behind a few overgrown banana leaves shooting from a pot half the size of my body. I'm not sure why I'm hiding, save for the fact they were a part of Olivia Montauk's entourage, and they might be talking about the murder for all I know—a murder one of them might have *committed*.

"Just don't make waves," the dark-haired woman says to the blonde as they pause within a couple of feet of me as they admire the offerings in the boutique window. "This is Olivia's last show. It has to go just right. She'll never have another one."

The blonde sniffs into a wadded-up tissue. "You're right. I'll do whatever I can to make sure things go smoothly. But I'm not going to lie, this show and life, in general, will run a lot smoother without her in it."

"You are terrible." The brunette swats the woman playfully on the arm as they take off chortling amongst themselves.

I scoff in their wake. That *was* terrible. And how dare the brunette laugh? Her behavior was equally repugnant. Clearly, they have no idea what a treasure to the art community was lost.

Without letting another distraction weigh me down, I step into the Queen's Boutique. It's light and bright and there are enough articles of clothing to cover up a nudist colony much to my delight, especially since I'm on the cusp of becoming a nudist myself.

Tank tops, T-shirts, colorful skirts, and dresses abound, and there's a glitzy jewelry counter up near the register and a section for formal gowns toward the back.

A couple of younger girls tend to the registers while that blonde I met yesterday sorts dresses on a rack.

"Elodie," I say with a little wave as I head her way. Her blonde hair is neatly coiffed back with a bright red bandana, and she's wearing a navy button-down blouse with a matching pencil skirt in keeping with the *Emerald Queen's* uniform policy.

"Well, if it isn't Trixie Troublemaker." She gives an impish grin. "I heard they found your ex-husband's body in your suitcase. I like you better already."

"It wasn't my ex. And he's not even my ex yet." I wrinkle my nose. "But believe me, I would have much preferred him over her." In less than a minute I give her a complete rundown of the events that have turned my life upside down in the last two days, starting with the nude trio I found in my bedroom eager to please my husband, the fact Handsome Ransom felt up my padded panties, and the fact I found one of my favorite artists dead in my husband's suitcase.

"So you see"—I take a deep breath— "that's why I need a whole new wardrobe and maybe a competent legal defense team."

Her eyes narrow over mine. "I say your hubby is darn lucky he's not here with you, or the odds are it might have been him in that suitcase. Hey, you're not one of those sleepwalking killers, are you? I mean, you could have gone down for a nap, drifted off into some comatose state, and killed that poor woman thinking she was your hubby or maybe one of his floozies."

"Not a chance. I didn't so much as blink for more than three seconds yesterday. I would have loved some serious sleep, but it's been a longstanding practice to deny myself anything that would be reasonable—like fresh bread and afternoon naps. And considering how things turned out, I'm grateful that I denied myself a little shut-eye. That carb-a-thon I was taking part in requires me to be horizontal for at least an hour afterward. I'll have to fit that into my schedule next time." I sigh again as I look around. "Ah, muumuus," I say, stepping over to the next rack and snapping up a white dress with red hibiscus flowers stamped all over it. "I'll take ten or twenty of these."

"Are you kidding?" She takes it from me and promptly hangs it back on the shelf. "Not unless you want to run around looking like Nettie Butterworth."

"Well, I'm not wearing jeans either. I'm determined to leave this place emulating the ship I'm standing on. Now that I don't have my husband breathing down my neck about maintaining his good image by way of my waistline, I'm going to unleash the beast and eat everything in sight."

"All right, fine. Can't say I blame you. This ship has some of the best food. I should know. This is the eleventh ship I've worked on."

"Eleventh?" I balk. Elodie looks about my age or younger. "How long have you been working on a cruise ship?"

"For the last twenty years."

"No." I laugh in disbelief.

She nods. "It's true. Let's just say I was running from my demons, literally. Anyway, I've been with the *Emerald Queen* for the last three years."

"So, Bess and Nettie beat you by a year." I bite down over my lip as I examine her. She's pretty. Scratch that, she's beautiful. I can't help but wonder if she's a part of Ransom's happy harem. "How about Ransom? How long has he been on the ship?"

"He came on board about the same time I did." She makes a face. "And yes, I'm well aware of his dashing good looks, but I haven't been bitten, mostly by choice. That man has gone after every pretty thing that shakes her tail at him. I have a strict no playboy policy."

"You're not into playboys?" A sense of relief fills me, and I don't know why.

"I *am* a playboy—*girl*." She winks. "Ransom and I are essentially the same in that respect. I like to do the hunting." She pulls back and takes me in. "You have a crush on him."

"No," I'm quick to deny it. "I swear I don't." I take the dress back off the rack and shove it at her. "Ten of these, please." I'll take ten of anything to change the subject right about now.

"Not on your life," she says, taking it from me once again. "You need something gauzy, something that clings to you a little, something sexy that I know Ransom Baxter will enjoy taking off."

"*Elodie.*" I laugh as she spins around and plucks a white gauzy number off the rack behind her. It's long, holds the promise of holding to the curves I'm eager to acquire, and has a scoop neckline and capped sleeves.

"I love it."

"I have this dress in seven solids and four prints. It's one size fits all." She averts her eyes. "I don't approve of that sizing. Do you approve of the price?" She turns the tag around so I can see it.

"Hmm." I shrug. "A little spendy, but I love nothing more than spending my newly minted ex's money. Give me one in all the colors and prints, and I'll need underwear, bras, something for formal nights, a few light jackets, maybe a skirt and a thin sweater, too. I hereby give you permission to spend his money for me."

My phone beeps and I look down to see a message in the group chat from Stanton.

I bought tickets for you to fly home from Oahu. Enough is enough. Your little tantrum is over, Trix. Don't be a witch about this.

This is the group chat! I gasp. What a dodo.

The dancing ellipses pop up and Abbey sends a text. **Mom? Are you on the ship alone? Dad? What the heck is going on?**

Parker pops into the group chat. **I'm about to hit the pillow. Is there something I should know about?**

"Oh no," I groan as I close my eyes for a moment.

"Hey"—Elodie leans in—"is everything okay?"

"No, actually." I take a ragged breath. "Everything is a disaster. Elodie, would you mind picking out a few more things for me? I think I need to get some air."

"Don't you worry. I'll get everything listed and send it straight to your room."

She jots down my cabin number and everything from my bra to my shoe size and I sail right out of the boutique as if the walls were about to close in on me.

I quickly tap my fingers over my phone. **Abbey, Parker, things are not ideal at the moment, but I'm safe and I promise everything will be fine.** I hit send, hoping I didn't just spout off a lie to my children. **I just need a minute, but I will give you more details very soon.** I hit send again then get straight to typing out a private message for Stanton.

You are a moron! I hit send one final time and the tears start flowing right here in the middle of a faux cobbled street that feels more like an alternate universe—and thanks to Stanton I'll be living in an alternate universe for a long time to come.

"Trixie?" a deep voice says softly from behind and I turn to see Captain Crawford in his uniform, with dark stripes over his white dress shirt. "Hey"—he pulls me in and instinctively I wrap my arms around him as I try my best not to break out into an all-out sob. "What's going on? Is this about what happened last night?"

"No." I wipe my face down and shake my head. "Not at all. I'm having trouble back home, and it just compounded itself. I'm sorry. You're a busy man. I shouldn't unload on you."

"Are you kidding?" he balks.

There's a genuine sense of caring that pours from him. And it doesn't hurt that he's handsome as hell himself. What is it with this ship and its surplus of handsome men, anyway? His soft brown eyes take me in as he brushes a tear from my face.

"I don't mind in the least," he says. "How about coffee? My treat." He winks as he says it just as his phone bleats and he glances down. "On second thought, it looks as if the authorities need to speak with me about the body." He sighs. "I'd better take care of this. How about a rain check?"

"I would love that." I bite down on a smile and pull him in for another quick embrace. I can't help it, I've always been a hugger.

He pulls me in tight and from over his left arm I catch Ransom looking lean and mean in his suit, hands in his pockets, his features hardened as he looks our way.

"We'll talk soon," Captain Crawford says as he gives me a pat over the back and takes off.

I move in the direction I just saw Ransom standing, but he's vanished with the efficiency of an apparition.

"How's it going?" a voice trills to my right.

"Speaking of apparitions," I say as I grab ahold of the perky poltergeist's elbow, and darn it if she doesn't feel real. "You're coming with me."

CHAPTER 9

"Where are you taking me?" the older woman howls.

"The real question is, where are you taking my sanity?"

We stumble into my cabin to find the bed made and a bunny fashioned out of a towel sitting square in the center of it. The ocean glitters like liquid sapphires outside my window as I lock us inside.

"Who are you and what do you want?" I hiss at her without meaning to.

Her lips knot up on one side as she frowns my way. "My name is Maltadora Radcliff, but you can call me Malora." She traipses over to the desk and inspects it for dust with her finger.

She's dressed head to toe in the same green velvet jacket and skirt I saw her in yesterday, and seeing that repeating your wardrobe staples is a common malady around here, I can't fault her for it.

"So, you're really dead?" I ask.

"Oh yes." She nods my way, and that orange beehive hovers over her head like a dust storm as it wobbles. Her lips are painted the same color as her tresses. A peach ruffled blouse peeks out from under her jacket, and it matches the rouge circles staining her cheeks. "I guess you could say I've been to paradise and back." She leans in. "And believe me, I'd like to go back. But from what I understand, I've been sent to help bring Olivia's killer to justice."

"Really?" I marvel at the odd thought. "So, you knew the deceased?"

"Oh, heavens yes. She was my neighbor years ago. Just a little wee one then, but she'd come over and I'd read her a story and she'd call me Granny. Her folks were never home, and from what I could tell not very interested in their brood. I took all the Farris kids in as if they were my own. That was her maiden name, Farris. But my son put me in a home for the aged, and I don't know whatever became of the Farrises... well, except for Olivia. We both know what happened to *her*."

"Okay, wait, let me get this straight. You knew Olivia as a child. And eventually, you passed away, and now you're back to help solve her crime?"

"Yes," she says, walking over to the mini fridge and helping herself to a pack of peanut M&M's. "Oh, these were my favorite." She offers me one and I take it.

She pops a few in her mouth and crunches away.

"How exactly are you eating?" I marvel. "And why do you feel so solid to the touch?" I give her arm a few pokes, and sure enough, she feels soft and doughy.

"I can feel as solid as I like," she says before her body begins to dissipate into a translucent state and a smattering of miniature green stars spray all around her.

"Wow," I say, stepping back and the room spins slightly. "I'm suddenly feeling light-headed."

"Oh dear, don't faint." She comes into focus once again and it's not unappreciated. "There's nothing to fear in death. I'm still me. Although, I don't care much for the planet anymore. Paradise is well, *paradise*." She frowns my way. "Which is exactly why I need to get back. Now how do we solve this crime?"

"I'm afraid you've mistaken me for Ransom Baxter. He's in charge of the investigation as far as I know."

"No, no, I'm afraid it doesn't work that way. I was specifically assigned to help *you*. It's happened before, although not to me. Other souls have been sent back to help with an investigation or two themselves. And from what I understand, the connection comes from the fact that the deceased, in our case Olivia, has a fondness for me. Apparently, she loved me quite dearly and whoever the poor soul loved with all their heart, that person—or more often than not, their old *pet*—comes back to aid in the effort. Of course, they would have had to have crossed the veil for that to happen. And I meet the requirements."

She opens her mouth and pours the rest of the M&M's into her mouth, masticates for less than a second, and puts in a heroic effort to swallow them down. She gags for a moment and jerks and jolts before cupping her neck and flailing.

"Malora!" I shout as I turn her around and do my best to give her the Heimlich.

"Kidding!" she sings as she floats to the bed. "I can't choke. For goodness' sake, I can't even breathe. Now tell me a little about yourself. I've got about five minutes to kill before they put out the lunch buffet on the lido deck."

"Fine," I say and proceed to tell her all about my newly single debacle, Stanton's idiotic way of filling our children in on the disaster that's taking place in our lives, and my wardrobe dilemma that was recently solved.

"Fascinating," she trills as she inspects me from head to foot. "After I finish up with lunch, I'll see about haunting your husband. But don't you worry. I'll be back in plenty of time for your investigation," she says as she quickly grows translucent.

"My investigation? I don't have one."

"Well, you'll have to solve the crime." Her voice warbles from some unknown destination. "Or else you'll go to prison."

"I can't serve hard time," I shout into the ether.

"Well then, we have a little work to do, don't we? Until then!" She evaporates in a shower of miniature stars, and just like that, I'm all alone in my cabin once again.

Wonderful. Not only did I find the body, but now I have to find the killer.

Here's hoping I don't get killed in the process.

Speaking of killing, my clothes arrive, and I change into a gauzy yellow dress and head up to the promenade where I promptly find a cozy lounge chair, curl up next to the expansive blue Pacific, and research how to start up a blog. The air is both briny and balmy and I take in a much-needed cleansing breath in hopes to soothe my weary soul. The tension in my shoulders relaxes a bit and I feel alive, healthy, dare I say happy—sans that whole murder, divorce, ghost thing.

At least three different articles give me all the tips and tricks I need to get things going for my perspective blog. They all stress the fact I need to add a copious amount of hashtags to each post and recommend sharing a link of my new blog to relevant groups on the internet.

With just a few clicks on my phone, I've got *Suddenly Single—What a Trip!* up and running. I chose one of the freebie templates the site offered, with a dark background and sandy beach with crystal clear waters lapping over the shore as the picture for my header, and I dive right into penning my very first post.

A waiter walks by with a tray full of tropical fruity drinks and offers me a complimentary refreshment, no alcohol, but I can make up for lost vodka later.

I take a few delicious sips from the frozen concoction then dive right into my new quasi-literary venture. I can't wait to bare my soul—sans any talk of ghosts, suspect lists, or dead bodies, of course.

Hello! My name is Trixie Troublefield. So glad you stopped by! Not only am I suddenly single, but I'm spending the next eighteen days in the South Pacific. And since my cheating soon-to-be ex isn't along to enjoy the ride, I'm taking you with me.

The Emerald Queen of the Seas *is not only the grandest cruise ship I've ever been on, but she's the only cruise ship I've ever been on. Why in the world did I wait so long to take such a grand adventure?*

I give them a rundown on all the culinary masterpieces I've indulged in so far and even let them know how nice the crew is.

Thinking on it for a minute, I delete the word *nice* and replace it with the word *hot*. I hashtag the post with as many relevant terms as I can think of before hitting publish. Then I take the link to my shiny new pet project and share it in every divorce, travel, and I-hate-my-cheating-spouse group on the internet.

Here's hoping someone gets a kick out of it.

The ocean beckons my attention, and I sip my fruity concoction as I stare out the glass barrier between me and the grand sea that sprawls out infinitely before me.

What would Stanton think if he saw my thoughts on the hot crew aboard the *Emerald Queen of the Seas*?

I guess there's only one way to find out.

My fingers glide over my phone once again and I shoot him a link to my shiny new venture.

I take another sip of my fruity drink and relax like never before.

It takes exactly two minutes before my phone pings and I glance down to see exactly what he thinks.

You'll regret this.

I text right back.

No, Stanton. YOU will regret this.

And I'll make sure of it.

CHAPTER 10

Dinner in the main dining room is glorious.

I pulled on a red breezy dress that manages to look fabulous and yet remains comfortable to wear, a fashion feat in and of itself. Ransom couldn't make it to dinner, and Bess said it probably had to do with the case because he never misses a meal with his girls—his girls being Bess and Nettie.

The ice carving of the night is a giant hibiscus flower backlit in a wash of red and pink, and coupled with the Hawaiian music, it really feels as if we're crossing over into the tropics.

Dinner is as follows: almond-crusted fried Brie for the starter because the new me apparently runs off fried cheese, along with bone-in ribeye broiled just enough—something the old me would have found sacrilegious. But I'm glad to tell the old me that my chicken breast days are over. It's dark meat, *red* meat, and maybe even *raw* meat if I get the chance.

For dessert, I indulge in a toffee cheesecake that I wouldn't mind hunting down later and having another slice of—or six.

We wrap it up and Bess leads the way to the theater.

"You're going to love the show tonight," Bess assures me. "The cast is putting on *Grease*."

"*Grease*? The musical?" I marvel at the thought. "Wow, that's one of my favorite movies. I'm going to love every minute of it. I can't remember the last time I went to see a musical. Stanton wasn't exactly a fan."

"Bup bup!" Nettie waves a finger my way. "He shall not be mentioned by name. Don't you know calling someone's name out loud stirs up the forces of darkness until they deliver them to your feet?"

Bess grunts, "Robert Redford, Robert Redford, Robert Redford," she says as we head toward a glitzy hall with a sign showcasing tonight's musical number and already I'm excited. "Well, I don't see him." She looks my way. "I may have just disproved Nettie's wonky theory. Don't worry, it's not like he's going to pop up like a ghost."

I cringe at the thought. "Speaking of ghosts, I think I may have hit my head harder than I thought the other day."

"Are you seeing ghosts?" Nettie sounds both envious and terrified.

"Only a little?" I make a face because I'm pretty sure admitting as much qualifies you for a visit from the men with big nets.

Bess chuckles. "You're not seeing ghosts. This place has a mirror inside a mirror. Believe me, I know the feeling. My first week on the ship I thought I had a stalker and it turns out it was me."

We enter the spacious theater and I take a breath at its majesty. It stands three stories tall with black velvet curtains ensconcing a stage large enough to accommodate any Broadway production, and the plush crimson seats are filling in quickly. The carpets are dark forest green, and there's enough brass lining the rails and stairways to fashion seventy-six trombones for every person here. From the ceiling blooms an elegant chandelier the circumference of a swimming pool as it glitters under the duress of its own light.

Nettie leans my way. "You see any ghosts?"

I give a quick visual sweep of the room. "No, but the night is young yet."

We're about to step deeper inside when I glance back in the hall and spot that dark-haired woman I saw earlier today talking about Olivia with that blonde. She has her hair pinned back on one side, and has a red dress on that looks as if it was melted onto her body. For reasons unknown to me, I can't seem to fight the urge to speak with her.

"Save a seat for me, will you?" I ask. "I'll be back in a minute."

Bess points out the row they like to camp out in, and I take note before ducking back into the crowded hall. It's like trying to swim upstream as I forge my way against the grain, but the woman is standing near a small concession stand and I catch her just as she collects a frozen red concoction reminiscent of the one I had this afternoon. I have no idea how to broach the subject of the dead with her, so I do what comes naturally, I bump into her and pretend to be horrified.

"I'm so sorry," I say, holding out my hands. "You didn't spill your drink, did you?"

"Nope." She holds it up victoriously. "I'm good."

"Hey, didn't we meet yesterday while boarding?"

She blinks back. "Are you with the ship? I'm sorry, I met so many people. I'm here as a part of a team. We're doing an art show in a few days."

A spray of green miniature stars appears from my left as Malora materializes in all her velvet glory.

"You know what they say"—Malora elbows me and I try not to react— "the show must go on."

I choose to ignore the disembodied among us for a moment as I look at the brunette. "So, you're still doing the show? I mean, I sort of heard what happened to that poor girl."

She takes a quick breath before glancing over her shoulder. "You *know*? They're going to make an announcement in one of the newsletters. Oh, it was awful. Olivia and I have been friends for years."

"Friends?" Malora lifts a brow. "Or enemies?"

I make a face. She's got a point but a distracting one at that.

"My name is Trixie Troublefield." I hold out my hand and the brunette gives it a shake.

"Isabella Bessinger. I'm—or I *was* Olivia Montauk's agent. She was supposed to be doing a showing here. And well, her husband thought it would be a waste to let all her beautiful pieces sit in storage, so we've decided to go ahead with it—as sort of a tribute to her."

"Well, that's very sweet. Do you paint?"

"Me?" she balks at the thought. "I'm no artist. I can hardly coordinate my clothing, let alone colors. How about you?" She quickly knocks the ball in my court.

"Oh yes. I paint myself, so of course, I'll be there. In fact, I used to keep up with Olivia. You can't imagine my surprise when I found out she was on the ship."

Malora nods. "And an even greater surprise once you discovered she was in your husband's suitcase." She swipes a finger through Isabella's drink before shoving it into her mouth and moaning with delight.

"Well, she's *still* on the ship." Isabella shrugs. "Temporarily, of course. They're taking her to the morgue once we arrive in Oahu. But since the show isn't scheduled until we head back to port, the rest of her entourage and I have decided to stay on and make sure the show goes as planned. We're all devastated." She winks as she takes a sip of her drink, and I can't help but frown.

Malora balks, "She's not all that broken up about it, is she? Ask her why she wrapped her hands around the girl and snuffed the life out of her."

I shake my head just enough. "Isabella, I heard they found her stuffed in a suitcase. Is there anyone in your entourage she was having difficulty with? Who would do such a thing to her?"

The woman takes a deep breath and the seams on her dress threaten to burst.

"I don't know. But I doubt it was someone in the entourage at all. Olivia has fans all around the world. And she has a creeper or two. Who's to say they didn't book a ticket? She always has her events laid out on her website. I bet they found it and showed up just to do the deed."

"I guess that's a possibility." I shudder at the thought.

I just started a blog. What if I get a creeper or two and they show up to stuff me in a suitcase?

"Don't go dark on me," Malora says as she butts into my shoulder. "I can tell you're internalizing. There's no time for that, we've got a suspect to grill."

I bite down over my lip. "Isabella, did you see anything out of place last night? I mean, you were probably with her for most of it."

She shakes her head. "That would be Amanda Charming, her public relations assistant. Blonde, about yea high." She holds a hand to her forehead. "It was her job to mind Olivia—sort of like a paid babysitter."

"And how about Olivia's husband?" I ask. "Is he here?"

She gives a quick nod. "That would be Dave. He's having a rough go of it, as you can imagine. But he's staying on for her final showing. He said he'd like to do something special for her while surrounded by all her pieces. I'm sure it will be quite sweet." She darts a glance past me. "It looks as if they're closing the doors. We'd better get in there if we don't want to miss it." She lifts her drink my way. "I'll look for you at the art show. Have a great time on the cruise."

"You, too," I say as she takes off.

"Well?" Malora huddles in close. "What do you think?"

"I think we need to speak with Olivia's glorified babysitter. She might—" I stop short when I see a tall man in a dark suit looking like a demigod about to conquer every woman in the vicinity—or let's be honest, they'd like to be conquered by him. And sure enough, every last straggler with a pair of functioning ovaries is craning her neck to get a better look at him.

"What's caught your eye?" Malora turns that way and groans. "My, *my*, he is a looker. Why don't you see about pulling him into a dark corner? That ought to teach your husband a lesson or two. Or better yet, teach the looker a lesson or two." She begins to evaporate in that shower of miniature stars that seems to accompany her. "Oh, and I forgot to mention, Stanton nearly fell down the stairs when I began knocking down picture frames in your bedroom. He thought it was an earthquake. I really need to step up my haunting game."

And with that, Malora Radcliff is no more, and if she steps up her haunting game, Stanton may be no more as well.

"Trixie," Ransom says my name as he steps in close. His eyes ride up and down my body and I can feel it as distinctly as if he was touching me. "I see you found yourself a new wardrobe. You look…stunning," he says that last part under his breath as if it wasn't meant for me at all.

"Thank you." My cheeks heat. "I'd say you clean up nice yourself, but I've never seen you looking anything less than impeccable." Shockingly sexy is more like it, but I'll keep the commentary to myself for now.

"That's very kind of you." He tips his head to the side. "I believe I owe you some lava cake. How about we head to the lido deck and you tell me all about the conversation you just had with that woman." He looks at me sternly, and I can't help but feel I'm about to be reprimanded. "I've got a few questions I'd like to ask."

I nod his way.

Lava cake, Handsome Ransom, and an active homicide investigation—three things I never thought I'd crave, and yet here I am, hungry as can be.

"Lead the way, Detective," I say. "I'll tell you anything you want to know."

Unless, of course, he wants to know about ghosts—in that case, he'll have to get his own disembodied spirit. Malora Radcliff is my dirty little supernatural secret.

Good luck trying to get that out of me, Detective. He'd have better luck taking off my shiny new underwear. And if he's lucky, he just might get the chance.

CHAPTER 11

"You see ghosts?" Ransom Baxter's brows hike a notch as we sit across from one another in the pleasantly dimmed Blue Water Café.

Who knew the buffet on the lido deck could provide such romantic ambiance?

Have I mentioned how scrumptious the lava cake is?

As soon as we arrived, Ransom took us straight over to an entire section dedicated to this amazing, ooey, gooey dessert, which is warm, melted chocolate buried in a warm, luscious, dark chocolate cake. Each lava wonder sits snug in a ramekin no bigger than a few inches, which would explain why we grabbed four apiece. Yes, four. And sadly, I'm on that fourth one right now.

"Of course, I don't see ghosts. It's my go-to answer whenever anyone asks me if I killed a woman I've never even met."

Ransom's first question out the gate was just that—asking me if I killed a woman, point-blank. He said he was obligated to ask as a part of the investigation, but that's beside the point. So, I blurted out that I didn't do it—but maybe the ghost that's traveling with me felt compelled to do the deed herself. And my goodness, if the fact I'm hopped up on carbs and sugar didn't have something to do with the otherworldly confessional. If Ransom wanted to lead me to his room, I doubt I'd be able to refuse, and I'm not so sure the carbs and sugar would be to blame either.

I lean in a notch. "How did she die, anyway?"

"Strangulation." He's back to frowning at me.

"Well, there you go. I don't have the stomach or the strength to strangle anyone, so you can wipe me off your suspect list."

His lips curve a notch as a curious look grows on his face. "Not even your husband?"

"He happens to be an exception," I say. "And I don't think a jury in the land would convict me for that."

"You'd be surprised. Which brings me to my next question. Do you think Olivia Montauk knew your husband?"

"As in she was one of his floozies? Nope. Besides, Isabella just told me that Olivia was married. Did you know that her husband is on this ship? I say we shake him down for all he knows. I mean, the poor guy is grieving, but surely he must know something. The woman is dead. Clearly, someone had a problem with her—about who knows what. Hey? Maybe she was cheating on him? Maybe *he* was cheating on *her*? I bet if we look, we'll find him in the casino with a floozie of his own sitting on his lap."

His brows dip low as his frustration only seems to deepen.

"Trixie," he growls out my name, and an explosion of heat filters through me. I've never quite heard my name growled out in that manner before, and I'll be darned if I'm not craving to hear it again. "You will not go looking for Mr. Montauk. Yes, I'm well aware he's on this ship. But this is my investigation and I'm going to handle it. The safest thing you can do is steer clear if you see either him or Isabella. I don't want you mixed up in this any more than you already are."

Now it's my turn to frown. "All right, fine. But since it's your investigation, I've got a few nuggets I think you should know about."

I fill him in on the fact Olivia was in front of me when we boarded the ship, the fact the gray-haired man was holding her, and that I think she had eyes for the big, beefy wall of muscles that was with her, too. I let him know that I saw the gray-haired man and Isabella arguing that day—and while they were tussling, Olivia was *hustling*, embracing the aforementioned big, beefy wall of muscles. And I also tell him the fact that the last time I saw Olivia alive was when that blonde carted her off by the elbow.

"You saw all of that?" He looks amused and a tad bit morbidly alarmed.

"And then some. This afternoon in front of the Queen's Boutique—" I stop short because something else happened in front of the Queen's Boutique that I don't want to remind him of—and I'm not sure why it matters to me if Ransom saw me in Captain Crawford's arms or not, but I digress. "Anyway, the blonde? Turns out, her name is Amanda Charming. She was Olivia's public relations assistant." I tell him all about how I saw her and Isabella walking by and heard Amanda say that life would run a whole lot smoother without Olivia in it.

He inches back, his eyes flitting to the corner of the room as his thoughts run rampant.

"Thank you for letting me know. And I can't state it enough, if you see any one of those people, Trixie, you should walk in the opposite direction."

I scoff at the thought. "If you think they're so dangerous, why don't you arrest them all?"

His cheek flinches. "We can't rush the process or we risk missing out on who the killer might be altogether. I've already spoken to Dave, Olivia's husband, and Craig, her security detail."

"*Ooh*, is Craig Mr. Muscles?"

He nods and manages to glower while doing it. "I mean it, Trixie. Stay away from them."

"I will," I say it lower than a whisper.

"Trixie," a deep voice calls out from my right in a jovial manner, and I look up to see Captain Crawford heading this way, in a navy suit with a glowing white dress shirt underneath. His hair is slicked back and he looks more than happy to see me. He glances over at Ransom and that smile glides right off his face. "I see you have company."

Ransom's chest expands as he looks my way. "We were just finishing up." He nods. "Thank you for your time, Mrs. Troublefield." His eyes linger on mine for a moment, and I can feel the burn long after he rises from his seat. He doesn't say another word before heading for the exit.

"Captain Crawford." I force a smile as he falls into the seat in front of me.

"Please, call me Wes," he says.

"Wes?" I tease and I take another bite out of my lava cake.

Captain Crawford is sweet and handsome, and perhaps a lot less edgy than Ransom Baxter. And he has that whole man-in-power thing going on. It's hard for me to believe he's not taken.

"Weston," he says. "Is everything okay?" His countenance reflects his concern.

"Everything is fine. I mean, it's not really fine. My husband cheated on me and I'm staring down the barrel of an entire string of divorce attorneys—but all in good time." My shoulders hike a moment. "My soon-to-be ex, the one I left behind in Maine, he sort of dropped the separation bomb on our children. They're both in college, a boy and a girl. Do you have any kids?"

"Two sons, Owen and Carter. Twenty-four and twenty-three. Owen is headed to med school and Carter is headed to law school."

"Wow." I can't help but laugh. "That is really impressive. You're impressive." I toast him with my fork before finishing up my last bite of this lava dream. "So, tell me something about yourself."

"I'm from Maine as well," he says with a smile. "Ballast Bay."

"Hey, that's really close to Castle Point, where Ransom is from."

His features darken as if on cue, and I wrinkle my nose.

"Why do I get the feeling there's some serious tension between the two of you?"

He hitches his head to the side and chuckles. "That's because you're intuitive. Nothing serious, and certainly nothing worthy of mentioning." He frowns so hard, for a second I think he's glaring at me. "Tinsley tells me you'll be helping with the art show." A slight smile curves his lips once again.

Whatever is going on between Ransom and Wes is clearly a fresh wound. They can't stand each other from what I can tell. I'm shocked they're on the same ship.

"Just the crafts class. And I'm happy to do it. Oh, and I'm blogging now." I pull out my phone in a spurt of energy and pull it up. "What in the—" My mouth falls open as my thumb scrolls over the screen. "It says here I have over six hundred comments. That can't be possible. I just published my first post less than six hours ago."

"Can I see?"

"Sure." I hand him the phone and his brows hike in amusement as he reads my post. "This is gold, Trixie." He shakes his head. "My ex would be cheering you on. Only I didn't cheat." He says that last bit under his breath. "Didn't seem to matter, though." He scrolls down. "These comments look like the real deal. No spam detected. It looks as if you're on your way to blogger stardom." He gives a playful wink as he slides my phone back.

"I guess that's lucky for me *and* for you. I plan on doing less husband bashing and far more praising of the *Emerald Queen*. You have a magnificent vessel here—not to mention the ocean, the food, the duty-free shopping, tropical ports of call, the molten lava cake, which is in a category all on its own."

"I happen to agree with you."

And just like that, we start in on a pleasant conversation that lasts well into the night.

"Just hearing about your seafaring adventures makes me want to underscore the fact you are one lucky seadog," I tell him. "I could get used to this, you know."

He nods. "You should. You could complete Bess and Nettie. You'd make a fabulous trio and that way we'd get to have more lava cake in the lido deck." He points to the empty ramekins we've amassed since he's arrived. As soon as the staff saw the captain sitting here without anything to nosh on, he asked what I wanted and the lava cake has been flowing all night. "We reposition about every three months, so it's never boring. We're headed up to Alaska in late spring."

"From the tropics to the fjords? You might be able to sway me. Although I'm pretty sure by then I'll have a very fixed income. I'll have to figure out how to survive financially to a ripe old age, and I doubt a fancy cruise ship will be in the budget."

"I'm sorry," he growls as if he were angry about it.

"No. I'm sorry," I say, giving his hand a quick pat then quickly pull away. I've taken far too many liberties with the man already.

"Well, Trixie, I hope you're hungry." He waggles his brows, and for a second, I think the captain himself has just propositioned me, and to be honest, I don't know that I would turn him down. Darn carbs and sugar high.

In fact, I might just shoot off a few pictures of the two of us while in the throes of passion and send them to Stanton. If he could have a slipup in both the coital and texting department, so can I.

"I'm not sure how hungry I am, but I am certainly up for a culinary challenge," I say. "What do you have in mind?"

That devious gleam in his eyes makes me think I may be right back on the menu.

"Everything," he says as he helps me out of my seat and leads the way to the third deck, the same deck where my cabin is located. This isn't really going to morph into a one-night stand, is it?

I mean, on the outside, Wes seems like a genuinely nice guy. And have I mentioned he's the captain?

But then again, plenty of psychos have held grand positions before—I'm running off an assumption. And really? Would shaking the sheets with this handsome man really be the worst thing that could happen? I bet he'd let me wear his hat all the while, although at the moment not even *he* is wearing his hat.

But once we get off the glittering elevator, where we populated it with a disturbing echo of our reflections, he doesn't lead me in the direction of my cabin. Instead, he threads his arm through mine and leads me with his head held high as we enter the main dining room where a grand party seems to be taking place.

Jazz music plays over the speakers as throngs of people circulate around the grandest spread of culinary fare I have ever witnessed. And the carvings! Not only are they made of food—chocolate dolphins, watermelon transformed into exotic flowers—there's even a large *lard* sculpture of a pig in the middle of it all. But the real showstopper is what looks to be miles and miles of both hot and cold dishes, everything from burgers to a freshly carved prime rib. They've even got the eggs benedict I missed out on this morning.

Wes and I indulge in any and everything our hearts and stomachs desire.

But all the while Ransom Baxter haunts the back of my mind as sure as if he was an apparition.

And he's one ghost I can't seem to shake.

CHAPTER 12

The next few sea days fly by in a flurry of buffets, midnight buffets, musicals—a cabaret and *Beauty and the Beast*—dizzying nights drowning my sorrows in molten lava cake, and thankfully a small reprieve from Malora Radcliff. And unfortunately for me, it's mostly been a reprieve from Ransom as well. I did see him at dinner, but he refused to discuss the case. He's not off the hook by a long shot. I plan on wearing Ransom down before we ever dock back in LA—regarding the case, of course.

I've logged an amazing amount of hours on the promenade deck with my e-reader catching up on books I never thought I'd have time to read. It's been tough keeping my eyes glued to the proverbial page because every few minutes it seems as if we are passing a pod of dolphins. It's been one magical moment after the other.

And you can bet the last dollar I'm going to swipe from Stanton that I blogged to my heart's content. Who knew divorcees would be so eager to connect with the like-minded and equally disgruntled?

Each day as we inch our way toward the South Pacific, the

weather has grown increasingly warmer and that much more humid. Surprisingly, I don't mind the humidity. It feels like a hug, and right now I'd take a nice, strong hug from anywhere I can get it.

But, for now, all thoughts of the case have been cast aside. It's our first day in Hawaii and I could hardly wait to open my eyelids this morning. The first thing I do is scoot to my window—and wow—I'm transfixed by everything I see.

First and foremost, Oahu, the island we're visiting first, surprisingly has a big city appeal with all of its high-rises, major highways, and bustle of humanity, but just past the glittering towers stand emerald green mountains and sheer hillsides that are covered with translucent gray clouds. But despite the patchy precipitation that seems to hug the greenery as if they were old friends, it's bright and sunny out and I can't wait to set my feet on Hawaiian soil.

Since I've never been before, Bess and Nettie told me they'd give me a condensed tour of all their favorite things to do on the island. And since the ship is docked here for two days, we'll have plenty of time to do them.

This morning, Elodie sent three bathing suits to my room—red, white, and black—each a one-piece with a tiny skirt attached, all of them exceptionally pricey. She's much better at spending my husband's money than I ever was. Props to her for that.

I choose the red one and toss a red gauzy dress over it that ties in the front, so if I get too hot, I can open the front and grab the sunscreen she sent down along with it. As soon as I'm ready for the day, I hightail it to the lido deck for a quick bite. There's not a chance I'd eschew the gargantuan breakfasts I've grown accustomed to.

Bess and Nettie already indulged while I was getting ready, and we're due to meet up at the atrium to disembark and begin our tropical adventure.

For the first time since we've left Los Angeles, I have a rather demur breakfast comparatively of lox and bagel—more than a few pancakes slathered with butter and syrup. At this point, I'm not sure what would happen to my body if I denied it its daily sugar intake at regular intervals.

And once I'm through, I waddle straight to the atrium. The elevators open and I'm glad to see it's not all that crowded. The ship has been offloading passengers for over an hour, and Bess and Nettie recommended we wait at least this amount of time to miss the chaos.

I spot Captain Crawford near the exit as he sets pale yellow leis on the passengers as they take off for the day. Clinging on his left is Tinsley, and Elodie stands to his right as she passes out pamphlets to anyone who wants them.

Bess and Nettie pop up, waving and skipping as if we were about to head to a party. They're both dressed in colorful dresses, a green shift for Bess and a floral muumuu for Nettie with coral and blue hibiscus flowers.

Nettie pulls me close by the arm. "Are you ready to get *leid* by the captain?"

I laugh at her very purposeful double entendre. "I guess I am."

"I'll take pictures for you," Bess volunteers, and I give her my phone.

We head over, and Elodie seems to be biting down on a smile.

The closer we get to the open maw of the exit, the increasingly hotter and far more humid it grows. It feels as if we've been thrust into a dryer with a load of wet towels and yet I find the blue skies and the floral scent of the tropics energizing.

Elodie steps in close and whispers, "Rumors are swirling."

"About?" My eyes widen a notch because I might have an iota of an idea. Let's just say more than a few heads turned when I showed up on the arm of Captain Crawford that night at the midnight buffet.

"We'll talk later." She shakes her head my way and buttons her lips. "You go have a great time."

"I will," I say as Captain Crawford holds up a lei my way.

"Trixie Troublefield, you are next," he says as I step in and he lands the perfumed wreath around my neck.

"Oh my word," I say as I inhale deeply and pick up the delicate butter-yellow blooms. "What in the world are these? They smell divine."

"Plumerias," he says with a pained smile. "You've really been missing out. We'll have to make up for lost time."

Tinsley clears her throat. "A tour of the island should fix that up. Why don't I book Mrs. Troublefield the deluxe package on the house? I'll have her so scheduled she'll hardly have time to miss a thing." She snarls at me as she says that last half.

I bet she'd love to schedule me to the hilt.

Bess scoffs. "You do that and Nettie and I will never see her again." She shakes her head my way. "Don't take her up on it. Not only is it exhausting, but you have to schedule your potty breaks."

I make a face. My bladder has a mind of its own these days. If anything, I schedule life around *it*.

"*No one* will have time to see you," Elodie says it sternly before giving Tinsley the side-eye. "And I'm sure some people would love it that way."

"I'm fine." I shake my head at Tinsley. "But thank you. And I'm very excited to teach the upcoming art class. In fact, I can't wait to do it." I look up at Captain Crawford. "I'm hoping to pick up a few art supplies for myself this afternoon."

"I hope you find what you're looking for," he says. "I'd offer to give the grand tour myself, but I'll be meeting with city officials as soon as this wraps up. How about a rain check? The second one in a week."

"Well, I took you up on the first one, I don't see why I wouldn't take you up on the next."

"All right, pictures!" Bess calls out and Captain Crawford

wraps an arm around me as we smile for the camera. Bess clicks away and I turn to thank the captain just as he leans in to say something and our lips bump over one another.

"I got it!" Bess cries out.

Nettie belts out a whoop. "Not only did you get leid by the man in charge, but you snuck in a smooch. I like how you work, kid."

A low growl comes from Tinsley, but my fingers rise to my lips as I look at the captain.

"I'm so sorry," I whisper.

"It was an accident," he says. "And it was purely my fault." He glances over my shoulder and frowns. "May I help you?"

I turn that way to see Ransom glaring at us—or more to the point, glaring at Captain Crawford. Ransom's dark hair is slicked back, he's wearing a white T-shirt, jeans, a pair of sneakers, and has a pair of sunglasses clipped to his shirt. Shockingly, he looks equally as stunning in casual clothes as he does in those suits he traditionally wears.

He looks alarmingly sexy, vexingly so, and the women in line behind me are all fanning themselves twice as frenetically as they were before while they gawk his way.

"Detective," I say without meaning to. I mean, technically, he is a detective, but it sounds so cold and impersonal. Although, let's be real, we haven't spent any time together since he introduced me to lava cake. And in all honesty, lava cake and I have been having a rather intense relationship ever since.

Stanton might be noshing on naked hussies, men, in general, might come and go, but I'll always have chocolate.

"Trixie." Ransom's lips flex with a momentary smile—you blink and you miss it. "Captain." He nods. "I've got a meeting with the Honolulu Homicide Division in twenty minutes."

"I'll be there." Captain Crawford looks my way. "I'm up to my eyeballs in red tape and it'll take the next three islands for me to untangle myself from it. Maybe when we get to Kauai I can show you a few of my favorite things? Kauai is a jewel."

"Captain Crawford," I say, pressing a hand to my chest. "That would be very nice of you, thank you."

I step aside so the next people in line can have a turn at bat.

"Ransom." I head his way. "What you saw back there—that was an accident," I say, hitching a thumb back at the captain and his crew. I'm not sure why I thought I needed to bring that kiss up, but I did.

His lips twitch. "Considering it's Wes at the helm, I have no doubt." He leans in a notch. "Just know that when I kiss a woman, it is always on purpose."

Every last cell in my body catches fire with the proclamation. His eyes linger over mine and my heart does its best to evict itself right out of my chest.

"It's good to know you're deliberate in your actions." The words quiver out of me, and suddenly I regret opening my mouth. "Good luck with the investigation."

He nods. "Have fun on the island. Nettie says you're going snorkeling."

"I am?" I glance back at Nettie and Bess. "I've never been snorkeling in my life."

"I'm glad that's going to change for you." His lips purse. "I'm afraid I'm booked with the precinct for the next two days. But if you have a little time when we get to Maui, I wouldn't mind getting together. Maybe a sunrise hike? Breakfast somewhere not on the ship. We can nap on the beach afterward. Maybe grab lunch at one of their famed food trucks. We can play it by ear if you like."

My mouth falls open. "I would love that."

Sunrise with Ransom? The *beach* with Ransom? A helping of Ransom for lunch? I couldn't construct a better day if I tried.

He tips his head my way. "I'll get in touch with you tonight and give you the details. We'll have a great time." His eyes bore into mine when he says that last part just before he shoots right out the door.

We part ways and Bess, Nettie, and I start in on our adventure as the sun sears us from above.

"Come on, girls. We gotta hurry," Nettie says as she hooks her arms through ours. "Our tour bus leaves in ten minutes."

"It's your lucky day, Trixie Troublefield," Bess shouts as we do our best to sprint down the gangway.

"Luck and I don't exactly get along these days," I shout back.

"Ha!" Nettie laughs at the thought. "Says the girl who just got leid by the captain."

"And asked on a date by the hot detective," Bess adds. "Face it, Trixie. Your luck just did the hokey pokey and turned itself around."

Maybe it did.

And here's hoping it lasts.

But if the second verse is the same as the first, something tells me it won't.

I shoot Stanton that rather steamy-looking picture of Captain Crawford and me engaging in a lip-lock—accidentally as it were.

I hope he gets seasick just looking at it.

CHAPTER 13

Bess, Nettie, and I hustle down to the loading zone and soon we're seated on a plush passenger van, headed onto the main road on our way to a magical place called Hanauma Bay.

I can't tear my eyes from the window as we drive by miles of white sandy beaches. Everywhere you look people are in bathing suits and flip-flops. Every now and again you can see kids and adults alike enjoying snow cones the size of their heads in a rainbow of colors.

"Those look amazing," I say as I point to a family huddling over the treats.

"That's shave ice," Bess says. "It puts any other frozen fruity treats to shame."

Nettie nods. "We know a gal on the beach who makes them the way God intended."

Bess rolls her eyes. "We are not getting schnockered again in the middle of the afternoon. I had a hangover for days and I missed out on two islands."

Nettie makes a face. "That only happens if you're evil."

"What's evil is you trying to steal the woman's vodka."

I chuckle at the thought as the scenery grows more exotic by the second. Every few feet there's another plumeria tree covered with the same delicate blooms we have on our leis.

Before we know it, we've arrived at our destination and file out of the van after locking our valuables in a cooler with a lock. We were told the bus driver would protect it with his life, and for whatever reason, that gave me the courage I needed to step away from my phone—the only lifeline I have to my children. And sadly? If I ever did lose that modern wonder, I doubt I could contact anybody. It's been three decades and a day since I've bothered to remember anyone's phone number.

Our tour guide outfits us each with a towel, fins in our respective sizes, and a breathing apparatus before taking us to a ridge from which the entire bay down below can be seen.

"Magic," I breathe the word out as I take in the beauty of the glittering cove that sits at the bottom of a steep hillside. Hanauma Bay is filled with tourists enjoying its pale blue waters. The water is so clear near the shoreline you can see the dark outlines of the coral reef below.

"You think this is magic?" Bess ticks her head to the side. "Just wait until you see what lurks beneath the water."

"Sharks?" I ask half-heartedly, but a part of me wonders.

Nettie shakes her head. "Men in tighty-whities. Now come on, girls. We've got skivvies to inspect."

Bess rolls her eyes as we start walking down a rather steep walkway toward the beach. "Ignore her. We're not here for the skivvies. We're here for the turtles."

"Turtles?"

"Sea turtles," Bess trills as if they were her favorite kind, and I have no doubt they are.

We make it down to the bottom, strip to our bathing suits, and Bess and Nettie help me put on my flippers as we walk like a trio of ducks a few feet until the water laps over our feet.

"Oh, it's warm," I cry out, mostly from relief. As beautiful as the water looks, I hadn't planned on taking a dip this entire cruise. It seems without Stanton, I'm not only broadening my horizons, but I'm actually enjoying them, too.

"We gotta walk in backward until we're about waist deep," Nettie says, taking me by the arm as the three of us do just that. "The dark patches to our left and right are the coral reef. It's *verbatim* to stand on them."

"Verboten," Bess corrects. "And she's right."

"I'm always right," Nettie grouses.

The water hits my midsection, and I let out a yelp.

"Not so warm now, is it?" Bess brays out the laugh of an evil villain as I gasp and scream until I'm able to catch my breath once again.

"All right"—Nettie says as she holds out her mask— "this is where it gets *Trixie*." She winks my way with the play on my name. "Go ahead and spit in your mask and wipe it around the lens with your fingers." She proceeds to demonstrate.

"Don't listen to her," Bess says. "These masks have already been wiped down with an antifog solution. Just put it on and put this doohickey in your pie hole." She points to the mouthpiece. "Remember—no breathing through your nose. We need you in shipshape for the luau tonight."

"Luau?"

"That's right," Bess says, plopping on her mask. "The cultural center puts on the best show in town, and the food is amazing. They have a six-island village we'll explore beforehand and the dancers will knock your socks off."

"You'll even get to see a volcano in action—albeit a safe and sane version. Bess and I always hit the show when the ship docks on the island."

"Well then, I can't wait to see it." I look out at all the snorkels sticking out of the water and my stomach does a flip-flop. "I'm not so sure I can do this."

Bess waves me off. "If we can do it, anyone can do it." She

helps me put my mask on just as a wave tries its best to thrust us toward shore. "Go ahead and put your head in the water and start breathing."

"Head in water, start breathing," I say as I shove my face in the water and open my eyes to a whole new world. A school of tiny gray minnows swims by followed by a pale blue triangular fish with yellow stripes. I try to alert Bess and Nettie to the tiny cutie when I come up for air.

"What are you doing?" Bess calls out as she does the same.

"I can't breathe," I shout as I gasp and gulp for oxygen as if I just escaped a burning building.

"Yes, you can," Bess shouts back. "We've got to get out farther if we want to see the real show. You can do it, Trixie. I believe in you."

"Stan the Cheatin' Man probably wouldn't." Nettie gives me the side-eye as she says it.

"Way to weaponize my ex into a dare, Ms. Butterworth," I say, snapping back on my mask. "All right, let's give it another go."

And another go, and another go as I kick, flail, and scream, trying to convince myself to breathe underwater.

I can't help it. It's not like I'm trying to be resistive. It's unnatural to breathe underwater. And just as I'm about to let Stanton win this imaginary war, I do it. I take a breath through my mouth and don't accidentally drown myself in the process. Once my heart rate slows to a trot, I start to relax.

Bess leads the way as we pass every colorful fish imaginable, orange fish with stripes, rainbow-colored fish, spotted boxfish—my personal favorite—fish with long snouts, fish with huge lips that today's girls pay good cash money for. Entire schools of yellow and blue fish flutter before us in what looks like a perfectly choreographed underwater ballet.

Bess begins to flap her arm and point hard to our left, and I look over just as a sea turtle the size of a coffee table floats this way.

Nettie howls while doing her best to clap underwater and I can't help but laugh.

The creature is glorious in every capacity. And if I'm being honest, its face strongly resembles that of my great uncle. He swims by with his flippers extended and he looks like an underwater sea angel.

I want Abbey and Parker to experience this. How have we never done anything this exciting as a family? Of course, I know the answer. It was Stanton and his work-alcoholic tendencies, and probably his extracurricular coital partners that stood in the way. But that's no more.

As soon as I can, I'm booking a cruise on the *Emerald Queen of the Seas* for Abbey, Parker, and me.

There's a giddiness that rises in me when I think about the kids meeting all of the wonderful people I've had the privilege of meeting on the ship. In the short time I've been on board, these people have felt like family to me. It's nice to know there's a world of kind people out there. And as much as I love Brambleberry Bay, a part of me wants to take one trip after another, seeing what else might lie outside of its borders.

We finish up, head back to the ship, and get ready for our foray into cultural appreciation and fine luau dining—not to mention solid ground and the ability to breathe without a tube sticking out of my mouth.

I don't see a single thing that can go wrong.

~

STANTON SHOOTS me a text just as the tour bus lands at our destination.

Way to keep it classy, Trixie. Don't worry. Me and my lawyers will keep it classy, too. You keep this up and you'll be working at the feed shop just to make ends meet. Don't do anything stupid. You have a ticket home, plane leaves at nine

in the morning your time. Get on it. Enough of these sick shenanigans.

I show the text to Bess and Nettie and the three of us have a good laugh.

Nettie tosses a hand in the air. "I guess he didn't care for you kissing the captain."

"Wait until he sees you with Ransom," Bess adds. "Do you want me to stalk you like the paparazzi? I can get a few good shots in, if you let me."

"Yeah." Nettie nods. "And you get a good smooch in while you're at it."

"No thank you," I tell them. "I'm pretty sure we're going to keep it chaste. I didn't plan on kissing Captain Crawford, and I don't plan on kissing anyone else either. We're just going to have a good time—as friends."

My insides contort themselves as if protesting. All right, fine. Every last bit of me is protesting, but only because a man like Ransom demands it.

I try to shake all thoughts of Stanton, Captain Crawford, and Ransom out of my mind for now. I'm somewhere new and I want to soak in every last tropical minute of it.

The cultural center is a vast sprawl of acreage that indeed showcases six Polynesian islands, each a decent walking distance from one another as historically accurate huts made of palm fronds and other available materials are dotted around the property.

First up is the island of Hawaii—or at least a grouping of the Hawaiian islands all at one station where we watch a group of gorgeous Hawaiian women in traditional long canvas skirts printed with red dye in various patterns, paired with tan strips of cloth that wrap around their bosoms. You can see the art in every inch of their accouterments. They have fitted leis around their wrists and one sitting on top of their head comprised of verdant ferns. It's a feast for the eyes as they treat us to a hip-swaying hula, and once they're through they pull us up on the makeshift stage with them and teach us how to swivel our hips with the best of them.

Next up is Aotearoa, with a group of strapping, young, shirtless men with bodies fit for Mount Olympus. Each one has a series of unique black stripes and swirls running over their faces to mimic the traditional Maori tattoos, and their grass skirts look as if they're about to treat us to something a little more traditional to men the world over. They start in on a ferocious dance that consists of howling and growling, and Nettie howls and growls right back.

"Do you mind?" Bess elbows her. "You're going to get us kicked out before we get to the haupia pudding."

Nettie waves her off. "I've got men to appreciate. I've got all the pudding I want back on the ship. Hey? You just gave me a great idea. We should buy a suitcase and stuff one of these hunks into it."

"That's a terrible idea." I shudder.

"See?" Bess muses. "Even Trixie thinks it's a bad idea."

"Only because of the memories," I say.

Next, we hit the station marked as *Fiji* and visit their traditional abodes. Another group of men comes out with half their faces painted red and holding long spears. There's an older gentleman with a cap of gray hair among the shirtless crew and Nettie's tongue starts a waggin' at the sight of him.

"No," Bess says. "Down, girl. You can't take him back with you."

"Eh." Nettie tosses that nest of gray sitting on her head. "I've got other plans for the chief."

Once we're through, we walk to the next island display, Samoa, where we watch a young man in red shorts and little grass skirts attached just above his ankles as he climbs a forty-foot coconut tree and puts on a show as he plucks one from the top. He teaches us how to carve it, open it, and make a fire with the husk. And before we leave the area, we each pony up ten bucks to buy a cold coconut with a straw sticking out from the top. And boy, is it refreshing.

Tahiti brings more gorgeous women and shirtless men entrancing us with their smooth moves. And finally, Tonga where a handful of men beat on impossibly large drums and we feel every vibration right through our thoracic cavity.

The sun quickly sets and a bell rings alerting us to the fact the luau is set to begin. We're herded in a giant thatch tent where a buffet of every Hawaiian delicacy tempts us—and we give in.

I load my plate with all the kalua pork, lomi lomi salmon, rice, shoyu chicken, and poi I can eat. Okay, so I can't eat much poi, but the clear noodles definitely have my attention. For dessert, Bess loads up on fruit and haupia pudding, and I indulge in the white opaque pudding myself. Come to find out, haupia is a coconut custard that tastes like the personification of this magical island.

Once our bellies are full, we're navigated to an amphitheater where we watch a show that tells the stories of the islands. The dancing women, the shirtless men, the giant makeshift volcano that explodes and oozes lava at the end, it all leaves us spellbound.

"Well, that was just the best of everything," I say.

Bess nods. "No matter how many times I see it, I swear the show just gets better and better. Isn't that right, Nettie?" She leans past me. "*Nettie?*"

Bess and I search high and low until we see a woman stumble from the bushes, her gray hair standing on end, her muumuu more than slightly askew, and that chief from Fiji adjusting his skirt as they break in two different directions.

"You floozy!" Bess calls out as she reels Nettie in by the arm. "I can't take you anywhere. If I were your mother, I'd lock you in your room."

"It wouldn't be any use," Nettie says, raking her fingers

through her hair in an effort to tame it. "I'd just climb down the balcony like the good old days."

Bess huffs at the thought, "If you climb down the balcony from your cabin, you'll be getting frisky with a bottlenose dolphin."

Nettie ticks her head. "If he can shake his hips like the chief, it might be worth the trip."

We take the tour bus back to our floating home, and just before we hit the harbor, a text pops up on my phone.

Ransom here. Looking forward to our time in Maui. We can meet at the gangway at six forty-five a.m. the first morning we arrive.

I text right back. **I wouldn't miss it.**

We head back to the ship and I hit the sheets, hugging the elephant fashioned out of towels left on my bed.

All night I dream of swinging my hips next to a shirtless chief who looks a lot like Ransom Baxter. We do things in those bushes that would make even Stanton and his horny harem blush.

In fact, they make me blush, too.

Ransom Baxter has the power to make any red-blooded woman blush from head to toe by simply looking at her, and here I get to spend the day with him.

Maybe I'm not so unlucky after all.

Although something tells me the universe is about to set the record straight.

CHAPTER 14

In the morning, I pen a missive on my new travel blog *Suddenly Single—What a Trip!*

I tell them all the hilarity that ensued with me flailing and howling as I struggled to breathe underwater and the amazing time Bess, Nettie, and I had at the cultural center. I leave out the details of Nettie's bush-whacking good time but do tell them I saw one gray-haired cutie stumbling from the bushes with a certain man of the coital cloth. It's just too juicy to leave out. And much to my chagrin, I tell them about the captain's kiss. Then I fill them in on the last day of our time on Oahu.

Yesterday Nettie, Bess, and Elodie—my new friend and famed ship stylist—went to Pearl Harbor. I was never so moved in my life. I shed tears as we stood on the platform and learned about the history from the tour guide. It's important that we never forget history in hopes to never repeat it. That's something I can carry into my own life. Afterward, we hit Waikiki Beach and slept on the pale sandy beach. Every now and again clouds would mercifully cover the sun and give us a reprieve from its searing heat. It rained for a few minutes, here and there, but it was so warm we didn't mind that at all. Later, we had shave ice the size of our heads then took another long nap on the beach. I've never felt so relaxed in all my life.

I never thought I'd be on a cruise ship, let alone on one in the South Pacific all by my lonesome—leave it to Stanton to make all of my unwanted dreams come true. But you know what? I kind of want to pen him a thank you for this. Who knew the worst moment of my life could lead to one of the most magical? Sometimes life can be a trip, too. Until next time!

Once I wrap things up, I get ready for my hot date with the hottest detective I know. The only detective I know, but I'm pretty sure if I knew them all, he'd still be the hottest.

We sailed for Maui last night, and that's where we are currently. As much as I loved Oahu, I'm ecstatic to see what the famed island of Maui has to offer.

The atrium is dark and sparsely populated when I spot Ransom near the gangway looking heart-stopping in a white T-shirt, black shorts, and ball cap.

"Detective." I give a cheeky smile. "Good morning."

"Good morning yourself." He takes in my gauzy pink dress. I've got a pink bathing suit on underneath and a pair of sparkly flip-flops that Elodie chose for me. I'll admit, it's nothing the old me would have picked out, but the new me seems up for anything, even sparkly flip-flops and heading off to watch the sunrise with a handsome man who isn't my husband. I glance down at his waist. "Hey, you don't have your gun on you."

"It's my day off. I don't need it. Besides, I don't foresee anything going wrong today."

"You're with me," I tell him. "And lately, I'm a walking broken mirror—bad luck city, twenty-four seven."

"I think your luck is changing, Trixie. And I'm determined to prove it."

"Someone likes to fly in the face of the universe." I was going to say *someone likes a good challenge*, but that might have made me out to sound like a sexual conquest and I'm still not sure he doesn't see me that way. I'm well aware of his reputation. But now that he's well aware of mine, I feel like we're on an even playing field.

"Shall we?" He hitches his head into the darkness that waits outside the door.

"We shall."

Since Maui is a no-go as far as having a cruise ship dock in the harbor, we catch a smaller boat that delivers us to land, something I just learned that is referred to as *tendering*.

Ransom already has a car waiting for him not too far from the dock. He tells me he much prefers to drive himself around the islands so he can explore the nooks and crannies.

"Each island is unique and has its own charm," he says. "Maui is great. Not only does it have some of the best beaches, but you can get a close-up of some of the smaller islands surrounding it."

"I bet you've done everything there is to do here after years of visiting."

"You'd think so, but I'm not even close. I doubt if I lived on the island full time I'd be able to see it all. But the best way to introduce anyone to the island is to witness the splendor of the first kiss of morning. The next best thing is sunset."

"I can hardly wait for both." And what kisses lie in between.

We drive through darkness for a little less than half an hour until we hit a sign welcoming us to Kamaole Beach. We park and walk down a sandy road with the flashlight from Ransom's phone leading the way. I stub my toe on a tree root and trip, causing Ransom to grab me by the waist in order to stabilize me.

"Whoa," he says. "Here"—he holds out his hand— "I promise I won't bite."

A small part of me is disappointed by the fact he won't be biting, but I blink a smile his way despite the fact.

I thread my fingers through his strong, sure hand and a spiral of heat rides from my hand, straight up my arm, and right through my body.

Holy wow. Not once do I remember holding Stanton's hand and having that effect—having any effect. This feels like a relief, as if I was always meant to hold Ransom's hand, as if I've always craved it.

Ransom firms his grip over mine as we continue down the trail, and I feel assured and safe as we come upon the waves lapping the shore.

A pale glow illuminates the horizon as he rolls out a beach towel and we take a seat side by side and watch as the sky turns salmon, casting its orange light over the ocean. To the right, I can see landmasses rising from the water and they look so close you'd think you could touch them.

"That's Molokini, Kaho'olawe, and Lanai," he says, pointing to three different islands. "They make for an incredible view."

"They sure do," I say breathlessly just as the sun peeks out from the horizon in all its blazing glory, and soon the world around us lights up with a majesty that I could never imagine. The ocean quickly turns an aqua shade of blue, the waves roll like pearls onto a white sandy shoreline, and I can see bushy trees behind us surrounding the trail we walked down from. "This was the most beautiful sunrise I have ever witnessed." I can't help but smile as I say it. "I'm glad I got to see it with you."

"I'm glad I got to see it with you, too. How about a walk by the water?" He helps me up and we take a walk along the shoreline, shoes in hand, feet in the cool water, sand between our toes, and it feels like I've stepped into another world, another dimension. It feels like heaven. He asks about my time in Oahu and I spill every last detail. We share a laugh about Nettie's wild escapade, but I have a feeling it's not the first he's heard.

We opt for breakfast next and he drives us to one of his favorite haunts, a place called Griddle Cakes where you make your own pancakes at a grill right there at your own table. Ransom and I each order a breakfast fit for a lumberjack, and along with our bacon, eggs, and hash browns, we're each given a squeeze bottle of pancake batter to make our own culinary creations.

I spell out Maui with my batter and take a picture of it as it puffs up a golden brown. I'm about to send it in the family group chat, but I don't want Stanton mucking up the waters while I'm on a date with Ransom so I think better of it.

The thought stops me cold. I'm not really on a date, am I?

"Everything okay?" Ransom asks, taking a sip of his coffee.

"It's fine." My shoulders curl toward my ears like a cat. "I'm just trying to soak in every moment. My life back in Brambleberry Bay keeps trying to rear its ugly head, but I'm holding my own so far."

"Holding the past at bay isn't easy." His brows sink low and I get the feeling he's speaking from experience.

"And how about your past?" I ask with the utmost caution and suddenly regret every word. "You know what, never mind," I say. "If I don't want to rehash mine, I don't see why you need to rehash yours. My mistake."

"I don't mind," he says it low, his eyes boring into mine. "Ask anything."

And just like that, I have carte blanche, and I'm not sure I want to use it.

I shake my head, trying to stop myself, but I can't seem to do it.

"Have you ever been married?" I shrug a little, feeling guilty that I went straight for the jugular.

"Once. We ended it amicably. She's on her second divorce."

"Do you have any kids?" It's clear I'm not stopping anytime soon. I can't help it, I'm twice as hungry to know more about him than I am my breakfast.

"A daughter, Emerson. She's twenty-two and just started law school out at Magnolia University."

"That's so impressive. And she's a Georgia peach now," I say with a laugh, leaving out the part of the Georgia peach back on the ship, Layla Beauchamp from guest relations. "You did good."

"Thank you." His lips curve a notch. "You're doing great as well."

A part of me wants to ask about the strange beef he seems to have with the captain, but I know that's none of my business.

"What is it?" He nods with genuine curiosity.

"Nothing." I clear my throat. "Are you enjoying your time on the ship? How long do you see yourself doing this?"

"I love my job. And to answer your next question, right now it's indefinitely, but that could all change given the right circumstances." He rakes his gaze over my features and my face lights up like a flame.

A part of me wants to be that right circumstance, but that's just a wild fantasy—which is more than easy to have when you're thousands of miles away from the disaster you left behind.

We indulge in small talk about the ship. I ask about his adventures on board and he tells me a few stories of thievery, a few wild parties gone awry, and a bachelorette party that almost landed the bride-to-be overboard.

We finish up our breakfast, and Ransom takes care of the bill much to my protest. We're about to step outside when his phone rings.

He winces. "I need to take this. It's the port authority. Why don't you stay inside where it's cool? I'll be back in a minute."

He steps outside and a small gift counter catches my eye. I spot a pair of silver earrings in the shape of hibiscus flowers that would look stunning on Abbey and a postcard of a gorgeous sunset here on Maui, so I collect both and head to the register. I hand the girl at the counter my credit card and she runs it with a smile. But the cute brunette's smile quickly dissipates as she runs it again.

"I'm sorry, ma'am, but your card isn't working."

"Oh?" I quickly produce another. "Try this one."

She repeats the effort, only to come up with the same results, so I give her my third and final card.

"Still no luck." She shrugs. "Don't feel bad. Most people have their credit cards frozen if they don't tell their credit card companies that they're traveling. I'm sure a simple phone call will clear it all up."

"I'm sure it will," I say without the assurance I need to back that.

I called every credit card company myself and let them know we'd be in Hawaii. I'm sensing a devious ex at the other end of this fiscal melee.

Ransom steps back in and I head his way sans the purchases I was hoping to make.

"Everything okay?" he asks as his forehead wrinkles with concern.

"I think my ex just cut me off from all the credit cards," I tell him. "So much for getting those art supplies I was hoping to score."

"Well, I can't have a tortured artist on my hands." He bites down on his lip. "I know how to fix this."

"I do, too, but hiring a hitman to take out Stanton might land us both in prison."

His chest vibrates in lieu of a laugh. "How about we start slow and build our way to the hitman? That should give you some time to cool your heels."

"Good luck with that," I say. "I might cool off, but not anytime during this century."

"I like your determination. But that won't stop me from trying to get your mind off it."

Ransom drives us out to a place called Front Street where businesses that sell everything from T-shirts to fine art line the street on both sides. Of course, there are restaurants, too, and lots and lots of tourists. We stop at a place called the Rainbow's

End Art Shop where they feature work from local artists and even have an art supply section in the back.

"Go ahead," Ransom says. "Shop until your heart's content. My treat."

"That is far too kind. But I couldn't accept it."

He frowns hard and looks ten times comelier while doing so. A couple of women to our right sigh hard in his direction, and one looks as if she's about to faint at the sight of him. Can't blame her. I'm not too far off from fainting myself.

"You should pick out what you need or I might end up buying every wrong thing," he says. "It's either me or you shopping here today. Take your pick." He nods. "Pick you."

"Fine, but only because you drive a hard bargain. And as soon as I get back on the ship, I'm straightening this mess out and paying you back. He can't keep my money from me forever. Although my sanity is another thing entirely."

I quickly collect a pack of those alcohol markers I've so greatly missed, a medium-size notebook with paper made for mixed media. I pick up gouache, a water-based pigmented paint that has recently usurped my love for acrylics and oil because it's just all around easier to use. I also pick up a few basic brushes, and true to his word, Ransom ponies up at the register.

We take off and I thank him profusely all the way to the car.

"Where to next?" he asks. "We could hit the road to Hana, a dazzling display of the tropics on a winding road to a wild version of paradise, or we could snorkel, nap on the beach, anything you like. It's your day."

My fingers tap over my lips. "The winding road to paradise sounds nice, but I'm craving a beach. Snorkeling sounds fun. I think I'm all through with the panic attacks as far as convincing my brain that it's okay to breathe underwater. And that beach nap sounds like a dream."

"Then that's what we'll do. I know just the place to take you."

CHAPTER 15

Ransom and I drive along the stunning Maui coastline and I marvel at the palm trees and the water that at times seems to be a few steps outside the car right up until we reach our destination.

We drive north for about twenty minutes and stop off at a rental shop where we pick up our gear for snorkeling before heading to a place called Honolua Bay. We park and walk down a dirt trail under the protection of a canopy of fruit trees and flowering trees in every color until we hit an aqua glowing cove.

"Oh, Ransom," I say as I try to take in all the beauty at once. There's a catamaran anchored in the bay and dozens upon dozens of tourists snorkeling away. The breeze is warm and perfumed from the trees nearby, and the teal water looks as if it's doing its best to seduce us into diving right in. "This truly is paradise."

"It gets better," he says, leading us down the rocky shoreline as we pile our things under some shrubbery and he lands a few stray branches on top of it.

He strips off his shirt and my jaw unhinges.

First of all, it's not fair that he gets to go through life with the face of a deity, but the body of one, too?

I'm not all that surprised. Ransom is heavily chiseled, his six-pack has a six-pack and his skin is perfectly bronzed.

He glances at my dress and lifts a brow before pretending to busy himself by zipping and unzipping the backpack he brought along.

Oh, good grief, it's my turn to strip.

Why does this feel so wrong?

I peel off my dress and flick off my flip-flops. "All ready to go," I say, sucking in my stomach with all the strength I can muster, suddenly regretting the miles of lava cake I've inhaled since I was introduced to the chocolaty wonder.

"Let's do this," he says as we head to the water, put on our fins and snorkel gear—and to my surprise, I catch onto that whole breathing underwater thing as if I didn't nearly need a sedative just the other day.

Ransom and I swim side by side as we come upon an endless parade of sea turtles, schools of orange striped fish, yellow and black striped fish, pale blue angels, and a few strays that are as long as they are fat. An eel shoots out from between a few rocks and my entire body jerks as I begin to panic.

Ransom grabs me by the waist and buoys us to the top and we spit out our mouthpieces.

"Are you okay?" he asks as he flips his mask onto his forehead.

I give a frenetic laugh. "I think so. I wasn't expecting that little guy. I'm not a fan of his slithering land cousin either, so my reaction is no surprise."

We rise with a wave that barrels past us and Ransom pulls me close for a moment before letting go.

"Sorry." He frowns. "I didn't mean to—"

"No, it's okay. Believe me, I'd much rather you hold onto me than I drift my way to Tahiti. I'm a beginner, remember?"

"You're doing great," he says as he holds out his hand. "Ready for another run along the reef?"

I take up his hand and nod. "I'm in."

Ransom leads us seamlessly through the underwater splendor as we continue our magical journey along the coast. But I won't lie, the fact he's holding my hand, the fact it feels as natural as breathing—above water—it worries me a bit.

Am I actually falling for this handsome man by my side?

Is that even safe in my emotional condition?

Is this a classic rebound brewing?

And the worst question of all—would I mind?

We finish up our foray into the deep blue sea and Ransom drives us down to a food truck where we each pick up poke bowls and indulge in the best tasting sushi I've ever had in my life. Stanton is more of a burger and steak guy, but the country club we belong to has recently brought in a sushi chef and I've indulged a few times with my girlfriends.

Once we're through, he takes me to a place called Kapalua Bay and we head down to the sandy beach, each with a towel in hand, ready for that nap under a palm tree. There's a fair share of tourists out and about and the bay is just as magical if not more so than that of Honolua.

"Just when I thought Honolua was the best show in town, you give me a perfect bay with a sandy beach," I tell him as he hunts for a place to hunker down.

There's a grass belt up above the beach with a smattering of trees, spreading their branches wide as if they knew it was their job to offer shelter from the sun.

"That's the thing about this island. It just gets better and exponentially better." He cranes his neck past me. "I see shade if you're up for lying under a tree."

I turn that way and my attention is quickly hijacked, but it's not the trees I'm looking at. It's a woman with blonde curls running down her back. She's standing with a pink backpack and not much else on. Okay, fine. She's wearing a two-piece barely-there bikini that shows off more skin than she would if she were naked—if that were at all possible. She has a wide-brimmed hat on and a pair of sunglasses, but I recognize her despite the mild disguise.

"Ransom," I hiss as I scoot in close. "There's that woman from the ship—the blonde." I quickly point her out and his chest depresses when he sees her as if he were disappointed. "That's Amanda Charming. Isabella said she was practically babysitting Olivia that last day."

"It is her, isn't it?" a female trills from behind and I glance that way, only to see the shifty specter that's been haunting my world as a shower of miniature green stars dissolves around her.

"Malora," I hiss her name low like a curse because she's the last person I wanted to see this afternoon—and let's be real, she's sort of a curse at this point, too.

"Bless you," Ransom says. "And as far as Ms. Charming goes, I've yet to question her. Leave her to me. I'll get to her when we're back on board, and I'm sure she'll tell me everything I need to know."

"He wishes," Malora balks. "If you were a killer, would you fess up to a strong, handsome detective the first chance you had? Doubtful." Her mouth falls open as she inspects his chest and she reaches over and gives it a little scratch.

I won't lie, for the first time ever, I'm envious of the dead.

"She brings up a good point," I say, then immediately regret it.

Ransom squints my way. "Who brings up a good point? Isabella?"

"Yes, her—Isabella." I'm not exactly ready to fess up about my newfound ability to see through to the other side. "I bet I can get a little info out of her. People are guarded when they speak to the authorities. She might tell me a thing or two. Besides, I should probably go over and introduce myself. Not only did Tinsley ask me to help out with the auction, but I'm doing a tutorial on how to paint like Olivia."

He closes his eyes a moment. "No."

"No?" A laugh gets caught in my throat and I'm equally amused as I am annoyed.

"No, this is an active homicide investigation. Your point person for the art show and the tutorial is Tinsley. This woman could be the killer for all we know. I refuse to put you in danger."

"Oh well." Malora tosses her hands in the air. "He has a good point. I'll be back on the lido deck if you need me."

I hold a hand her way, signaling for her to wait. "I'm sorry, Ransom, but I have to say hello. It feels natural given the circumstances. You don't have to come along. I'll just be a minute." I traipse past him, and soon he's right back by my side.

"Trixie, wait," he says. "Think this through. Haven't you had enough trouble lately? Believe me, you don't want to go compounding it by befriending a potential killer."

I make a face at him as we draw close to the woman.

"Oh look, honey," I say loud enough for her to hear. "There's a spot in the shade right there." I point to a bald patch of sand no more than six feet away from where she's standing examining the scenery. "Why don't you go put down our towels?" I say, shoving my things in his arms.

"Anything you say, sweetie," he says back without an ounce of amusement. He frowns from Amanda to me and mouths the words *be careful* as he does as he's told.

Finally, a man who knows how to obey.

If Ransom wasn't worth his weight in gold already, he's worth twice that now.

"Come on." Malora pushes me along and I trip over a stray flip-flop and almost knock the poor woman over.

"Oh my goodness," I say as I back up with my hands spread wide. "I'm so sorry. I really need to watch where I'm going."

The blonde laughs. "I'm fine. And the view is so spectacular, I'm sure collisions are common on this beach."

"I bet you're right." I bounce back a notch. "Hey, I think I recognize you from the ship. Are you here with the *Emerald Queen*?"

"That I am." She laughs. "It's nice to meet a fellow passenger. I just rented a car as soon as I got off the ship this morning, and this is where I landed. I can think of worse places to be."

I nod. "Like back home with my ex."

She offers a pained smile. "Sorry about that. But here's to new beginnings, right?" She glances past me in Ransom's direction. "And from what I can see, you've hit the jackpot."

My lips press tight as Ransom offers up a quick wave while lying back on his elbows.

"That I did." I sigh because it's a lie that somehow feels like the truth.

"Now, now, don't get distracted." Malora tries to block my view of Ransom, and yet I can still see the outline of his body right through hers. "Let's shake her down so I can shake down that jerk chicken they're serving today."

I'm not sure why or how she can eat, but she's been noshing to her heart's content ever since she arrived so I'm not questioning it.

I force a smile at Amanda. "My name is Trixie Troublefield. I think I recognize you because you were with Olivia Montauk. I'm actually assisting the ship with the sale of her pieces and the art class she was scheduled to do." I cringe. "I heard what happened."

She grimaces. "They're keeping it hush-hush, but there's going to be an announcement this evening, along with an invitation to her private soiree—they're calling it An Art Affair to Remember."

"A soiree?"

She nods. "We thought since we had all of her pieces on board we may as well proceed with the sale. And Dave, Olivia's husband, thought it would be a way to memorialize her. He and Isabella came up with the name. It coincides with a formal night, so it made sense. Not only did Olivia love a good party, but she was all about the drama."

"Drama?" I quirk a brow. "I bet she had a lot of that going on. I mean, she must have, to get herself killed like that."

Amanda shudders. "Oh, she had drama." She gives a quick look around before scooting in. "She also had a secret."

"A secret?" both Malora and I say at once.

Amanda nods as a devious smile plays on her lips. "But it's not mine to tell."

Malora waves her off. "Oh, for goodness' sake, the girl won't mind. She's dead."

True as gospel.

"Well, if Olivia isn't here to repeat it, I don't see what the harm is." I tip my ear her way, hoping she'll take the bait.

Amanda shakes her head. "Olivia might not be here to spill the beans, but her security guard is."

"Her security guard? As in Craig?" I ask, surprised by her answers.

"You know Craig?" She inches back as she marvels at the fact.

"Go with it," Malora insists and I plan to.

"Just a little." Very little. "So he knows her secret?"

A husky laugh brews in her chest. "Does he ever." She looks back at the water and her expression darkens.

The day Olivia died, it was Amanda I saw carting her off by the elbow. And those words she spoke the morning I saw her in front of the shops—that the show and life in general would run smoother without Olivia in it? This woman had a beef with her. I have a feeling this whole secret thing could be a ruse.

"Amanda, I had heard Olivia could be difficult to work with," I say. "Did you have any problems with her?"

"Ha." She shakes her head. "Who didn't? Olivia put the D in *diva*. And I was essentially her handler, so I got the brunt of her tantrums." She gazes off a moment and her expression goes dark. "We were friends, though. She came through for me a time or two when I needed it most." Her expression hardens. "If you'll excuse me, I think I'll take a quick dip." She glances back at Ransom lying there like a chiseled piece of steel. "And I think you've got better things to do than talk to me." She takes off with a wave.

Malora floats in close. "She said Olivia came through for her when she needed her most. I say we investigate and see exactly how Olivia came through for her."

"I think you're right. I get the feeling Amanda wasn't Olivia's fan."

"I'm off to the lido deck." Malora snaps her fingers and explodes in a vat of stars. "Go get a snack yourself, Trixie," her disembodied voice trails behind. "I'm talking about the snack looking at you from the beach towel in case you need directions. Not only does he look ripe, he looks delicious."

I fall onto the towel next to Ransom, but I don't take a bite out of him. Instead, I tell him everything that just transpired.

His lips purse. "Do me a favor and leave Craig Jackson to me."

I nod his way. "He's all yours, Detective. All I want is a nice, long nap." And in less than two minutes, I drift off with Ransom Baxter less than two feet away and all seems right with the world.

But all is not right in Olivia Montauk's world.

Olivia is dead and someone out there decided to pin me as the prime suspect.

I may not be the luckiest girl in the world, but one thing is for sure—the killer's luck is about to run out.

CHAPTER 16

You can bet your bottom dollar I spelled out every moment of my romantic trip with Ransom on my new blog *Suddenly Single—What a Trip!* sans the romance of it all.

I didn't have the heart to come across like some love-struck teenager in the event Ransom happened to stumble across my site. And believe me, I wanted to amp up the romance just to make Stanton squirm. Each day I've dutifully sent him a link to my latest and greatest post.

After Ransom and I got back on the ship, I shot a text to Stanton, called him a few choice expletives—not my finest hour—and demanded that he allow me access back to my credit cards. I visited the ship's ATM services department, only to find out that he's cut me off at the pass there, too.

Stanton's response? He'll have a ticket home waiting for me once the ship arrives in Kona. I let him know I won't be taking that plane either.

I'm determined to finish this cruise.

I've got a murder to solve—my name to clear—a class to teach, friendships to maintain, and perhaps *two* budding romances. Although I seem to be veering hard in Ransom's lane, not that anything will come of it. In less than a week, we'll be back in Los Angeles, and I'll have a plane to catch for sure.

The thought of Ransom, Captain Crawford, Bess, and Nettie sailing back to Hawaii without me doesn't seem fair. And in a few months, they'll all go off to have an adventure in Alaska, then who knows where after that. My heart aches at the thought of not being a part of the fun.

Ransom mentioned at dinner that he was making strides in the case but would try to catch up with Bess, Nettie, and me on the Big Island if at all possible.

But I digress. Before I went to bed, I checked with the purser at guest relations, a young man by the name of Neville Wager who originally hails from Montana, and he let me know that even though my initial credit card was disconnected, that another credit card kicked in and was covering all of my expenses.

Either Stanton is unaware of this credit card miracle or there is some mystery credit card that he doesn't know about. I didn't want to push it. The last thing I want is to go picking around, only to have my last lifeline on the ship disconnected. So I accepted what the purser told me and left it at that.

I did check in with Abbey and Parker and made sure their credit cards weren't tied to my ship purchases and they assured me they weren't. Curious.

So just like that, I have another mystery on my hands, albeit one that doesn't involve a corpse—unless you count the corpse that is my marriage.

Here's hoping Stanton doesn't pull the final rug out from under me. For once, I'm rooting for an entire bevy of naked floozies to keep him occupied for the next few days. While he's busy collecting STDs, I'll be busy having fun in the sun.

Today, we're docked on the Big Island, Hilo to be exact, and since Bess and Nettie insist on showing me a good time, I've given in to their itinerary. I tried to bow out after I explained my credit card debacle, but that only made the two of them more determined to make sure I have a good time. So I caved but let them know I'd be tallying up how much I owe them. And I'll owe them plenty.

Come to find out, the ship is only in Hilo until six p.m., and the one activity Bess and Nettie insist I can't miss out on happens a little after the ship sails. So we'll be spending the night in a hotel, then meeting up with the *Emerald Queen* over in Kona where the ship will dock next. This is the only island where the ship relocates for its two-day stay, but thankfully we won't miss the ship altogether. And since Ransom and Captain Crawford are both obligated to sail with the ship, they won't be able to join us for our overnight adventure.

"It's warm and sunny," Bess says once we climb into our rental car, which she'll be commandeering for the duration of our stay.

"Thanks for the weather report, Captain Obvious," Nettie says from the back seat.

"Oh, you know what that means." Bess waves her off. "It means we need to get to the Rainbow Falls first." She glances my way. "You can only see rainbows at the falls when the sun is to your back, so it's best to go early. They're gorgeous. And this place has always had a unique way of connecting me to nature—spiritually."

Nettie gives a husky laugh. "I've got a way of connecting you to nature in a unique way." She leans my way. "I know a guy in Kona, who knows a guy."

"Say no, Trixie," Bess balks at her offer. "Believe me, the last time she started a sentence with 'I know a guy, who knows a guy,' we ended up in a jail cell."

Nettie waves her off. "Ransom bailed us out—with a little help from the captain. And now we've got quite the tale to tell."

"Maybe next time." I wince at the thought of ending up in a jail cell. I'm sure Stanton would somehow weaponize that against me, as I'm sure he'll see my blog and my refusal to listen to his odious command of abandoning this trip.

We land at Rainbow Falls fairly quickly since it's located right here in Hilo. The sign reads *Wailuku River, Rainbow Falls Area*. The first thing I notice about the Big Island is how much hotter it seems to be and how much drier it is, too. The humidity is still present, but it's less of a hug than it is a distant hello.

The rocky crags that surround this part of the island are blackened, and the fingerprints of its volcanic origin are everywhere. The palm trees line every free space and they sway gently with the tropical breeze.

There's a short hike of less than half a mile that takes us from the parking lot to the lookout above the falls as we increase our elevation by about forty feet. We pass glorious banyan trees with their multitude of leggy branches that drip to the ground and create one large tree trunk as they meld together in the middle. And we enjoy the respite from the sun as they provide the much-needed shade for our trek.

But once we hit the top—wow. The air is knocked right out of my lungs as I take in the beauty and the majesty this place has to offer.

The falls are over eighty feet tall and they spill into a pool of sapphire. The rush of water, the power of each drop forming a thunderous fugue of energy is awe-inspiring, and my soul will now be forever tethered here.

Bess was right. This is a spiritual connection.

"There's a rainbow." Nettie points to the right where the mist from the falls meets with the sheer wall of ferns, and sure enough, we see it—a colorful display that acts as a wink from nature, assuring us she knows how to balance the beauty and the power. And then, as if on cue, there's another, and another, and yet another.

My heart sings just witnessing it, and no matter how many

pictures I snap to send to the kids, I know for a fact they will never do it justice.

So I put down the phone and soak it all in with my eyes, my heart, and my soul. I feel whole here. Healed.

Next up on our hit list is the Hawaii Volcano National Park.

We gobbled a little time by grabbing lunch then taking in the vistas from a rocky beach where we saw plenty of sea turtles on land and in the water. Then we did a little inadvertent shopping after Nettie spilled shave ice onto her primarily white muumuu—Nettie said she needed another dress anyway, and evidently didn't pack one in her overnight bag. So, by the time we get to Volcano National Park, we still have a couple of hours to kill before the sun sets and the real show begins.

We explore the dirt trails with their narrow passages as the trees once again provide a canopy. We explore Thurston Lava Tube, a five-hundred-year-old cave that was formed by a river of lava. We stick to the areas that are lit up by the park and avoid the pitch-black shadow lands, mostly because the flashlights on our phones are not recommended for that non-illuminated zone. The walls, the ceiling, the floor, it all feels so very sacred knowing that it was born of fire and sheer determination of a wild flow of lava. My heart thumps every step of the way.

And finally, we gather at the Kilauea Overlook Point and secure our spots as we wait for the sun to go down. According to Bess and Nettie, the real show takes place at the Halema'uma'u Crater where we'll be able to see the active lava flow glowing with our naked eyes.

"I've never been this close to something this exciting," I say, giddy as the sun begins its descent for the day.

Bess chuckles. "That's saying a lot considering the fact you were married for twenty-five years."

"*Eh.*" Nettie shrugs. "We were leashed to men for a good spate of time ourselves, and we know what you're talking about."

"Hear, hear," Bess says as a hush comes over the crowd as the sun dips below the horizon. Then slowly, minute by minute the view grows that much more spectacular.

Out in the distance, on a dramatic black backdrop, a fiery red glow emerges from the center of the crater along with a plume of smoke that rises to the sky.

From this vantage point, the smoke looks like a whisper, a love letter to the stars, as it swims effortlessly upward. But the fire at the heart of it, that's where the real power lies, the incessant burning, the unstoppable flame that burrows into the night and makes the darkness its own.

"It's so beautiful," I choke out the words and both Bess and Nettie wrap their arms around me. "So powerful yet silent."

"Group hug," Nettie says as she holds on tight. "You know, Trixie, as women, we're a lot like that volcano. There's a lot of power inside of us, and for the most part, the world—we don't always see it even though it's always there."

"She's right." Bess ticks her head at the thought. "And when it goes dark in our world, that's when we discover our own light, our own undeniable strength, our—"

"Ability to attract a hot man or two," Nettie finishes for her.

Bess grunts. "Okay, fine. You're right about that, too. But this isn't about finding someone else to complete us. It's about discovering that we were enough to begin with."

Nettie scoffs. "Who said anything about completing us? Try *satisfying*."

Bess shakes her head at me. "Before she goes porno on us, let's get a picture of the three of us."

"I agree," I say.

We find the nearest teenager to take several shots with the volcano behind us and we each do a few selfies as well.

"This is magic," I say as Bess, Nettie, and I link arms and look out at the sheer beauty of the fiery lava lighting up the sky.

"This is power," Bess counters.

"This is making me hungry for pancakes," Nettie bleats.

"To magic, power, and pancakes," I call out and Bess and Nettie repeat the refrain.

We stay for what feels like an eternity, soaking it all in, then we head for the first all-night pancake joint we can find and drown ourselves in carbs.

This day equaled perfection in every single way.

But Ransom flits through my mind and so does that body.

Things will be perfect once we catch Olivia Montauk's killer.

And a deliberate kiss from Ransom wouldn't be so bad either.

CHAPTER 17

The ship's next stop is Kona, and since the passengers still on board can't get up close and personal with the Big Island from this angle, they'll need to tender once again.

Ransom sent a group text to Bess, Nettie, and me and asked how things were going. So Nettie let him know that she slept in a queen bed last night with Bess, but that my queen bed had a *vacancy* next to me—then asked if he knew someone who could fill it.

Not funny, but it was true. The motel we stayed at was no-frills, and come to find out, both Bess and Nettie snore like a couple of foghorns. But I'm not saying a word.

Bess invited Ransom to meet up with us today and he said he'd love to, but there was a thief on board, and Ransom and his team needed to stomp out that fire, in addition to tracking down Olivia Montauk's killer. I've never been so angry with a thief and a killer in all my life.

I blogged yesterday's fabulous adventure and woke up to find that the comments nearly tripled. I'm not sure what's happening, but I'm pretty sure it's some internet glitch that will correct itself sooner than later. Although I did see in a few of those comments that I was starting a revolution, and others called me their traveling queen. Some called for Stanton to be tarred and feathered and burned at the stake—others had far more visceral and grisly suggestions. No one was pleased that I was cut off my credit cards, and I dare say I loved the camaraderie.

But after Bess, Nettie, and I left our motel, Bess drove us down to the nearest coffee plantation where we eschewed the tour for the fresh coffee they served and we picked up some coffee cake to go along with it. Never in my life have I tasted such fresh, such determined to imprint itself on my soul, *java*.

It's as if the islands are determined to rewire my brain, revive my resolve and my spirit, and give me the strength and energy to live a Stanton-free existence with all the vigor each day deserves.

Our final destination of the day is the City of Refuge, a stretch of coastline along the west coast of the island at the Pu'uhonua o Hōnaunau National Historical Park. Blue ocean meets up with black rocky crags along with a sandy alcove. Replicas of thatched huts are dotted about where various demonstrations are being given regarding local customs and culture, and loads of wooden tiki statutes and sacred poles are scattered about the area.

On the way over, I've regaled Bess and Nettie with takes from the pits regarding my fiscal situation and Stanton's stubbornness to cut me a break.

"Don't you worry," Bess says, pulling out her phone and tapping over the screen. "I just sent you the name of the shark I used when I went through my own divorce. She doesn't specialize in divorces per se, but when she takes on a case, she makes sure the opposition feels the pain. My ex is still limping from the wallop she gave him. Her name is Fiona Dagmeyer. She works out of Ashford County back in Vermont—that's pretty close to my hometown of Honey Hollow. You get on the horn and sic her on Stanton Troublefield, and he'll be sorry he ever met you. Trust me, there's a reason they call her the Dagger."

"The Dagger? I like her already," I say. "I'll contact her as soon as we get back to the ship. The more trouble I can stir up for Mr. Troublefield, the better." I look around at the vast rocky expanse as it meets the churning sea. "Should we try to hook up with a tour?"

"We'll be your tour guides," Bess insists with a nod as the pressing heat engulfs us. The trade winds are scant today and the lack of humidity is noticeable, too.

Nettie nods. "Tours, in general, are great if you're a newbie, but they add up pretty quickly. I've told Bess we should get into the tourist business ourselves and charge half of what the tour companies want, but she threatened to sue me if I did it."

Bess grunts, "I didn't threaten to sue you. A major player in the tourist industry dropped you a note threatening to sue and Captain Crawford had to come and tell you to knock it off." She looks my way. "It was a liability issue. That and the fact no one wants to be undercut by two older and wiser women who know how to have a good time for half the price."

"Don't worry," Nettie tells me. "You've still got the best. See this place here? This barren lava field has enjoyed more than seven hundred years of good times by the innocent and guilty alike. Back in the day, if you even looked at the chief crooked, it could lead to a death sentence. Step on his shadow? You're twice the hound of hell. You'd end up here, living it up with other rebels. And you and I both know a good time ensued."

"They did not." Bess shakes her head at her counterpart. "Those people were basically imprisoned. But seeing that those who broke those sacred laws were punishable by death, this place was their only option. Because this is considered sacred ground, they couldn't shed any blood here. So, it became a haven for those who needed it." She glances to the blue sparkling water. "Although let's face it, this was no Alcatraz. There's a mausoleum adjacent to this place that creates a boundary line between the royal grounds and this place. And that's where the chiefs were buried. Their bones are thought to have protected the area."

Nettie twists her lips. "Seeing that there's a thief on board the ship now, along with a killer, I think we should dig up a bone or two and take it back with us. We're going to need some serious protection. This trip might just be our last."

Bess narrows her eyes over at her counterpart. "The only person we're going to need protection from is *you*. Remember that time you hauled back a sack full of lava rocks onto the ship? We nearly died in a hundred different freak accidents." She nods my way. "It's a known fact that you don't take any lava rocks with you. They make run-of-the-mill bad luck look like a winning day at the races."

"How was I supposed to know that?" Nettie squawks in her own defense.

"Because the tour guide told us so," Bess says, tossing her hands in the air with exasperation.

Nettie gives a dark laugh. "And that's why we don't take tours."

A group of, ironically enough, *tourists* move into the area led by a brunette with a ponytail wearing khaki shorts and a pink polo top that glows against her tan skin.

"Ooh, look." Nettie shakes me by arm. "Another tried-and-true tactic to getting a free tour—hang out on the periphery."

Bess nods and shrugs. "It works for luaus, too—only you don't get the food."

"We've got food on the ship," Nettie points out. "And who needs a bowl full of poi when you can get an eyeful of beefy shirtless men?"

"I'm in," I tell them.

A couple meanders our way, talking about a ghost tour they just finished up.

Nettie snaps her fingers with a look of regret. "That's what we forgot to do. We forgot to take Trixie on a ghost tour."

"Oh, I'm fine with skipping it," I'm quick to tell them. "I've sort of had it up to my eyeballs in specters lately."

"Lately?" both Nettie and Bess say in unison, and I swallow hard at the thought of how close I came to divulging another supernatural tidbit.

"What can I say?" My shoulders hike a notch. "I've got Halloween on my mind."

"Halloween is ten months away," Nettie says, cocking her ear my way.

"Nine, but same difference," Bess says. "But don't you worry, Trixie. There are no such things as ghosts. The locals just like to play it up because it makes for great tourist traffic."

"I'd have to disagree with that," a distinctly female yet elderly voice chirps from behind and I cringe because I have a feeling that distinctly female voice also happens to be disembodied. I turn around to see a spray of miniature green stars surrounding an orange-haired granny with a smile of the same hue, dressed in emerald velvet from head to foot. I'm getting twice as hot just looking at her. "Oh dear," she cranes her neck past me, "it seems we've got another one here this afternoon."

"Another one what?" I hiss as I turn around, half-afraid I'll be treated to my second poltergeist of the day, but as far as I can tell the only person in Malora's visual field is that brunette tour guide.

"Another person who can see me."

The woman does a double take this way before dismissing the tourists she's in charge of and the crowd shoots off in four different directions.

"What's that?" Bess asks as she cranes her neck in that direction with me. "Oh, another tourist group, you're right." She waves it off dismissively. "I'd tell you that you'll eventually get used to them, but that would be a lie."

"That's not what she meant." Nettie squints so hard my way she's giving me the stink eye. "You're seeing that ghost again, aren't you?"

I suck in a quick breath as I look at the ghost in question.

Malora chortles like the fiend she's turning out to be. "For a woman who can't see me, she sure is intuitive. But don't worry. She doesn't have the gift."

I bite down on my lip to keep the flood of words I'd like to have with Malora at bay, but it's no use. The lava on this island has nothing on the words about to spew from me.

"How do you know?" I whisper to Malora. What if Nettie has been seeing ghosts all along?

Bess shrugs. "Believe me, I thought I'd get used to the tourists, too, but I need to side with some of the locals on this one. The tourists can get annoying."

Malora chuckles. "Nettie can't see me, and neither can she." She hitches her thumb at Bess. "Strangely enough, I don't know how I can tell, but regardless I can. For instance, I knew immediately that *you* could see me. Just like I knew immediately that *she* could see me as well." She points hard just past me, and I spin on my heels to see the brunette in the pink polo shirt giving a meager wave in this direction.

"No," I say, surprised and not altogether convinced.

"No what?" Bess says as she grabs ahold of my arm. "Trixie, are you all right? I think maybe the sun is starting to get to you."

Malora grins my way. "Don't mind her. Talking to the dead is a lot less lethal than any ramifications that cancerous ball of fire can have."

Bess grunts at Nettie, "Once and for all, she is not talking to the dead."

"I didn't say anything," Nettie says, digging through her tote bag and producing a folding fan for each of us that she bought at the gift shop back at the coffee plantation—and Bess and I happily accept.

My mouth falls open as I look to Malora because I'm pretty sure Bess is onto her.

"Oh dear." Malora taps her fingers to her lips. "I think maybe she heard me."

"Of course, I heard you," Bess says to Nettie before her eyes expand. "Wait a minute. How did you do that?" She inches back as she inspects Nettie with a scrupulous stare. "Are you throwing your voice? And how is your voice sounding different—sweeter and saner. What is going on?"

Malora gasps. "It must be your arm, Trixie. Look, she's holding onto you. I bet that's why she can hear me. Maybe have her let go."

"Would you stop?" Bess squawks at Nettie. "The only thing that's going to happen when I let go of Trixie is that you'll stop putting on the ventriloquist routine." Bess lets go. "See there? I hear nothing."

Nettie juts her chin forward. "Wait just a minute. Are you trying to tell me that if I hold onto Trixie here, I'll be able to hear a ghost for myself?"

"Fancy that," Malora marvels. "She's a smart cookie after all."

Nettie grabs my hand and Malora chortles up a storm.

"I hear laughter in the hereafter," Nettie shouts.

"Of course, you do," Malora trills. "I'm right here next to you, dear. *Boo!*"

"Would you stop?" I say to the ghost before me as I shake Nettie free.

"No way, no how, Missy." Nettie gloms right back onto me again. "She said boo, and I heard her. What's your name, and what do you want?" Nettie asks at top volume while looking frantically all around.

"Don't you dare." I point a finger at the specter who holds the keys to the ghostly kingdom.

"Trixie"—Bess shakes her head— "I highly advise you not to egg Nettie on. Before long, you won't be able to shake her. Not only will she move into your cabin, but she'll be spooning with you all night whether you want her to or not."

"You liked it, and you know it," Nettie grouses.

It's true. I heard them arguing about spooning last night and well into the morning.

"I did not like it," Bess says. "I liked it about as much as I like pretending there's a ghost among us."

"Shall I make her a believer?" Malora asks and Nettie nearly jumps out of her skin—with *excitement*.

"I heard her! It's a she! It's a girl ghost! I can hear ghost people! My ghost is better than your ghost," she shouts to the open ocean and a handful of people turn our way.

"Would you mind?" Bess swats the air between them. "You're causing a scene. There are no ghosts. Now let's get on with the self-guided tour before we all faint in a heap. Next time we're bringing our wide-brimmed hats." She nods my way. "And I'll make sure you get one, too."

"We're not going anywhere." Nettie grabs ahold of Bess' hand and clamps it onto my arm. "Go on, haunted hot stuff, tell us what you want and how many naked men we're going to have to sacrifice to get it."

My mouth squares out as I look at Malora. It's bad enough having a ghost I can't control, but I can't seem to control Bess and Nettie either.

"I can explain everything," I blurt the words out at top speed. "There is no ghost. I'm the one throwing my voice. And I—"

"Are quite the fibber," Malora adds and both Bess and Nettie look in her direction as sure as if they could see her. "Oh, just come out with it already. Trixie sees ghosts. I'm her first, in fact." She fans herself with her fingers with a look of pride on her face, and I let out a hard groan.

Bess shakes her head at me. "Boy, you're good. You could have your own show. We've had a ventriloquist on board now and again, and I've always seen their mouths move at least a little. If I were you, I'd take this act on the road. You're going to make millions, kid."

I'd smile at the fact Bess just referred to me as a kid, but the truth is, I'm far too traumatized by the horror taking place to care about my ill-conceived youth.

"That wasn't Trixie," Nettie says. "And look, she's not even denying it. That's because she can't look us in the eye and lie to our faces."

"She just denied it five seconds ago," Bess howls.

"Oh, they're great fun, aren't they?" Malora honks out a laugh. "Don't worry, girls. I'm not here to cause any harm. In fact, I'm here to help Trixie with the investigation."

Another hard moan evicts from me.

"I knew I liked you." Nettie points right at the surly specter as if she can see her. "Not only are you the *ghostess* with the *mostess*, but you're an amateur sleuth like me."

"Trixie?" Bess says it sternly. "Please set Nettie straight, or she's going to be unbearable from this moment until she turns into a ghost herself."

"Not if you go first," Nettie tells her. "And if you do, you've got to promise to come back and haunt me. You owe me and you know it."

Bess rolls her eyes. "Now that's one promise I'll keep." She nods my way. "Please, Trixie, I'm imploring you."

Nettie holds a finger my way. "If you lie twice to a couple of old ladies at the City of Refuge, the spirits of ancient chiefs will cause the ground to open up and swallow you whole."

I avert my eyes. "That might be easier than the present state of my life."

"Come now," Malora says. "Whatever you're going to do, do it quickly. I sense a shiny new suspect in the vicinity."

"Where?" Nettie calls out as she looks every which way. "Let me at 'em." She looks back at the ghost among us. "What's your name, hon?"

"Maltadora Radcliff, but you can call me Malora."

Bess frowns my way. "Trixie Troublefield. You have no idea the Pandora's box you're unleashing. Nettie might just follow you all the way back to Maine. She's going to eat your last nerve for breakfast. Never mind what she's going to do to your sanity."

A sickly moan evicts from my throat.

"Excuse me?" a friendly voice chirps from behind and I turn to see that brunette tour guide. The brass nameplate pinned to her shirt reads *Holly* and I groan again because if Malora is right about this woman, Bess is about to lose both her last nerve and her sanity. Nettie has all but accepted my absurd new reality at this point.

The perky brunette nods. "I was standing over there and noticed you were talking to this fancy-looking lady." She pauses to give Malora a quick wave. "It's so rare I see a ghost in the wild —well, outside of the ghosts that I see on the tours I give. That's why I took the job." She smiles our way as if this were a perfectly normal conversation one might have with a group of strangers. "So, are you all transmundane?" She looks to the three of us before glancing down at my arm, which is still being strangled by both Bess and Nettie. "Oh, it's you," she says, looking right at me. "The hand-holding thing should have given you away right at the bat. I didn't discover that little tidbit until a few years back. Can you believe it? One day my boyfriend was holding my hand, and just like that, he could hear the ghosts around me, too. Anyway, let's just say things didn't end well between us. He was more than a little *spooked*."

"What's happening here?" Bess' voice drops an octave, and I can tell she means business.

"Would you hush?" Nettie tells her. "Holly here just let Trixie know she's something called transmundane. I bet that means she can see the dead."

"And hear them." Holly nods. "But actually, transmundane is just an umbrella term for a subset of powers. *Supersensual*—that's the correct name for those who can see the dead—it's just one of many. Let's see, there's telesensual—being able to read minds. There's sibylline—having the ability to see into the future—it's like those phony fortunetellers would have you believe. It's more or less a peek into tomorrow for that specific person given straight from the man upstairs." She frowns my way. "Don't you hate the way the world sensationalizes our abilities and makes us sound like freaks?" She shakes her head at the annoyance of it all. "Anyway, I thought I'd pop by and say hello. I'd better go hydrate if I want to finish out the last leg of my tour without passing out."

She starts to take off and I panic.

"Wait!" I pull her back. "How did you get like this? How did *I* get like this?"

I cringe because in less than ten words I just officially outed myself to Bess and Nettie.

"Knew it!" Nettie whoops and hollers, but I choose to ignore it for a moment, and ignore the fact she's currently dancing a jig.

Holly sighs. "You know, I've heard it's something we're born with, but sometimes it can lie dormant until something jars it out of us."

Bess scoffs. "Like a bonk on the head with a bottle of backyard vodka?"

"That would definitely do it." Holly laughs at the thought. "I fell off a swing when I was eleven, and it's been hairy-scary times ever since. But I don't mind so much." She gives me a quick pat on the back. "I run tours throughout the island. Holly Cantrell. Look me up whenever you want. I gotta run."

She takes off and I choke on a river of words.

"Holly Cantrell," Nettie says, typing the woman's name into her phone. "Don't worry, Trix. I've got it down for you."

"Thank you." I wince over at Bess. "Are you okay?"

"Am I okay?" she marvels. "Are *you* okay? I can't get my head around it."

"That makes two of us," I mutter.

"Look, here he comes." Malora motions to my right, and I look that way to see a man about ten years on me with a wreath of gray hair and I take in a never-ending breath.

"I think that's Olivia's husband," I say.

"Good work, sister," Nettie says, holding a hand up to Malora, and sure enough, the ghost gives her a high-five.

Wonderful.

Bess and I are worried about the fragile state of our emotional health and Nettie is high-fiving a woman who crossed the veil years ago.

"All right, fine." Bess tosses her hands in the air. "Why is this ghost here to help solve the case?"

"She said she was sent to help me," I tell her. "It's not all that uncommon for someone to return from the other side to help out with an investigation."

"That's true," Malora says and I quickly pick up Bess' hand once again. Nettie, however, is still holding on and about to cut off my circulation. "I knew Olivia when she was young. And apparently, whomever you loved the most is the one they send down to help out if your life is cut short via a homicide. It could be anyone, it could even be a pet they send—the only other qualifier is that you have to be dead."

"Good grief." Bess closes her eyes a moment.

"Here he comes." Nettie elbows me, and sure enough, Dave Montauk has inched his way over and is studying the sea with his arms folded tightly. He's dressed in a gray T-shirt, plaid shorts, with sunglasses pressed to his face, and appears to be mesmerized by his surroundings. Can't say I blame him.

"Let's go," Nettie says, pulling us forward. "I've got a plan."

Bess moans, "Typically, it takes less than an hour for us to get arrested after she says those words."

"In 1492, Columbus sailed the ocean blue," Nettie calls out at top volume before ramming us into the poor man and causing him to stumble backward.

"Oh goodness. Are you okay?" I ask him as I try to regain my own footing.

Dave staggers a bit before chuckling softly. "I'm fine." He nods to the three of us. "Are you ladies all right? I heard the chorus you were singing. Semantic memory is a wonderful thing. I used to be an elementary teacher." He offers a faint smile. "But I quit to help my wife out with her career a while back. My wife was an artist."

"You don't say." Nettie scoots in. "She wouldn't happen to be that artist who bit the big one on the *Emerald Queen*, would she?"

Both Bess and I groan at that one.

Malora shrugs. "Sure, she's crass, but she knows how to get somewhere."

Bess turns in Malora's general direction. "I'm liking you more by the minute."

Nettie chuffs. "At my age, crass is a compliment."

Dave looks momentarily confused. "I'm sorry, yes, that was my wife. And you'll have to forgive me for not being able to keep up with the conversation, but I've had trouble concentrating ever since I lost her. I would have flown home by now, but the authorities keep asking me a few more questions every time I turn around. And the ship is loaded with her work."

"We're so sorry for your loss," I tell him. "I'm actually helping the ship out with the classes Olivia was set to teach. I'm not an artist on any level compared to her, but I've studied her style. It's so very beautiful, and unique."

A dull laugh bounces through him. "That sums up Olivia in a nutshell. If you need any assistance with teaching, just let me know. A member of the staff that's with us is trained in Olivia's technique herself."

"Oh? Is that Amanda?" I wrinkle my nose. "Actually, she's PR, isn't she?"

"Ah"—his expression brightens a notch— "you are familiar with the troops. Yes, Amanda Charming is PR. Isabella was Olivia's agent—she's the one trained to assist if you need her." He ticks his head to the side. "You'll have to excuse me, I don't think I'll ever get used to speaking about Olivia in the past tense."

A moment of silence pulses by.

"I met Isabella on the ship," I tell him. "Thank you for the heads-up. I'll touch base with her if I can before the class starts. Amanda let me know about the memorial you're planning."

"Ah yes—the ball." He looks reluctant about it. "That was Isabella's idea. Always the thinker when it comes to squeezing an extra dime from the auctions. We've coordinated it with a formal night, so it will have all the glitz and drama that Olivia would have loved. I'm hoping we sell out of every piece."

"Why is that?" Malora leans in. "Doesn't he want to keep a few pieces for himself?"

"Why is that?" Nettie echoes the dead. "Don't you want to keep a few pieces for yourself?"

"Atta girl." Malora nudges her. "You're far easier to work with than Trixie."

Bess rolls her eyes again.

"I don't know," Dave says. "Lord knows I have enough of her work hanging on the walls back at home. But I suppose I'll offload those as well. This might sound strange, but she was a part of each of her pieces. It would be like looking at a ghost."

"That's understandable," I tell him. "Dave, when I spoke to Amanda, she hinted that Olivia has some sort of a secret. Do you think that's what got her killed?"

"A secret?" His eyes widen a notch before he flits a glance to the ocean and he takes a deep breath.

"He knows the secret," Malora insists. "I've caught my husband with a secret a time or two, and he always shifted in the same manner, looking away and blowing up his chest right before he lied to my face.

"No," Dave says as his chest expands. "She didn't have any secrets. That's just Amanda being Amanda—always trying to build an air of mystery about my poor wife. It was a lucrative endeavor while she was still living. I'll have to tell her not to perpetuate such rumors given the circumstances. If you'll excuse me." He nods as he barrels past us.

"That ended abruptly," Bess says.

"Yeah," Nettie says. "I'm with you, Malora. That man knows exactly what secret his wife was keeping."

I nod as we watch him blend into the crowd.

"And I know who might be able to fill us in on this so-called secret," I say. "Craig Jackson, Olivia's private security detail."

"It sounds like we've got another suspect to question," Nettie says with a little too much enthusiasm.

"Ransom won't like it," I tell her.

Bess balks, "Have you learned nothing from your experience with men? We don't let them dictate what we can and can't do."

I bite down on a smile. "I like how you think. But we'd probably better keep that as our little secret." I glance to the velvet-clad woman among us. "And I'd prefer it if no one else knows about the esteemed Malora Radcliff either."

"Have it your way," Malora trills. "I'm off to haunt the lido deck. I prefer my hot lava in the form of chocolate." She lifts her hands and disappears in a spray of miniature green stars, much the way she appeared.

"Save some for me, Toots!" Nettie calls out.

"So what do you ladies say?" I shrug their way. "Is my secret safe with you?"

"You bet," Bess is quick to assure me.

"I swear her life on it," Nettie says, hitching her head toward Bess. "I'm not saying a word."

We carry on with our self-guided tour of the City of Refuge, but I can't get my mind off of Olivia Montauk.

There's a killer out there, most likely still a passenger on that ship, who might just want to run to a city of refuge themselves sooner than later.

But it won't do them any good.

Justice will be served, and if Malora is right, I'll be the one to dish it out.

CHAPTER 18

It's getting increasingly tricky not to bring up the case when I'm penning a missive for my blog.

I regaled my readers with the antics that took place yesterday —such as what can go wrong when you have far too much Kona coffee then find yourself in the middle of a historical preserve without a restroom in sight. Thankfully, there was no drama regarding Stanton to report on, but I'm still making phone calls, trying to untangle that fiscal knot. And speaking of things that are near impossible not to bring up—a ghost by the name of Malora Radcliff would be one of them.

When we got back to the ship last night, we hit the lido deck hard and found Malora there front and center in a bed of chocolate lava just the way she threatened. Bess had enough of her ghostly shenanigans, but Nettie linked arms with me and she and Malora had a molten lava cake eating contest. Okay, so I participated. When in Rome—or the Big Island.

Then, true to my word, I contacted Fiona Dagmeyer, shark extraordinaire, and we hit it off pretty well. To quote her, she's committed to helping me *stick it to Stanton*. The first thing she's going to do is get me access to my credit cards as soon as possible and then put him on notice that his balls are about to be skewered.

I like her already.

Ransom was a no-show last night at dinner. A sure sign he's up to his eyeballs in work—Bess told me as much.

I won't lie, I missed him. I missed seeing his searing blue eyes seated across from me at the table—chitchatting about our day, talking about any and everything. There's such a warmth about him and yet such a surly stubbornness. I've never met a man quite like him.

And the fact he was a part of an FBI behavioral unit? A part of me wonders if he's breaking down my psyche every time we speak. If he's figured me out, I'd appreciate it if he gave me a clue as well. Some days I look in the mirror and I think I'm seeing a complete stranger. And you know what? I like this version better.

The old me was a carpet that I let Stanton walk all over because I wanted to be a good, submissive wife. He made the money; he paid the bills. I let him own me in ways that I vow no one will ever own me again.

All thoughts of Stanton and the doormat I had been aside—this morning we've docked at a whole new island and I have a date of sorts with the captain.

According to the *Sea Breeze Daily Newsletter*, Kauai is known as The Garden Island for all its rich flora and fauna. And from what I can see out my window, with all of the tall, mountainous formations and the verdant thickets covering every square inch, they are most assuredly right.

Captain Crawford sent me a text last night asking me to meet him in the atrium at nine-thirty, but when I get to the gangway, it's not Captain Crawford I see. It's Ransom.

He's wearing a pale blue dress shirt with his sleeves rolled up and a pair of slacks that could easily be a part of a suit and I have no doubt they are.

"Trixie." His lips curve and his chest expands at the sight of me. "You look lovely this morning." There's something very cat-who-swallowed-the-canary about him today and I don't know why. But with his dark hair slicked back, those come-hither bedroom eyes, and the face of a Roman statue, about ten different women are listing this way, wishing with everything in them that *they* were that canary. Me included.

"Thank you," I say, plucking at the sunny yellow dress I've thrown on. "I can't wait to see what the island has to offer."

"Then I insist I give you a personal guided tour." His lips twitch another notch, and this time I'm certain he's up to no good.

Someone clears their throat from behind and I turn to see Captain Crawford looking unlike his usual self. He's donned a T-shirt and shorts and has a ball cap and sunglasses in his hand. His wavy hair is combed neatly and his amber eyes glow against his tan skin. He's comely, there's no doubt about it. Any woman would be lucky to have either him or Ransom by her side. And at the moment, I'm twice as lucky because they're both less than a foot away from me.

"She's busy," Captain Crawford growls at him before manufacturing a smile just for me. "Good morning, Trixie. I'm sorry if this bozo was bothering you." He glances at the bozo in question. "We're spending the day together, but you already knew that because I mentioned it to you at the debriefing last night."

"Yes." Ransom glowers at him a moment, his lips knotted up, presumably to keep from saying what's really on his mind. "Come to think of it, you did mention it, didn't you?" His brows hike a notch as he looks my way and I can feel those blue eyes searing through me as sure as a brushfire, and if I had to guess, there's a smidge of hurt in them. "Have a wonderful time, Trixie. As an artist, I'm sure you'll find the beauty of the island inspiring."

Captain Crawford nods his way. "I'll be sure to hit all the highlights with her."

Ransom looks fit to kill.

"*Ooh*, speaking of kill…" I wince because I didn't mean to say that out loud. "I mean, killers—I ran into Dave Montauk yesterday while we were on the Big Island."

"What?" Ransom looks more than mildly alarmed. "Please tell me you didn't speak to him."

"Not initially." I'm back to wincing. "But after Nettie rammed us into him, I basically had no choice. He's a real nice man. And his grief was palpable."

"Trixie," Ransom's voice softens a notch, "remember what I said about staying away from anyone remotely connected to the case? This is still an active homicide investigation and we're not taking anyone off the table as a suspect just yet."

"That includes you, Trixie." Captain Crawford winks my way before looking at Ransom. "You mentioned that last night, didn't you?"

Ransom stiffens, the steam coming from his ears only rivals my own.

"Ransom," I hiss his name without meaning to. "You can't be serious. I'm no killer. I don't even have a motive."

Captain Crawford shrugs. "He hinted that you might have a motive."

My mouth falls open as I suck in a quick breath, but before I can ask Ransom a single question, the captain hooks his arm through mine and we're descending the gangway.

The warm air gives us that old familiar humid hug and the faint scent of plumerias clings in the breeze.

"Welcome to Kauai, Trixie," he says. "Don't give the case or the investigator another thought. In fact, I hereby declare a moratorium on all things relating to the two. How about it? We have a great day and focus on the beauty all around us."

"I'm in." I give a heartfelt nod his way. "I'd like to forget every single one of my troubles. And I want to thank you for this. I mean, you're the man in charge, and I'm just one passenger. Your kindness to me has been more than generous. Thank you for that, Captain Crawford."

"It's my pleasure, and please, call me Wes." He presses his brown eyes to mine and warms me with them.

"Okay then, *Wes*. I'll try to get used to it," I say. "So what's first up on the agenda?"

"I thought we'd take a drive along the coast for a while before heading over to the Fern Grotto, then round out the day at the Wailua Falls."

"Sounds perfectly magical."

His lips curl at the tips, but he doesn't break his gaze from mine. "It will be."

Captain Crawford—*Wes*—already has a car waiting. He whisks us away from Nawiliwili Harbor and down the coast as he treats us to miles of sandy beaches. We drive through quaint small towns before hopping onto the highway.

"We're going to make a left up here," he says, getting onto a smaller road and I see a pizzeria, an ice cream shop, a candle shop, and a tiny grocery store that looks family-owned. "And this road is going to lead us to the Poipu area. But before we get there"—he motions to the canopy of greenery up ahead. "This is the famed Tunnel of Trees." No sooner does he say the words than the sky is covered with tree branches stretching on either side of the road as they conjoin overhead to create just that, a tunnel.

"Oh my word, this is stunning," I say as I marvel at the verdant beauty interweaving above us like a curtain of emerald lace. "What kind of trees are these?"

"Eucalyptus," he says. "A long while ago a wealthy rancher donated hundreds of trees that he didn't need and the tunnel was born. This is one of my favorite stretches of highway on all the islands. There's just something peaceful about it."

"I'll say, I can't take my eyes off of it. The first thing I'll do when I get back to my cabin is sketch this out."

"You should. I knew the artist in you would appreciate the beauty. Just wait until you see everything else this island has to offer. Words can't do it justice, but I have a feeling your paintbrush can."

We drive down to Poipu and he takes us to three different beaches, and each time we get out and walk along the warm sand as equally warm water trickles over our feet.

After another forty-minute drive, eating some of the best cheeseburgers known to man and taking in the wall-like mountains, we arrive at the Wailua Marina State Park and hop on a boat as we travel up to the Fern Grotto. The tour guides in charge on the covered pontoon ask the women to stand and instruct us to point right and left—and before you know it, they've finagled us into doing the hula. One of the guides pulls out a ukulele as another guide comes around and makes sure we're swiveling our hips just the way the Hawaiian gods intended.

Everyone has a good laugh about it, and once we dock and jump ship, Captain Crawford—Wes—wraps an arm around my shoulders and chuckles.

"You were amazing," he says as we fall behind the crowds zooming off ahead of us.

"I was so embarrassed." I laugh. "I've never swiveled my hips for anyone—a sad but true story. I felt like I was giving you a lap dance."

Did I just say those words?

Can I control nothing that comes from my mouth?

He laughs twice as hard. "Seeing that I've never had one of those, I wouldn't know. But you were a natural." He winces. "Not to say I recommend you go into the lap dance business."

"I think I'm doing the world a favor by abstaining from that career path. Speaking of career paths," I say as we follow a dirt trail through a covering of exotic green plants with leaves the size of our heads. In addition to that, there's a plethora of tall, furry-looking bushes that look perfectly foreign to me with both purple and red blooms that may as well come from a different planet. "How did you get into the cruising business?"

I pause to take pictures of the glorious greenery around us and he motions for my phone and he takes a few pictures of me next to the verdant glory.

"I've always been interested. My father was a fisherman. So I guess you could say I'm in the family business in a roundabout way. Got my master's in marine science, and from there worked on various ships, became a senior officer on a few, eventually got my captain's license, and here I am."

"Wow. That's wonderful that you were so laser-focused. You've certainly spent a lot of time on a boat. Was that hard on the family?"

He blinks over at me, and I freeze.

"I'm so sorry." My fingers rise to my lips. "That's certainly none of my business."

"No, it's fine." He steps in close and I scoot in next to him and snap a few selfies of us next to a tree with coral-colored flowers in the shape of a horn. "The boys were just about to turn into teenagers when I started the heavy lifting. My wife and I had been steadily drifting apart at that point. I went home every chance I could, but it wasn't nearly enough to save anything left between us. The boys have been away at school for years now, and I've been here. My wife is now my ex, and that's all she wrote."

"I'm sorry. But you seem to have a wonderful life now. Each day must be a new adventure."

"Believe me, it is. It can be overwhelming at times, but I've got a phenomenal crew. We all work together, and we're all family on the *EQ*."

"I can see that." I nod. "I mean, I don't have a lot to reference, this is my first cruise, but everyone is so nice." Tinsley comes to mind. She might be a little too nice where the captain is concerned. "And they all seem to adore you." Especially her.

"I wouldn't say all." His brows flex as we continue down the path. "But you know what they say, you can't please all of the people all of the time."

It's just gnawing at me to know what's going on between him and Ransom, but I don't want to dampen the mood more than I already have.

"Well, you please *me*." I shrug. "I think both you and your crew are wonderful."

His eyes soften as he takes me in. "Thank you, Trixie. That means a lot."

We meander our way through dense jungle thickets filled with bamboo shoots that seem to touch the sky until we hit a cave-like structure with hundreds of ferns growing right out of the stone cave wall, and the best part? There's a waterfall set in the middle of it. A million leafy ferns hang like chandeliers as they sway in the breeze.

"Wes, this is gorgeous," I purr as a trio of ukulele players strum a melodic rhythm on the concrete platform facing the emerald wonder.

"It's one hundred percent natural," he says, stepping in close as the tour guide in the front orients the lot of us to the history of the place.

"In addition to being one of many of Kauai's crown jewels"— the short redhead with a pixie cut continues— "the Fern Grotto serves as a premier wedding destination. Is anyone here celebrating an anniversary?" She looks out at the crowd, but nary a hand rises.

"Ironic," I whisper to Wes. "It's actually my anniversary today." Something that apparently I was repressing until this very moment.

"What?" He inches back. "Trixie, I'm so sorry."

"We'll need a couple of volunteers," the woman calls out.

"We'll do it," Wes says, waving her way before taking up my hand and leading us to the front.

"What exactly is it that we'll be doing?" I whisper to him.

"I'm not sure," he whispers back. "But if it gets your mind off your troubles, it's worth it."

"That's very kind of you." I give his hand a squeeze and he sheds a quick grin my way.

"Hey, it's the captain," someone shouts from the crowd and Wes nods and gives a cheery wave to a welcoming applause.

"The captain?" the redhead says with a smile. "Why don't you and your lady friend both hold hands, look lovingly into one another's eyes, and our band will serenade you with a traditional wedding song from the islands."

We do as we're told as the ukuleles change to a melodic rhythm.

"As you can see," the redhead calls out. "The Fern Grotto creates a stunning backdrop for a wedding venue, a renewing of the vows ceremony, or anything in between." The crowd laughs at that one. "Captain, you may now kiss your bride," she shouts and both Wes and I look at one another stunned.

Kiss?

Do I want to be kissed today? No less in front of a couple of dozen people? People from the *ship*. But then again, I don't want to be known as the woman who turned the captain and his kisser down flat. Wes is certainly attractive, and so very kind. Those warm melted chocolate eyes that he sees the world through have only ever made me feel comfortable.

"It's just for fun." I shrug, my heart beating a million miles an hour.

"For fun." His lips twitch, but his eyes never leave mine. He leans my way and I give a last-second glance to the crowd and note a tall, beefy-looking man, built like the grotto itself, and a breath hitches in my throat.

It's him! I turn my head his way. *It's Craig Jackson, Olivia Montauk's security detail.*

Wes lands a kiss to my cheek, just shy of my lips, and good grief, had I not turned my head, he would have struck paydirt. Not that I would have minded—wait—why wouldn't I have minded? I haven't kissed anyone other than Stanton since I was in college. An applause breaks out, and soon the tour dissipates as everyone breaks into small groups and a thousand conversations all at once.

"I'm sorry." I wrinkle my nose at poor Wes. "But thank you for that. I certainly wasn't expecting to get a hug today, let alone a kiss."

He gives a pained smile. "Well, since I've done one, would it be all right if I did the other?" He holds out his arms.

"Are you kidding?" I wrap my arms around him and we exchange a hearty embrace. "I'll take a hug from you any day of the week." I pull back and sigh.

"You're a good woman, Trixie. And you deserve to be happy. I hope in some small way, I was able to make this day a little more bearable for you."

"It's certainly a day I couldn't have imagined." I glance toward that beefy man once again as he stands at the overlook all by his lonesome. He's wearing a tank top, board shorts, and those rippling muscles of his look as if they could double as flotation devices.

A group moves our way, and soon one of the gentlemen has struck up a conversation with Wes while a few of the women angle to get a picture with him.

Never one to look a gift horse in the mouth, I slink away and make a beeline for Mr. Muscles.

"That's some view," I say just as a smattering of miniature green stars appears and Malora Radcliff appears in all her ghostly glory.

"Ooh, lookie what we have here," she trills as she pokes him in the biceps with her finger. "Nettie would really like this one."

She's probably right about that. Malora and Nettie not only have quite the bond going, but they seem to have the same taste in everything—men included.

He slaps the exact spot she poked as if he were killing a mosquito.

"Sure is a good one." He sighs wistfully. "Congratulations on the nuptials," he says. His tone is low, and there's something all around morose about him.

"Oh, actually, the captain and I aren't really married. We were just a stand-in for the real deal. I guess the tour guide wanted to drive home the point that this is quite the romantic locale." I shrug. "And it is," I say as I look into the darkened grotto in front of us. "You know today would have been my twenty-fifth wedding anniversary."

He pulls back and looks my way, seeing me for the very first time. His skin is tan, and he has a thick nose and light eyes. His body is so thick and cumbersome, even his muscles have muscles.

"I'm sorry," he says. "When did your husband pass away?"

Malora balks, "Honey, she's not that lucky."

I make a face because she's right.

"He didn't pass away," I tell him. "He cheated. This was supposed to be our honeymoon cruise. And well, I took it without him." I glance back to see Wes mobbed by a group of women and my stomach squeezes tight.

That's not a pang of jealously, is it?

"A cheat, huh?" Craig growls as if he's fit to kill. And believe me, I'd pay good money to watch Craig rip Stanton limb from limb. "I can't stand a cheat." His expression darkens as he looks to the grotto. "But I've certainly seen women put up with one. I'm glad to see you're not one of them. A woman should know her worth, know that she deserves better than to have someone stepping out on her—disrespecting her right to her face." He shakes his head aggressively. "It's not right."

"I certainly agree." I shudder. But enough about me. "That was the captain of the *Emerald Queen of the Seas* back there," I tell him, hoping to steer his attention back to the homicide at hand. "We're just friends, of course."

"Hey, I'm on that ship." He brightens a bit when he says it, and then just like that, a look of grief fills his eyes.

"Oh, he's mourning her, isn't he?" Malora tsks at the thought. "Say, you don't think he's mourning the fact he killed her, do you?"

I give a little shrug. He's certainly strong enough to have pulled it off.

Amanda Charming alluded to the fact that Olivia had a secret, and that even though it wasn't her place to spill it, she said that Craig knew about it, too. I just have to shake it out of him somehow.

"Did you hear what happened on board?" I lean his way. "A woman was killed—stuffed in a suitcase. It turns out, she was a famous artist. I'm an artist myself and I happened to follow her. As a fan—not some sick *stalkery* way."

"I know all about her." He pinches his eyes shut a moment. "Olivia and I were pretty close. I worked security for her."

"Security? Was she having trouble with obsessed fans?"

"No, no, nothing like that. I was taking care of the paintings for the most part. I watched over the work while the shows were happening. I helped move the pieces to make sure they weren't being manhandled, things of that nature."

"Then you must have been close to her."

"Very—very close." He swallows hard, his eyes welling up with tears.

"I'm so sorry," I tell him. "I can't imagine how terrible this must be for you. I know for a fact the ship is going on with the show. I'll be there helping out with the crew. What do you think happened? I spoke with Isabella, her agent, and she seems perplexed."

Malora waves me off. "She wasn't perplexed, she blamed Amanda."

She practically did.

"Isabella?" he growls out her name. "Some agent she turned out to be. Olivia hasn't been well in the last couple of years."

"She wasn't well? Can I ask what happened?"

"She had crippling arthritis. She had carpal tunnel, too. But when surgery didn't fix her troubles, the doctors recommended she try a variety of medications. She changed her diet, took all the meds, but none of it worked. She was pretty down about it, too."

"How did she possibly paint?" I shake my head at the thought. I've thanked the good Lord on several occasions for all ten of my fingers. I *need* to paint like I need to breathe. I need to spend time expressing my thoughts onto whatever medium I have in front of me. I may not have known Olivia, but I know on a cellular level it was the same for her.

"I have no idea how she did it." His face burns a dark shade of red.

"Oh, he's an angry one, isn't he?" Malora chitters. "Ask him if he killed her. I think you should be getting back to the captain." She nods toward Wes. "Give it another minute and that mob of women is going to take off with him. But hopefully not before they take off his clothes. I'd like a little show myself."

I glance that way, and sure enough, she's right.

"So, who are the police focusing on?" I ask him. "I mean, you said you weren't here to ward of obsessed fans so it must be someone else."

"She had a few groupies." He shrugs. "But you know what they say, in these cases, you don't have to look too far."

"I heard she had a secret." I nod up at him. "Isabella mentioned something about it." I bite down on my lip hard because it was actually Amanda, but if I tell him that I've been prodding everyone in their circle, he might think *I'm* an obsessed fan. And at this point, I basically am.

"Isabella said that? Well, isn't that rich." He chuckles to himself as he rocks back on his heels. "Olivia and everyone around her had secrets. Isabella has them. Heck, her PR woman had a whopper."

"Amanda?" So much for not coming off like a stalker.

He nods. "Mandy's PR firm took a nosedive last summer. She was let go by a few clients after they caught her double-dipping in their funds. Apparently, she owed a hefty sum in back taxes and said she was merely *borrowing* the money. She swore up and down that she never did that to Olivia. And Olivia believed her. In fact, it was Olivia who gave her a loan to get herself out of the financial pickle she was in."

"Olivia gave her a loan?"

He nods. "When Olivia cared about someone, there were no limits to what she would do for them. Too bad that same treatment wasn't granted to her."

"Ask about the husband." Malora nudges me and nearly knocks me into him. I think she has more strength than she realizes.

"How about her husband?" I ask, catching myself before I launch onto the poor guy. I'm sure knocking into his chest would feel like hitting a brick wall.

"He's pretty broken up about it." He glowers at the grotto again. "They were having some trouble toward the end. I don't know what it was about but Olivia wasn't happy. I think he was the one who pushed her to get back to work. He quit his job ages ago, and Olivia was the primary breadwinner. All I know is, she spent these last few weeks running to me and not to him. Something was up, but she never wanted to talk about it. She did say something to me a few days before we stepped on the ship." He pauses to take a ragged breath. "She said this would be her last show. She was putting her foot down."

My jaw roots to the ground. "I'm sorry she felt that way."

He nods. "I'm sorry it's true." He nods and wishes me a great rest of my trip before taking off.

Malora leans in. "So now what?"

"I don't know. I've got that class tomorrow. I'm hoping either Isabella or Amanda will be there. Amanda borrowed money from her…"

"I bet it was a substantial amount," she says.

"I bet it was, too."

She grabs ahold of my arm and gives it a squeeze. "Here comes the head honcho hottie. Good luck with him. They're having afternoon tea in the Lagoon Lounge and then we're having a rousing game of Bingo. I'll see you aboard the ship." She gives Wes' cheek a light pinch as he comes in close. "I'll be in your cabin later." She turns my way and winks. "It can't all be work and no play." And just like that, she dissolves in a vat of miniature stars.

"Everything okay?" Wes steps in my path and I nod his way.

"It's even better now."

He brushes the hair from my eyes. "I'm glad you're enjoying the grotto. If we're ever back this way again, I'd love to take you kayaking up the river. Once you get to a certain point, you can hike out a bit and eventually you'll hit a secret waterfall. It's gorgeous, and it leads to a pool you can swim in.

"Sounds magical." My stomach tightens again. "I would love to come back here with you one day." I don't believe the words that just came from my mouth. I think we both know that will never happen, it's just one of those things you say. But it felt right. And I'd like to think if I did come back—and Wes was here, we'd enjoy the day kayaking and hiking out to that secret waterfall.

We take our time at the grotto before heading back down the river and back to our rental car.

Wes drives us up a short canyon, and soon we're at the Wailua Falls, taking in the spectacular view from the top of the lookout.

We take pictures of ourselves, and I send a few to Stanton for posterity. I can't help it. If I had to witness him doing nude acrobatics in our bedroom, he can certainly handle seeing me have a good time with the captain—on our anniversary. This is what he gets.

By the time we get back on the ship that evening, Stanton has fired off over a dozen irate messages demanding that I return home right this instance. A few of his last straggling texts claim that he wants me back, he wants to right all the wrongs. He begs for just one phone call.

But I'm not giving in.

He's delusional in every capacity. And according to my credit card companies, he's reported all of our cards as stolen.

Stanton is playing hardball.

Whoever killed Olivia Montauk is playing hardball, too.

And if I have any say in it, they're both going down.

Aloha.

CHAPTER 19

Before I went to bed that night, I chronicled every last detail of my time with the captain on my blog *Suddenly Single—What a Trip!*

I also filled in my blog-happy peeps all about how Bess, Nettie, and I drove to Hanalei the next afternoon and napped on the beach surrounded by emerald mountainsides that shoot straight into the sky. It felt as if we were protected by ancient verdant soldiers.

I couldn't drink in the landscape fast enough. I brought my alcohol markers and my sketchbook with me and filled nearly half of it with the beauty of Kauai alone. On the way back to the ship, Bess and Nettie pointed out the Sleeping Giant, a mountaintop that's carved by nature to look like exactly that—a sleeping giant with his nose and chin pointed in the air. There is still so much of that magic island that I long to explore. I don't know when, but I'm coming back. Kauai is calling to me like a siren song, as if I belong there, and part of me believes I do.

By the time I get to the lido deck for breakfast, the entire ship is a titter all because of yours truly.

Who knew a mock wedding at the Fern Grotto would be

enough to fuel the rumor mill about my upcoming faux nuptials to Captain Crawford?

I'll admit, I chuckled the first few times people asked to see my ring, and without hesitation, I showed them my wedding ring, indeed—the one I hadn't even realized I was still wearing.

Isn't that something?

This ring has been so much a part of me, I hardly notice its presence. I suppose the time has come to take it off, and I guess I'll do that when I get back to my cabin. A part of me is mourning the ring far more than I am what it represented. It's an old friend that's been with me through meatloaves and manicures, the birth of my children, holiday parties, and those lonely hours when I felt all alone in the world and couldn't put my finger on why. I'll admit, I'm sad to see it go.

After a gorging breakfast of lox, more lox, and even more lox along with a bagel frosted with enough cream cheese to qualify as a birthday cake, I grab a latte from the coffee bar. I still have a few minutes before the painting class I'm teaching this afternoon, so I decide to add an addendum to my blog, which entails my newly minted status as the future Mrs. Weston Crawford. I hit send and head over to the crafts room one deck down, and before I ever get off the elevator, my phone pings with two different texts. The first one is from Abbey.

Mom! I just read your blog. That is hysterical! But on a side note: I know what happened between you and Dad was pretty crappy. But after giving it some thought, I'm glad you made the decision to go on the cruise without him. And I'm really glad to see you're having a good time. I hope you enjoy the rest of your time at sea. You deserve it.

The next text is from the devil himself, aka my soon-to-be ex-husband.

You're not really falling for this guy, are you? Just remember that you're in a vulnerable state and men like that prey on feeble women like you. I bet he sleeps with a different

woman every night. Don't think you're special. And who the hell is this Fiona Dagmeyer chick you sicced on me? You can't afford an attorney. Call her off before you sink yourself further.

My blood boils at his words and I quickly text back.

First—I am far from feeble. Second—it's none of your business who I am and am not falling for. And third—you're the one who sleeps with different women and makes me feel anything but special. Lucky for me, I'm not buying anything you shovel my way. And last but not least—Fiona Dagmeyer is here to stay. There's a reason they call her the Dagger. You'll find out why, shortly.

"There." I sigh as I hit send. If anything, I'm going to enjoy the heck out of the rest of my time at sea, if for no other reason but to spite Stanton.

The crafts room is light and bright and already buzzing with bodies as women and men of all ages chat while sipping coffee. Bess and Nettie show up and they help me distribute paints, brushes, and cups of clean water as we each set up a station to call our own. Thankfully, there are enough mini easels and a variety of canvases, canvas boards, and stacks of quality paper to choose from. I make the executive decision that everyone works on a sixteen by twenty canvas. That way not only will they get the full artist experience in the vein of Olivia Montauk, but they'll have a nifty souvenir to take home with them, or to ship to their respective residences if needed.

Last night I poured over as much of Olivia's artwork as I could find on the internet. Her cozy landscapes embraced all four seasons, and always included at least one tiny cabin with smoke puffing from the chimney and the warmth of lights glowing from inside. The true marker of Olivia's work was the stylistic way she put paint to canvas. Each stroke was curved into either a full circle or a C, and this technique very distinctly gave the overall painting a very rich and textured look to it. It's not something she advertised, or something that was ever mentioned, but a true artist could see all of the hard work she put into each and every piece.

For today's group project, I've chosen a verdant hillside that slopes toward the sea. And to the right of the water, there's a tiny cottage with a thatched roof, comprised of cobblestones, and a glowing light that comes from the window.

I take them step-by-step, having them paint a large swath for the expansive sky, the hillside is next, then the water. Because acrylic dries so fast, we don't have to wait long to add the cottage. And just as everyone is busy at work, Tinsley Thornton, cruise director extraordinaire, walks in.

She heads my way and I meet her halfway.

Her dark hair is pulled back into a ponytail and she's donned what looks like a hot pink tennis skirt paired with a lime green shirt. She's a visual riot, and if that fire in her eyes is any indication, she's about to riot quite literally.

"What's this?" She holds up a picture on her phone of myself at the Fern Grotto holding hands with Wes, and if I'm not mistaken we're looking lovingly in one another's eyes.

"Apparently, it's my wedding announcement." My lips pull back a notch when I say it. I'd give a full-blown smile, but that might cause her to blow a gasket faster than she's about to.

"You think this is funny, don't you?" She scoffs my way. "You'll be off this ship in less than a week. I wouldn't go ruining your reputation by doing something rash." Her lips cinch a moment. "Look, Wes and I have a thing. We're this close to making it official. I understand how easy it is to get wrapped up in the whirlwind of it all. But your time is short. None of this is real. So don't go mucking up the waters for the two of us." She lifts her chin a notch. "If you're in the market for something quick and dirty, I'm sure Ransom Baxter will be more than happy to oblige."

My stomach bites with heat at the thought of doing something quick and dirty with Ransom.

"I dated Ransom for a time myself." She gives a sly wink and my stomach is filling with heat again, only this time it's for an entirely different reason.

"You dated Ransom?"

"Hot and heavy." She shrugs. "We're more or less off and on, but now that I've got a clear shot at the captain, I've let Ransom go into the wild. But I could have him back at the drop of a hat if I wanted to." Her lips twist with pleasure.

"That's pretty amazing. I mean, they're both pretty amazing men." My heart sinks because Tinsley is the one living the high life with those two men, not me. It was just some delusion I chose to believe. She's right, I got wrapped up in the whirlwind of it all. None of this is real.

"Looking good," she calls out to the class as she drifts off to inspect everybody's work.

Bess and Nettie scuttle over.

"We heard the whole thing," Nettie scowls as she says it. "Don't mind her. You keep mucking up the waters with whomever you want. You can shake the sheets with them, too."

"She says she's serious with Wes—and that she has Ransom on the hook, too. Is that true?" I ask as the two of them exchange a quick glance.

"It's true in her mind," Bess says. "Captain Crawford, Wes"—she winks my way—"used to have a thing with her, but things fizzled on his end and continued to sizzle on hers. As for Ransom, that was mostly in her mind." She winces. "I think?"

"Oh, it doesn't matter," I say with a sigh. "I'll be a memory in just a few days—and all of this will feel like a dream."

Both Bess and Nettie sigh at the thought.

The class goes on, and just as we're wrapping it up, in walks Isabella Bessinger, agent to the artistic stars. Her dark hair fringes her neck like shards, her light eyes are glassy as she takes in the room all at once, and she's wearing dark shorts and a matching top that clings to her skin, making her look like that much more of a waif than she already is.

Craig mentioned that Isabella had a secret, too—that just about everyone around Olivia had one. Of course, he said the whopper was the secret Amanda had regarding the fact she owed Olivia money.

I wonder if I could squeeze a secret or two out of Isabella?

"Hello there." I put on a cheery face as I head her way. "What do you think?" I ask as I wave over the dozens of easels holding replicas of Olivia's work.

"One word—wow." She laughs. "You are phenomenal." Her eyes spin as she takes me in. "Before we leave, I am definitely giving you my card. If you could do this, I have no doubt you can paint up a storm yourself. I'd love to see your portfolio when you get back home. Just shoot me some pictures. I think a very lucrative relationship can be forged between the two of us."

My adrenaline spikes just hearing it.

"Thank you. I would love that," I say, suddenly star-struck by her. This could mean big things for me—such as carving out a living for myself and no longer being subject to Stanton's shenanigans.

Speaking of shenanigans, a spray of green miniature stars appears, and in pops Malora Radcliff in all her velvet glory.

"Lookie here, we've got another one." She sniffs the air between her and Isabella as she inspects the woman's clothing. "Oh dear, that color is all wrong for her. Why don't you offer to teach a class on fashion and the importance of color? Her skin is looking a bit too sallow."

I agree with the sallow part, but I won't have time to teach another class. The cruise is wrapping up and so is my stay here.

"Are you all ready for the art auction tomorrow?" I ask and Isabella twitches at the mention of it. "I'm sorry. This must be hard for you."

Her forehead fills with concern. "Harder than you know. At

the end of the day, Olivia was a friend. Tomorrow marks the end of an era—the first auction set to go forth without her."

"The first?"

She nods. "Luckily, Olivia has a warehouse full of pieces just waiting to go to market. It's practically a never-ending supply." She winks my way. "And now that she's gone, I've advised Dave, her husband, to charge twice their old value. It's a well-known fact that once an artist dies, their work is worth that much more."

"I know it all too well," I tell her. "I had a friend back home in Maine, a wonderful artist who specialized in mixed mediums—he passed away unexpectedly, and suddenly you can't even look at his work without ponying up the big bucks. But unfortunately for his estate, he only had a few pieces left to sell. How fortuitous for Olivia's husband to have a warehouse full of them. She must have been painting nonstop for the last few years."

She gives a frenetic nod. "She was practically unstoppable."

"Well, I mean, she must have stopped recently, right? I bumped into Craig the other day and he mentioned Olivia had health troubles with her hands."

Her eyes flash as a dull thump of a laugh stems from her. "I wouldn't believe a thing Craig Jackson says. If he says good morning, chances are it's night. The man has been spreading lies ever since Olivia died." She scoffs and shakes her head. "I can't believe he said that to you. He's telling everyone who will listen all sorts of nasty rumors."

"Why would he do that?" both Malora and I ask at the very same time.

Isabella glances over her shoulder before leaning in. "Because he wanted to have an affair with her. Word is, Olivia was giving him the brush-off." She nods. "Craig was furious. I don't know about you, but I wouldn't want a man of his stature angry with me. There's no telling what he could be capable of." She lifts a brow and both Malora and I suck in a quick breath.

"Why, he must have killed her." Malora is quick to cast the

first stone in the beefy man's direction—and she might have just pegged the killer with it.

I take a step toward Isabella. "Have you told the investigators?"

A tiny smile crimps her lips. "I spoke with that woman, Quinn something, this morning and let her know I had a few thoughts."

"Quinn Riddle," I say with a nod. "She's working with Ransom Baxter on the case."

She nods. "Isn't that Ransom a looker, though?" She fans herself with her fingers. "I need to keep my thoughts about Craig close to the vest for now. Please don't say anything. I'm still stuck on this ship for a few more days with him and I don't want to be the next person stuffed in a suitcase." She glances at my hands dappled with paint. "If I were you, I'd offer aprons for the participants to wear the next time. Acrylic comes off your fingers with enough scrubbing, but once it's on your clothes, you've got an unwanted work of art on your hands—and by hands, I mean shirt."

"You're one hundred percent right about that."

"I think I'll go offer up some tips to the class." She takes off and I watch as she does just that. She picks up a participant's hand and carefully guides it over the canvas like a seasoned pro.

"I guess she really does know her stuff," Malora says.

I nod. "She does, indeed. I guess that's what makes her such a great agent."

The class wraps up. Bess and Nettie take off for the promenade deck to nap in the sun, and I head to the atrium to guest relations to see if I can get any one of my credit cards to work again.

Here's hoping something goes right for me during this trip.

Deep down, I don't have a lot of faith that it will.

CHAPTER 20

"I'm sorry," Neville, the dark-haired looker, says as he squints at the computer screen in front of him. "Not one of them has been reactivated. Typically, when they're stolen, you'll have to call in and have them mail you new ones. It's happened on the ship on occasion. It'll cost a bit for shipping, but I can give you an address and you can have them waiting for you in Los Angeles if you contact your credit card companies."

"Oh yes! I would love that."

He gets right to jotting down the information I'll need while I take in the atrium with its foliage, the palm trees, the fern. I didn't realize when I boarded the ship how much it was mimicking the islands, and I love it even more for that now.

The makeshift street with all of the little shops and boutiques is swamped at the moment. I was toying with the idea of popping in and saying hello to Elodie, but I'm pretty sure she's busy.

A dark-haired cutie arrives and takes a seat next to Neville and I can see that it's Layla Beauchamp. She has her hair in a bun and she's wearing a navy sleeveless dress with a red and white scarf knotted around her neck and her nametag winks with the light. She's a stunner, all right.

I'm sure if Stanton had come along on the trip, he would have paid extra special attention to her—even thrown down breadcrumbs in hopes she'd follow him back to our cabin.

I shake my head at the thought of having Stanton here with me. If that was the case, I probably would never have met Bess and Nettie. And the captain would have been nothing but respectful to the two of us. He might have even sent over a bottle of champagne to our tables.

Then there's Ransom.

My heart drums just thinking about what a near-miss that would have been. I'm positive I would have noticed him. Not noticing him is like not noticing the Eiffel Tower in Paris or a lion charging at you from the Colosseum in Rome.

Of course, I would have chalked him up as an extraordinarily handsome man and gone on my merry way. I wouldn't have gotten to know him—not that I know him now. But still. The point is, Stanton would have ruined a perfectly good vacation without realizing it.

"Here you go," Neville says as he gives me a card with the ship's mailing info on it.

"Thank you," I say as I bury it in my purse. "Hey, I probably should leave well enough alone, but could you tell me which credit card my husband is using to pay for my onboard expenses?"

"Oh, it's not his credit card." He manufactures a brief smile. "It's someone else's entirely."

"What? Oh my word, you disconnect that right this minute. The last thing I need is to serve hard time due to credit card theft."

Both he and Layla share a laugh.

"You won't serve any time at all," Neville is quick to assure me. "It's on the up and up."

Layla nods. "Let's just say when the ship was alerted to your financial troubles, a senior staffer stepped in."

"A senior staffer? Who is it?"

Neville shakes his head. "We're not at liberty to say. Please, Mrs. Troublefield, enjoy the rest of your stay. I assume you have a lot waiting for you when you get home."

I make a face because I certainly didn't need the reminder.

I'm about to leave when Layla pulls a pin from her bun and shakes her hair loose.

"Well hello, Detective Baxter," she purrs like a kitten and I turn to see Ransom stepping up with a smile twitching on his lips, but he's not looking at Layla or how much body her hair has—or her actual body for that matter—he's looking at me.

"Neville, Layla"—he nods my way— "Trixie. What's going on?"

"She was just leaving." Layla pushes her chest out in an effort to garner his attention. "I've got a break in ten minutes, and I've got a few new yoga moves I'd love to show you."

Ransom frowns just a bit. "I'm afraid I'm swamped," he tells her. "My next order of business is to question Mrs. Troublefield. You wouldn't happen to be hungry, would you?"

I bite down on a smile that's threatening to take over my entire face.

"I am starving," I say.

"Great, I know a secret place that everyone should enjoy at least once before their trip comes to an end." He hitches his head, and I'm right there by his side.

Ransom takes us to the top deck to a restaurant called the Rim of the World, a glass and marble wonder with a view of the sea that makes you feel as if you're soaring over the world.

A blonde waitress seats us at what she refers to as Ransom's usual table.

"You have a usual table?" I marvel as we sit in plush seats where we're treated to views of the many aquatic facilities just below us. Titan's Revenge—a series of slides that tunnel both on the ship and over its borders, the wave pool, and we can see the zip line from here, too.

"I'm afraid I do." His chest rumbles with a thunder of laugher as he pulls my chair out for me.

"Thank you," I say as we take a seat.

"So what was happening at the atrium?" he asks as the waitress hands us each a menu before making herself scarce.

"I'm still trying to claw my way out of that mess with my credit cards." I quickly scan the menu. "You know what? I've never heard of any of these foods. What's good here?"

"Do you like spicy food?"

"Love it." I wrinkle my nose. "Stanton hated it. He had a delicate stomach."

His lips flex with a smile. "Then how does kung pao chicken tacos sound?"

"Like we're living the dream in two different countries."

The waitress comes back with glasses of ice water, and Ransom quickly puts in the order.

I wait until she's well out of earshot to lean his way.

"My credit cards are still a mess, but guess what? Neville and Layla told me that someone—a senior member of the staff here—has kicked in their own credit card for me."

His eyes widen a notch. "They said that?"

"Yes." I give a deep nod. "And I think I know who it is."

"Who would that be?" He cocks his head as if he were amused.

"Captain Crawford—Weston."

He leans back in his seat and his chest expands twice as wide.

"I mean, it sort of makes sense," I tell him. "He's been incredibly kind and accommodating."

"I bet he's been accommodating." His brows swoop in as if he were suddenly fit to kill. "I'd watch him if I were you. He's a smooth operator even if he doesn't look it. I might have the reputation, but he's got a few receipts himself."

My mouth falls open. "Well, thank you for letting me know. I felt bad about that whole fake wedding fallout."

He nods. "Congratulations on your upcoming nuptials. There's your smooth operator in progress."

A laugh bubbles from me at the thought then dissipates just as quickly.

"I just finished up my art class and it went well, but partway through it Tinsley showed up. She really peed a circle around Wes. Around you, too." I don't mind telling him. "It seems the two of you have quite the fan club." I'm half-tempted to get my verbal jackhammer out and bust my way into the dark past history he and Wes seem to share, but I don't want to ruin our meals just yet—especially not with tacos on the line.

"Please feel free to ignore her," he says it sternly. "Tinsley lives in a fantasy world. She's mostly harmless."

Mostly. I make a note of that.

"Isabella Bessinger walked in on the class, too," I say just as our food arrives.

Ransom's body goes rigid. "Did the case come up?"

"Just in a roundabout way," I say, pausing to take a bite out of my taco. "Oh wow, this is amazing." I take another quick bite before reaching for my water. "I mentioned that I spoke to Craig Jackson."

"Trixie," he growls out my name. "You spoke to Craig Jackson?"

"Yes, back in Kauai right after I fake married Wes. Everyone wanted a picture with the captain, and I saw Craig standing nearby, alone, so of course I went over to say hello."

"Of course." He's back to frowning. "Trixie, you realize this is an ongoing investigation. Did you talk about Olivia?"

"What else would we possibly talk about?"

"Are you talking about the case?" the voice of an older woman shrills as Malora pops up right next to me, already pawing at my plate.

She scoops up a taco for herself and both Ransom and I blink at the sight—for different reasons obviously.

I quickly grab onto the taco and he shakes his head.

Ransom cocks his head to the side. "I'd swear on my life that taco just floated right into your hand."

"It must be a glare from the window." I laugh a little too long, a little too hard. "That, or all the sea air is finally getting to you. Do you think you'll come back to Maine?" I take a bite and give Malora a lethal look lest she tries to test Ransom's sanity once again.

"All right, fine," Malora grouses. "I see a sushi burrito at the next table that I'd much rather have. Now go on and hash out all of the suspects, so I can be on my merry sushi-eating way."

If that's what it takes to get rid of her.

Ransom dips his chin a notch as he presses those daring blue eyes right at me.

"Are you trying to change the subject?" he asks.

"Not at all." I clear my throat. "In fact, let's lay out the suspects on the table and get it all over with." So my friendly ghost can harass some other poor, unsuspecting sushi burrito-loving soul.

"All right, I'll bite," he says.

"Do you hear that?" Malora nudges me. "You've got a biter on your hands. My third husband was a biter. He wasn't good at much else, but he knew how to—"

"Okay," I say, cutting her off before I'm treated to a soliloquy from Malora's sex life. "Where should we start?"

"What did Craig have to say?" Ransom looks livid that I spoke to the man at all.

"Let's see. He said that Amanda Charming owed Olivia money, that *she* owed the IRS, and double-dipped with a few of her clients in an effort to get herself out of the hole, but her clients caught on and she was fired. Apparently, Olivia came through for her. He said that Olivia gave her a loan."

"A loan." He nods to himself as if filing it away.

"That's right. And I bet if Olivia was demanding the money back, that might have been a motive to kill her. No Olivia, no loan to repay—that is, if Dave knew nothing about it."

"If he does, he hasn't mentioned it to me. What else did Craig say?"

"He said Dave and Olivia were having trouble. But what marriage doesn't? He also said that Olivia had been suffering from bad arthritis and carpal tunnel. It's a miracle we're having a show tomorrow at all. He said that she told him it would be her last show no matter what. But I bet she meant her painting days were over, because according to Isabella, there's a warehouse full of Olivia's artwork. Apparently, Dave is committed to selling it all. He told me himself it was painful to know he would have to keep seeing her pieces."

"Dave said so." His lids hood a notch because I can tell he's not amused in the least.

Malora nudges me. "Tell him what Isabella said about Craig."

"Oh, and when I spoke to Isabella today, my conversation with Craig came up and she said that I shouldn't believe anything that Craig Jackson had to say. She said he was essentially bitter because Olivia rejected him. I guess he was trying to lure her to the muscly side, which is strange because Craig distinctly told me that he couldn't stand a cheat."

A hard moan comes from Ransom, and for whatever reason, my insides heat when he does it.

About three different women cease all movement—mastication included—to turn their heads this way. Ransom demands the attention of all women at all times anyway, but throw in a moan like that, and you could stop a fleet of ships—or in the least rev an engine or two of the women in the vicinity.

"This is exactly what I didn't want to happen," he says as his jaw redefines itself. "I'm betting one of these people you've spoken to is the killer and they're manipulating the information they're giving you. Don't trust a thing any of them tell you, Trixie, and whatever you do, don't speak to any of them again."

"Sage advice," Malora says. "This is probably where you should tell him all about me and my role in all of this. He seems levelheaded enough. I'm sure once he realizes that the universe has chosen me to solve this case—and you by proxy, then he'll invite you right into the investigation."

I take a moment to glare at her. The only place Ransom Baxter would invite me to after I told him all about my crime-busting poltergeist sidekick is the funny farm. Ransom is level-headed, all right, and there's no way he could take that sort of information as easily as Bess and Nettie did. Come to think of it, poor Bess isn't taking it all that well either.

Nettie? Well, she was made for this supernatural moment.

I nod to Ransom. "You're right. I'll do my best to stay out of your investigation, Detective. Now that we've covered the bases as far as the case goes, I say we change the subject." I glare at Malora a moment before she gets the hint.

"Fine." She tosses her hands up. "But we've got to get cracking. We only have a handful of days before the killer jumps ship, and if that happens, they'll get away with murder—and you will most likely never rid yourself of me."

I gasp as she nods my way as if she's given me something to think about.

"I'll just be over here enjoying my sushi." She floats off and Ransom lands his hand over mine.

A spear of heat travels from his flesh right up my arm and jolts me right where it counts, the heart. His eyes hook to mine and we linger there a moment too long as his gaze sears every last part of me.

I have never felt these things once with Stanton's touch.

In a strange way, Ransom has the power to make me feel alive the way no one else has been remotely close to making me feel.

But then again, Ransom most likely invokes that same feeling in just about every woman.

Stanton is right. I'm not special. He might have been referring to Wes when he doled out the insult, but I suppose the same principle applies here, too.

"Are you okay?" Ransom asks softly. "You seemed to have drifted off for a moment."

"I'm fine." I shudder. "I was just thinking about things. You know, life." I shake my head. "When I was a little girl, I remember thinking that we just lived forever. And then my grandmother died and my mother had to explain to me that people generally only lived to a hundred if they were lucky. I must have mulled over that until I was a teenager. I couldn't believe that people worked so hard for things, then *poof* they were gone. Our time on this planet isn't nearly enough."

He nods. "That's a heady observation—especially for a kid. But then, you've turned into a brilliant woman. I'd expect nothing less."

Color heats my cheeks. "Toss around the word *brilliant*, and it will get you everywhere." A breath hitches in my throat. "I didn't mean that," I quickly recant. "What I meant was I haven't heard that term in connection to me—probably ever."

"Well, your intelligence certainly is worthy of the accolade." He lifts his water my way. "And I agree with you, our time on this planet isn't nearly enough."

"Now that I've depressed us, what other cheerful subjects should we broach? Taxes? The fear of a tapeworm taking up residence in our brains?"

We share a warm laugh over that one.

And just like that, Ransom and I talk about any and everything.

The conversation is easy and light. We don't talk about Wes and whatever haunted mysterious past the two of them might have. We don't bring up Olivia Montauk's killer, Stanton, or Maine.

And you know what?

It is bliss.

But all of this bliss is about to come crashing to an end.

My time on the *Emerald Queen of the Seas* is about to wrap up, and if I don't catch a killer and wrap up this case, I won't be headed back to Maine alone—I'll be dragging a ghost along with me.

CHAPTER 21

There is something to be said of the moon shimmering on the water, creating a river of light that spans the horizon like all of our hopes and dreams personified.

I took a walk on the promenade deck after I enjoyed a light dinner at the Blue Water Café. It's my first and hopefully my last *light* dinner on this floating banquet. But I plan on more than making up for it at the midnight buffet. Those molten chocolate lava cakes were calling to me like a siren song, but I held strong. Seeing that I'm assisting in tonight's art auction, I wanted to be shipshape, pardon the pun, to facilitate it.

An Art Affair to Remember is more or less doubling as the celebration of life ceremony for Olivia Montauk. Her *soiree*, as Amanda called it, happens to fall on a formal night, and Elodie sent me a red glittery dress to wear for the occasion. It's floor-length, sleeveless, not too showy of a neckline, but far showier than I like with its thigh-high slit—another feature I wouldn't have opted for. I told her I couldn't accept it since it would essentially be on the captain's dime, and she assured me that this was on her and that I couldn't stop it from happening if I tried.

I've already made a mental note to send Elodie a very big tip when I get everything straightened out. She's been an amazing friend. I invited her to the auction and she said she wouldn't miss it.

The Queen's Gallery is located on deck five, past the Queen's Mall, toward the stern of the ship. The floor is comprised of dark carpet with gold flecks, the walls are covered with a deep crimson velvet, and there's a stage up front with Olivia's pieces covering it from end to end.

Three pieces are set on top of one another in canvases of varying sizes. Each one tucked in an ornate gold frame ready to grace the home of its new owner. Each piece is a moody landscape portrait with a tiny offset cabin, giving it just enough light to give it that supernatural glow she's so famous for fostering in her work. Above it all hangs a black and white sign that reads *Welcome to an Art Affair to Remember as together we remember Olivia Montauk—a true original.*

The gallery is set up more or less like a lounge with thick velvet chairs surrounding glass tables. A waitstaff wanders throughout the expansive room, offering a flute of champagne to each of the guests.

An elongated table is situated to the right where guests sign up for the fun and receive their bidding paddles. The auction isn't set to start for another hour, but this is the prime time to see the work on display along with procuring prime seating.

I spot Tinsley offering up a manufactured smile for the guests as she monitors the situation from the front of the room, and no sooner does she spot me than that plasticine smile glides right off her face.

"Ooh wee," someone chirps from behind and I turn to find Nettie, with Bess holding up the rear, both in glittery black dresses that give their faces an unnatural glow in this dim lighting. "She's giving you the evil eye if ever there was one."

A laugh bubbles up my throat, but I don't give it.

"She's not too thrilled with me," I say. "But lucky for her, I'll be out of her hair in a few days."

"Yeah," Bess growls. "Unlucky for us." Her eyes ride over the ruby red number I'm wearing. "Goodness. Just wait until the captain sees you in this. I think he'll do his best to make that fake engagement a reality."

Nettie smirks. "He'll have to fight Ransom for you."

"Ransom isn't interested in me," I'm quick to refute.

"Says who?" Bess inches back at the thought. "The man has eschewed an ocean liner worth of hussies for the duration of the trip so far with no end in sight for his dry spell. And I think you alone are to blame for that dry spell."

I laugh at the thought. "It's doubtful. Besides, we don't know who's knocking on his cabin door at night."

"True," Nettie says. "But Ransom has been known to flaunt his honeys, and so far the only honey he's flaunting is *you*."

I wrinkle my nose. "You know what they say, keep your friends close and your prime suspects in a murder investigation closer. Besides, a man like Ransom wouldn't be interested in me. Trust me, I've seen the way Layla looks at him, and she's young enough to be my daughter. I'm not interested in competing with that."

Bess shakes her head. "I don't think you have to."

I spot Elodie up on stage adjusting the labels next to each piece.

"I'd better get up there," I tell them just as a spray of miniature green stars appears near the bar in the back. "Ooh, Malora is here, right by that tower of champagne flutes."

"That's because she's a smart cookie," Nettie says while swatting Bess over the arm. "Let's go say hello to our new favorite spook."

Bess grunts, "I've said hello to worse people."

They take off and I make a beeline for the stage, but before I can make my way to Elodie, my phone pings. It's a message from the captain himself.

Good luck with the auction! Maybe we can catch up afterward and you can tell me all about it. I'm afraid I have dinner plans with a group of executives and I can't get away from it. If I could, I would most certainly be there.

That's very kind of him. I don't mind meeting up with him for a bite later. And I'm sure tonight's event will leave us with plenty to talk about.

No problem. You enjoy dinner. We'll catch up afterward. I can't wait to tell you all about it!

I make my way up to the stage and give Elodie a wave as I head her way.

She's head to toe in a green jewel of a gown, her blonde hair looks platinum in this stringent lighting, and it's cute in a fresh cut blunt bob.

"*An Affair to Remember?*" She nods to the sign hanging above us. "That's one of my favorite movies. Two people meet on a cruise ship—both engaged to other people? They vow to meet up at the top of the Empire State Building six months later if they were still into each other."

"And were they?"

"You'll have to watch the movie." She winks my way. "Guess who I ran into on the way here?" She lifts a brow as she says it, and judging by the look of mischief in her eyes, I'm not sure I'm going to like where this is going.

"A body in a suitcase?" I cringe as I say it just as I spot a large framed picture of Olivia Montauk sitting on a round table to the right of the stage. Six electric candles flicker before her, and my heart breaks just looking at the poor woman. "Wow, that was crass of me. I'm sorry"—I take a deep breath as I revert my attention to Elodie— "what were you about to say? Who is it that you saw?"

"Handsome Ransom." Her shoulders do a little shimmy as she sets the next label on the work of art in front of her.

"Oh?" My body heats at the mention of him. "And did he proposition you before you managed to cross paths? Bess and Nettie tell me he's having a dry spell."

She cackles like a witch on Halloween night. "Ransom knows better than to come crawling my way." Her lips crimp as she gives me the side-eye. "In fact, it was you who was on his mind."

"Me?" My heart lurches unnaturally. I won't lie. I'm more than flattered. "Was he swinging a pair of handcuffs?"

"Why? Do you like it kinky?" she asks as she slaps another label down.

"Very funny. What did he say?"

"He said if you see Trixie, tell her that I'll be at the auction as soon as I can clear up a few things. He also said you should steer clear of certain people. That you would understand the message."

I frown at the thought. "I get it. But what *he* doesn't get is that certain people will be unavoidable for me this evening." The words hardly leave my lips when Isabella Bessinger pops onto the other end of the stage and begins henpecking at the artwork before her. "Ooh, speaking of which, I'll be right back," I say as I scoot my way over to the leggy brunette in a sleek silver gown. "Isabella," I say with a cheery smile. "These pieces are exquisite."

"You really think so?" Her eyes round out as she looks my way.

"Yes." I give a quick nod. "I mean, look at these gorgeous landscapes. It's classic Olivia. I'm not sure why, but I thought she was moving away from her hillside motifs. The latest work I had seen all had a little water in it."

"It was just a phase." She cuts a dark look to the crowd. "If they want water, they can head to the promenade deck. Tonight I need them to love landscapes." She gives a curt nod before stepping past me.

That was odd. I shake my head as I watch her move nervously

from one easel to the next. But then, her friend is gone. I'm sure she wants everything to go off without a hitch tonight.

I turn to inspect the pieces in front of me—a winter scene, a fall hillside, and a thicket in the woods with a tiny thatched cabin. They're all so beautiful. The lighting in here is so murky you're practically forced to squint at them. I lean in and can make out the brushstrokes, the smooth clean lines. The paint lies flat. Not something I would have thought she'd be into, but to each their own. Most artists like to build it up to give the painting some texture.

Elodie comes by and slaps a label next to the winter scene and I do a double take at the numbers after the dollar sign.

"Elodie, these aren't the starting bids, are they?"

"That's exactly what they are. Why?"

"Nothing. It's just—they're triple what her paintings were worth just last week."

"Well, she's dead now." She shrugs as she sticks on another label. "I guess that's what happens. Her value must have shot up overnight."

"Yeah," I say without a lot of conviction. "I guess that's what happened."

I wonder who set these absorbent prices?

I glance around and spot Craig near the bar. "Excuse me," I say as I make my way to him. He's a head taller than just about everyone else in the room and his suit is bunching around his shoulders, mostly because a standard suit isn't big enough to accommodate his muscles.

"Glad to see you here," I tell him. "We met in Kauai, Fern Grotto?"

"Ah yes." He cracks a smile. "The future Mrs. Captain of the ship."

"That would be me," I grimace as I say it, because from over his shoulder Tinsley just gave me another dirty look. I'm sure she wouldn't be pleased to hear me propagating the lie. "Can I ask if you know who's responsible for the pricing of tonight's pieces?"

His chest bucks with a silent laugh. "Why? Let me guess, they're about to gouge this crowd for all they're worth?" He gives a wistful tick of the head before knocking back his drink. "*Ah*, let 'em. What the heck. Olivia was providing nicely, at least while she was able to, for those around her. It's easy to get used to that kind of a lifestyle. I could see why they'd want the money—*need* the money to keep things status quo. And that money we were talking about that Amanda owes the feds? This is probably her way of getting that final installment."

My mouth falls open.

Had she planned this all along?

"Wait, but I thought Olivia gave her a loan to cover that."

"Olivia mentioned it was just the tip of the financial iceberg. Amanda kept wanting more and more." He nods. "Olivia had a way of surrounding herself with greedy people. None of which had her best interests at heart." He twitches the empty champagne flute in his hand and takes off.

"Oh my goodness." I pull out my phone and am about to text Ransom when I spot Amanda Charming stepping up onto the stage. I shove the phone back into the slim purse secured to my shoulder. It's a red beaded number no bigger than an envelope and just about as thick that Elodie sent over along with the dress. You'd think I was Cinderella going to the ball, the way she's been treating me.

I traipse my way up the three small stairs leading to the stage and glide past Elodie as I reach the woman with the long blonde curls. She's wearing a navy gown with spaghetti straps and looks like a work of art herself.

"They're beautiful, aren't they?" I ask as I try to catch my breath while stepping in beside her.

"You could say that." She glowers at the portrait of a fog-riddled mountainside dotted with log cabins. "They're something, all right."

My left brow hooks into my forehead.

She seems as angry as Isabella was edgy. But is she angry enough to kill?

"You weren't getting along with her, were you?" I ask just above a whisper.

Amanda turns my way, and her large blue eyes look cartoonish in this dull light.

"No," she flatlines. "But we were great friends once. Every relationship has its ups and downs and we just so happened to hit a slump. I'd like to think we could have straightened everything out if she lived." She shrugs as if she were indifferent to it.

"Amanda, the day we spoke on the beach in Maui, you said that Olivia came through for you when you needed it most. It was finances that you needed, wasn't it?"

Her lips part as she searches my features for a moment.

"I heard that you owe the IRS more than a fat nickel and that you went to Olivia looking for a loan."

She takes a quick breath as she steps back, but I'm not ready to relent.

"But that wasn't enough, was it?" I ask while closing the distance between us. "You needed much more. What happened? Did you ask her for another loan? And when she said no, you devised a scheme on how to come up with the rest? These starting bids are through the roof. No reputable art dealer would even consider this markup, posthumous or not."

She gasps. "Are you accusing me of what I think you're accusing me of?" She closes her eyes and a small laugh sputters from her. "Yes, my personal finances are out of control. I don't know where you heard that, but I can only guess." Anger flares in her eyes once again. "But no, I'm not in charge of these ridiculous prices. I'm PR. I don't dip my hands in the financial part of these shows. And to answer the question you're implying—I'm not responsible for Olivia's death either." She glances at that welcome sign hanging above us. "I have a sneaking suspicion I know who did the deed and why. But I'm not talking. I value my own life too much to get mixed up in this any further. Let's just say tonight is wrapped in a riddle that could solve this entire mystery. Solve the riddle and you'll have your killer. I'll give you a hint—it's not me."

She darts off into the darkness behind the stage and I'm left to stew on her strange words.

Malora floats over. "Well? Have we got a killer or not? If I'm not headed back to paradise this evening, I may as well map out the rest of my night."

"I'm afraid not," I say, pulling out my phone and pulling up Olivia's website in a fit of frustration. I quickly scan for her events page, but there isn't one. That's strange. How else would some nutjob know where to stalk her every move? I check her other social media channels and nothing—not a mention of a ship at all.

"I don't know what's going on." The words come from me exasperated as I study the painting before me. So smooth and flat. "I thought for sure Amanda was responsible, but after speaking to her, I'm not so certain." A thought comes to me. "Wait a minute..." I scan the crowd briefly. "Craig mentioned something about Olivia providing a nice lifestyle for everyone around her. But back in Kauai, he mentioned that she had crippling arthritis along with carpal tunnel." I look at Malora a moment. "Wait a minute..."

"You just said that twice."

I nod. "I think the number two plays into this nightmare more than we realize. Amanda said that tonight was wrapped in a riddle, and if we solve the riddle we'll have the killer. Malora, tonight's show is called *An Art Affair to Remember*." My fingers float to my lips as I recall a hearty embrace at the beginning of this trip that looked a little too friendly from the outset.

I suck in a quick breath as a certain conversation regarding how difficult paint can be to get off clothing runs through my mind once again.

My head jerks toward the artwork again, and then I see it plain as day.

"Oh, Malora, I know who the killer is—or in the least who *they* are."

"Who, who, who?" she cries out, doing her best impersonation of an owl.

I glance to the entry of the gallery and see the very couple I have in the forefront of my mind.

He puts his hand in the small of her back and quickly shuttles her out of the room.

"Come on," I say as I zip my way in their direction and Malora floats steadily by my side.

"Where are we going?" she howls.

"I don't know," I whisper. "But I'm betting it's akin to the top of the Empire State Building—because they are very much interested in one another." And I'm very much interested in garnering a confession from them.

CHAPTER 22

I follow the deadly duo as they make their way past the crowd and exit through a door that leads to an outdoor alcove.

With the deftness of an apparition, I step out into the dark and windy night. It's quiet, save for the din of music and laughter coming from the deck below. I glance down and spot an expansive hot tub extending well past this alcove that affords me a view of the people milling below. But the area we're standing in is devoid of any people with the exception of my two prime suspects.

Tiny blue lights illuminate this scant quadrant of the deck and cast a sickly glow over the flooring. Moonlight trails an illuminated path after us on the water, and I watch as Dave and Isabella head over to the railing before wrapping their arms around one another.

Dave is decked out in a dark suit, and it just so happens to match that dark look in his eyes. Isabella's silver gown shimmers like an entire constellation of stars against the navy sky.

"Fancy that," Malora growls and I jump at the sight of her. "Oh, come now." She waves me off, and I admire her a moment as her spirit glows with an emerald and purple aura that could make the Northern Lights green with envy. "He was cheating on that poor dead girl all along, wasn't he?"

I nod. I don't know the ins and outs, but I'm determined to discover them.

Ransom comes to mind... and those loose threats he lobbed my way all in the name of my personal safety, of course.

I pull out my phone to let him know I'm just outside of the gallery and implore him to hurry over because there are new developments in the case that he should be aware of. No sooner do I hit send than the door opens from behind and knocks into my back. My phone goes flying, someone mutters a brief apology before shutting the door again, and both Dave and Isabella turn with a start.

"Trixie?" Isabella takes a few steps over and picks up my phone.

"Thank you so much," I say, speeding over and scooping it out of her hands just as the screen lights up and I can see it's a message from Ransom.

Where exactly are you? And get back to the safety of the crowd NOW.

I quickly bury it back into my purse.

"I just came out for some air before things get underway," I pant, taking a moment to inspect the two of them.

"As did I." Dave gives his lapels a quick tug and clears his throat. "Isabella just followed me out here to tell me the show was about to begin."

"We still have some time," I assure him, not in the least amused by the fact he's covering his tracks.

Malora leans in. "What should we do with the two of them?" she whispers even though she doesn't have to. "Shall we throw them overboard?"

I shake my head just enough for her to see it. Although,

considering I know how it feels to be cheated on, it's mighty tempting.

"Well"—Isabella shrugs— "why don't we all get back in there and get this over with? I'm excited to see how much we fetch this evening."

Dave gives an enthusiastic nod her way. "I want this auction to set the tone for the shows we'll put on once we get back on land. Trixie, with the help of you and the crew, I'm sure we can break records this evening."

Malora scoffs. "Goodness. I bet he wants scads of Olivia's hard-earned dollars so he can toss them over his bed and roll around naked with his lover." She glances my way. "I've done it once myself and it wasn't all it was cracked up to be. Speaking of crack, all that rolling can land a bill or two in all the wrong places."

My lips crimp because I'm positive she's right.

"Don't worry, Dave." Isabella takes his hand and gives it a squeeze. "We'll make a fortune this evening—all in memory of Olivia, of course." She pinches a smile my way as she says that last half.

"It's a show, all right," I mutter as my blood boils just looking at the two of them. And as much as I know I should wait for Ransom, or *listen* to Ransom in the least, and head back inside, my anger far outweighs my good senses. "Isabella"—my voice shakes as I say her name— "the other night when we ran into one another in front of the theater, you mentioned that you didn't think a member of Olivia's entourage could have killed her."

The woman sniffs. "That's right. I firmly believe this was an outside job." She pats Dave's hand as she says it.

I sigh as I nod. "You said she had a number of creepers following her, that they knew where she would be because it's all detailed on her website. But I checked and Olivia doesn't have an events page. In fact, there was no mention of her appearing on the ship at all, across any of her social media channels."

"Oh?" She cuts a glance to her cohort. "I suppose we'll have to fire Amanda."

Dave gives a dark chortle. "She was never worth anything to begin with."

"I bet they'd like to fire the poor girl," Malora balks at the thought. "All the more money they can keep for themselves."

I nod because she's exactly right. But they won't need money where they're going.

"Isabella"—her name comes from me pressured— "yesterday when you came into my class, you mentioned that paint was impossible to get out of clothing. That's something only someone with firsthand experience knows, and it's often an error they're passionate about not repeating. You knew this because it's happened to you, hasn't it?

Her eyes widen a notch.

"I'm not an artist." She shakes her head frenetically.

"No, you're not," I say. "That's why those knockoffs in there are worthless. You didn't do a very good job. You missed one vital detail. Olivia always added a swirl to each of her strokes. It's blatantly missing in each and every piece. Those forgeries will never sell."

Dave growls her way before jutting his chin out a notch. "I can assure you, Trixie, that those paintings were indeed painted by Olivia herself. I'm her husband, I watched her do it. It's my word against yours. Now, if you'll excuse us."

"Your word is worthless," I hiss his way, and Malora breaks out into spontaneous applause.

"The look on his face is priceless." She gives a ghostly chortle. "Mind if I take a picture of it with your phone?"

I clutch onto my purse in an effort to block her at the pass. I'm making strides here and I don't want to ruin my pace.

"Dave." I scoff as I say his name. "Craig Jackson will gladly refute anything you have to say. It was him who Olivia was confiding in during these last few weeks. He knew she couldn't paint. She had carpal tunnel surgery. The doctors told her she had crippling arthritis. I'm sure it's well-documented."

His eyes burn with fire. "Craig Jackson was doing his best to land my wife in bed. Nothing that man says can be trusted."

"Maybe Olivia was more interested in him than you think," I tell him. "After all, she had to know that you were cheating on her with Isabella here."

The two of them seize.

"Olivia hasn't painted in a year," I seethe. "She produced a nice lifestyle for the two of you, and once the money dried up, you grew desperate. That's when the two of you concocted the plan to produce your own cheap knockoffs. I saw Olivia stepping onto this ship. She wasn't happy. Not only that, but I witnessed an argument taking place between the two of you that afternoon as well—just hours before Olivia turned up dead. My guess is, she was going to cancel the show. She couldn't defame herself with Isabella's lousy work. She wanted off the forgery express because she was an honest person. And that's exactly why her life ended that afternoon."

Dave's chest pumps as he struggles to catch his breath. "Yes, that's why I killed her. But Isabella told me I had no choice. She said we'd go to prison, that Olivia had enough on us to destroy us."

"Would you stop." She shoves him in the chest. "You idiot. You just confessed to this nitwit. Now, what are we going to do with her?"

"That's easy," he says, and in one fell swoop I'm in his arms and half of my body is dangling over the side of the railing.

"Stop, thief!" Malora shouts. "Wait, he's more than a thief, isn't he? Stop, *killer!* Oh, why am I shouting? It's not like anyone can hear me anyhow."

The whitewash from the ship's wake looks as if it's miles below as I stare down at the briny sea waiting to welcome me into its icy waters.

My life flashes before my eyes—the good parts, Abbey and Parker. Bess and Nettie and all the fun we've had flits by in a blur, then I see Weston's smiling face, our conjoined hands—then Ransom appears looking decidedly angry that I've gotten myself into this pickle to begin with.

"I can't die," I shout as I spin and latch onto Dave's head with all my might.

A scream rips from me as I do my best to claw at his eyes and he jerks just enough for me to propel myself back onto the right side of the railing.

"Oh no, you don't." Isabella grabs ahold of my legs and proceeds to hoist me into the air while I hold onto Dave's head like a life raft.

"For goodness' sake," Malora grunts. "If you're not careful, you'll get yourself killed," she shouts, and I pause a moment to shoot her a look.

"Don't just stand there," I call out. "Do something!"

"Fine." She pushes up her sleeves. "I never claimed to be a lady anyhow." She lets out an egregious scream like that of a wild banshee and charges at Isabella, knocking the woman to the ground and my feet along with her.

"Good work," I say just as Dave hoists me into the air once again and I'm right back to staring at the churning Pacific down below.

The sounds of the door exploding open garners our attention. Dave turns that way, and so do I by proxy.

"*Freeze*," Ransom shouts, pointing his gun in this direction. His shirt is disheveled and his tie is askew as if he moved heaven and earth scouring this ship to find me, and I have no doubt he did.

His eyes drift to mine a moment, that stern look never leaving his face before he nods at Dave.

"Put her down then put your hands up or I'll shoot."

"They confessed," I shout while I still have the breath in my lungs to do it. "They killed Olivia to keep her quiet about the forgeries in the gallery. They're both guilty."

Dave drops me into his arms and quickly turns me into a human shield.

"You put that gun down," Dave shouts to Ransom. "I can toss her overboard with far more accuracy than it'll take for you to stop me. I'm the one in control here, not you."

"That's right," Isabella pants as she stands. "Put the gun down and slide it my way."

Malora balks, "They think he's an idiot, don't they?"

Dave spins me toward the water.

"*Wait*," Ransom shouts.

We watch as Ransom lowers his weapon, his eyes softening as they look to mine.

"Put her down," he says as he sets his weapon on the ground and lifts his hands away from it.

Dave's grip on me loosens just as Isabella dives for the gun, and with one herculean thrust, I push my way out of Dave Montauk's deadly arms.

Malora kicks the gun right out of Isabella's hand, and I dive over it.

"I got it," I shout as I jump to my feet, waving it victoriously over at Ransom. His eyes double in size.

"*Trixie*," he growls.

"Ooh, sorry," I say, waving the gun over at Dave and Isabella instead.

Ransom carefully takes the weapon from me and instructs both Dave and Isabella to put their hands in the air.

The door bursts open once again as Quinn Riddle and an entire slew of security officers pour out after her.

Ransom and Quinn quickly handcuff the dastardly duo and they're quickly led off by the swarm of officers.

Quinn steps my way as the alcove clears out. "You just couldn't stay out of his way, could you? You single-handedly endangered everyone on this ship. I am not amused, Mrs. Troublefield." She nods to Ransom. "I'll get them to the brig," she says as she takes off, and it's just Ransom and me, and, well, Malora.

A spray of miniature green stars ignites around the friendly ghost, as Malora quickly grows faint.

"How about that?" she muses as she begins to float toward the sky. "It looks as if I'll be back to paradise in time to enjoy a celestial buffet this evening. Good luck to you, Trixie Troublefield." She waves down at me. "Good work in bringing this case to a quick conclusion. I hope you nail your ex's cookies to the wall. And don't forget to make the best of what's left of your time on the ship. With two delicious men to choose from, you're bound to have the time of your life. You deserve it! Until we meet again!"

And just like that, Malora Radcliff is blipped right back to paradise in a wash of emerald stars.

"Goodbye," I whisper.

Ransom follows my gaze as he looks to the sky then back at me. "Trixie, are you hurt?"

"No, I'm more than okay." I shudder as I rub my arms. "I was just thanking my lucky stars."

That perennial frown returns to his face as he sears me with those blue eyes, and I can't help but note how unfairly handsome he is while doing so.

He takes off his jacket and wraps me in it before I can protest. Soon, I'm engulfed in his warmth and the spiced scent of his cologne. His body is less than five inches from mine, and there's something in me that demands to close the gap between us.

"I shouldn't be saying this, but you did good work, Trixie." His frown intensifies. "Don't make it a habit of tracking down killers."

"As long as dead bodies don't make it a habit of showing up in my luggage, you've got a deal."

His chest thumps with a dry laugh as he studies my features.

He leans my way a notch and I inch toward him just enough, my heart thumping wildly with expectation.

"There's something I think you should know." The words blurt from me before I can stop them.

"What's that?" he whispers with his lips dangerously close to mine.

"That day in the terminal when you caught me in your arms—I was wearing a butt pad."

Really? That's what my mind decided was so necessary to disclose? And at *this* junction in time?

Kill me now.

What the hell is wrong with my lips? Am I that afraid of kissing a handsome man that I'd rather suffer abject humiliation?

Although, in some weak way, I know for a fact I'm still trying to save face from that first humiliating episode the two of us had suffered through.

"A what?" His brows swoop low.

"You know, a *falsie*—to make my bottom a little shapelier. All the cool kids are doing it." And apparently, all the cool kids are lying, too.

I should throw myself overboard before I actually die of humiliation. I'd prefer a watery grave to a verbal horror of my own making.

He gives a brief nod. "Okay. For the record, you have a great shape with or without it."

My mouth opens with a laugh just as the door bursts open and Captain Crawford bolts in my direction.

"Trixie." He pulls me into his arms for a quick embrace. "Quinn just briefed me. You are far too brave for your britches, Trixie Troublefield."

A dull laugh thumps through me. "I'm not as brave as you might think."

"You're plenty brave," he says. "In fact, if you wouldn't mind,

I'd love it if you'd join me at my table in two days' time for the Captain's Ball."

I glance over at Ransom and catch him nodding to himself as if he were resigned to the fact.

"Of course," I tell Wes and his chest swells with pride. "Then it's a date." He pauses a moment to give Ransom a dark look. "Now, let's get you inside, Trixie. I'll do whatever it takes to get this night off of your mind."

Ransom's lips curve downward as he glares at Wes as if to say *I bet you will.*

And just like that, the moment is over.

I'm not kissing Ransom Baxter now or ever. I traded my magic moment to regale him with lies regarding my shapely bottom.

I blew it.

But not any more than Dave and Isabella blew it.

I might have to live with my humiliation, but they'll have to live with a couple of murder convictions.

Justice is on its way to being served for Olivia Montauk, and I played a tiny part in that—so did a ghost named Malora Radcliff.

Here's hoping there's not another disembodied spirit in my future.

But something deep inside of me knows I'm not that lucky.

If I were, I'd still be smooching with Handsome Ransom and not feeling the least bit guilty about it.

Now that would be lucky indeed.

CHAPTER 23

Suddenly Single—What a Trip!

As you've probably guessed, my cruising days were numbered and today was my final day at sea. I let Bess and Nettie talk me into the zip line. I screamed as if my hair was on fire as I crossed this behemoth ship. Okay, so I only crossed a portion of it. Nettie offered to give me a nip of her questionable vodka to calm my nerves beforehand, but I kindly declined her offer. Afterward, Elodie had some time off and we lounged on the promenade deck, and even though that warm Hawaiian trade wind hug is long gone, the weather is still miles nicer than it will be in Maine for months.

And that little kerfuffle about the art auction getting canceled that I mentioned the other night? Well, the cruise director allowed me to hold another painting class this morning. It was so popular I taught it back-to-back twice yesterday and this morning. It turns out, we've got more than one budding artist on board.

I'm going to miss this. I'm going to miss all of it. But there's still one more adventure to be had—I'm off to the Captain's Ball, as the captain's official date.

Wish me luck!
XO Trixie

I slip into the gold glittering gown that Elodie sent up this morning and inspect myself in the mirror. My face has a sun-kissed glow. I've finally harnessed my hair back from space once the humidity went down, and I look like a different woman.

I start to rub in the rouge on my cheek and my wedding ring winks back at me.

"My old friend," I say as I hold my hand out. "As much as I'm going to miss you—far more than the weasel who deposited you on my finger—I think perhaps this is where we part ways." I may have chickened out the other day, but this time I'm determined to do it. I run my thumb over the cool stone like I have a million times before. And then I do what would have been unimaginable just a month ago. I slip it off my finger once and for all.

It's as if the heft of the world has slid off with it.

And with that, I'm ready for whatever waits outside my cabin door—and back in Maine as well.

The entire ship has a frenetic energy about it this evening. Everywhere you look people are dressed to the nines, with women in formal gowns and men in suits and tuxedos alike. And even though we've already enjoyed two other formal nights, there is something special about this one. It's as if everyone has saved their very best for this evening, and they should, considering it's our final evening aboard the *Emerald Queen*.

A thick sadness grips me as I step into the main dining room for the very last time. Classical music plays overhead, and there's a clearing to the right where a few couples dance cheek to cheek. But my eyes snag on the ice sculpture sitting in the center of the room and I sigh at the sight of it. Two large glassy swans sit nose to nose, creating a giant heart with the shape of their elegant necks.

Love.

To think that's theoretically what brought me to this ship to begin with—that four-letter word, love. After twenty-five years with Stanton, all roads led to the *Emerald Queen of the Seas*. Ironically, in all those twenty-five years, I don't think I've ever felt so alive as I have these past eighteen days.

In an odd way, it took losing Stanton to find myself.

"Trixie." Weston heads my way in full captain regalia, a crisp white suit with enough stripes and gold stars to make any seafaring officer envious. His eyes expand as he takes me in from head to toe. "You are a vision." His soft brown eyes meet with mine. "You look beautiful tonight."

"Thank you," I say. "You look more than dapper yourself."

He holds out his arm. "Shall we?"

"We shall." I hook my arm to his as he leads the way to a large circular table behind the ice sculpture where a few familiar faces and a few unfamiliar faces greet us.

Tinsley is seated at the table looking at me with such disdain you'd think I stole her puppy. Bess and Nettie are here as well, and for that I'm relieved. But Bess had mentioned they would be, so I'm not surprised. What does surprise me is to see Ransom and Quinn Riddle seated at this table as well.

Ransom rises to his feet long before Wes and I get within a few feet of them. His eyes hook to mine and a spark goes off in my chest as sure as if he had touched me. I can't look away from him, not sure if I want to.

"You look stunning," he says it low as he gives a slight bow.

Wes and I take our seats, and it seems as if we're served every appetizer all at once.

"Hold onto your forks just a minute," Nettie says, picking up her wine glass and encouraging the rest of us to do just that until we all follow suit. "To Captain Crawford, well done on another successful voyage."

"Hear, hear," the table chimes at once.

"I'd like to make a toast as well," Ransom says with his eyes slit in my direction. "To Trixie Troublefield." A short-lived and rather pained smile crests his lips. "Your assistance in bringing down the criminals among us was invaluable. Thank you for that."

"You're welcome," I say as our eyes linger for a bit longer than necessary, and then just like that, everyone dives into the appetizers all at once.

Dinner comes and goes in a flurry, a surf and turf fest that I enjoy to the very last morsel. Being from Maine, I'm no stranger to a good lobster, and the filet mignon melted in my mouth like butter. For dessert, it seems the chocolate molten lava cake finally made its way onto the menu of the main dining room. And in celebration of that fact, I order two.

The music grows louder and moodier by the moment, and the lights from the chandeliers dim as the ball takes a turn for the romantic. Couples flood the dance floor, prompting Wes to hold his hand my way.

"How about it?" he asks.

I shrug up at him. "I thought you'd never ask."

He helps me to my feet and I spot Ransom cutting him a lethal look, or maybe it was me that look was meant for. I seem to incite the worst in him. Or at least the status quo.

Wes leads us to the dance floor, and soon he's holding me by the waist with one arm, his other hand in mine as we move to the melodic music.

"This is all so very grand," I tell him. "You're really living a dream life, you know."

He shakes his head, a hint of sorrow in his eyes. "The ship is great, but it's not everything."

"I get it." I bite down over my lip. "I hope you find someone very special, Wes. You deserve all the happiness in the world. And whoever she is, she's a darn lucky girl."

"I wish you just as much happiness, Trixie." He touches his forehead to mine. "And I hope you find it quickly. You deserve it."

I nod. "As do you."

A hand taps over his shoulder and he turns just enough for me to see Ransom standing there. My heart booms so hard I'm certain that Wes felt it, too.

The two of them exchange hardened stares for a moment before Wes reluctantly lets me go, and before I know it, I'm floating in Ransom Baxter's arms. And I won't lie—it feels like bliss.

"Mrs. Troublefield." Ransom nods my way.

A wry smile twists my lips. "You've caught me in more than one compromising position, I think we're on first-name basis by now."

His chest rumbles with a quiet laugh. "You're right. And no sooner do we get to know one another than it's time to say goodbye."

"Do we know one another?" I tease and he cocks his head as if to ask me to extrapolate. "Seeing that it's my last day, and it's doubtful that our paths will ever cross again, would you mind telling me why you and Captain Crawford seem to be archenemies?" I give his hand a squeeze as I say it.

Ransom tips his head back a notch, his chest expands wide as a wall, and I can feel every rock-hard inch of it against my own.

"He was my brother-in-law."

"He was your brother-in-law?" I blink as I try to wrap my head around it. "That's it?"

"That's it." His eyes flit in the direction where Wes is currently moving to the music with Tinsley and I'm pretty certain that's not it.

I bet it's not even the tip of the iceberg.

"So what happened?" I ask. "I mean, did something horrible happen to your sister?" I cringe at the thought of it.

"Nah," a female voice trills from our side, and we find Nettie in the arms of one of the headwaiters.

Bess comes up with a waiter of her own. "It's not your story to tell," she calls out to Nettie. "It's his." She shakes her head at Ransom. "Oh, what the heck."

Ransom goes rigid once again. "What the heck." His lips curve a notch as his eyes latch to mine.

A hand taps over his shoulder, and soon we've switched partners again. I'm dancing with Wes and Ransom has landed Tinsley in his arms and she doesn't look all that broken up about it either.

"Enjoying sparkling conversation?" Wes asks with a depleted smile.

"It *was* considering it was about you." I give an impish grin. "He let me know that you were once his brother-in-law. Small world," I say. "I guess after things went south with you and your wife, things went south for you and Ransom as well."

He nods. "It was a little more complicated than that. My ex and I didn't end so well. Let's just say Ransom blames me for that."

"I'm sorry." I take a breath. "I'm shocked he's on the same ship with you. In fact, why is he on the same ship with you?"

He cuts a dark glance to our left. "I've been asking the same thing for years."

"I was assigned this ship," Ransom says as he lands by our side while Tinsley floats in his arms. "And I don't back down from an obligation, unlike some people."

Wes drops his hands and takes a step back while glaring at Ransom. "I didn't drop any obligations. You know as well as I do that she left of her own volition."

"She left because you drove her away."

Wes raises a finger to Ransom. "I didn't drive anyone away." His voice hikes a notch. "I certainly didn't drive them to Central America into the hands of a drug lord where she could claim her throne by his side."

Bess and Nettie scuttle up by my sides like a couple of bookends.

"Did he say drug lord?" I whisper.

Bess nods. "And that's just the half of it."

Nettie nudges me. "It only goes down from there."

Ransom knocks Wes' finger out of his face, they exchange a few shoves, and before you know it, left hooks are being delivered. The room erupts in screams as Wes and Ransom continue to battle it out. Wes shoves Ransom into that elegant table with its sculptures of palm trees fashioned out of butter and that ice sculpture of swans with their elegant slender necks, and together they send the entire display crashing to the ground, save for one rogue swan neck flying like a Frisbee in this direction. Without thinking, I reach up and catch it like a football.

Bess and Nettie break out into applause.

Nettie leans in. "What do you get when you turn that swan's neck into a microphone and start singing?"

"I have no idea." I shake my head at her.

"A swan song," she says.

Bess, Nettie, and I have a good laugh over it.

I may not have gotten the man in the end, but I got to sing my proverbial swan song on this cruise and that has to count for something.

~

Suddenly Single—What a Trip!

Well, travelers, my time has come to say goodbye. Thank you for embarking on this adventure with me. This was a journey that was started alone but finished with a cast of thousands. Thank you to each and every one of you for coming along for the ride. Last night's Captain's Ball was a perfect way to end this luxury cruise, even if the night did have a few bumps and bruises.

Until we meet again.

Safe travels. And wherever you are, wherever you go, remember you are worthy of happiness.

Find it and share it with the world.

XO Trixie

Not one to miss out on the last breakfast, I went up to the Blue Water Café as soon as the buffet opened and indulged in French toast, pancakes, and an omelet made to order loaded with cheese, sausage, and bacon.

Of course, I couldn't say a proper goodbye to the café without a bagel loaded with as many lox as I could fit on it—the cream cheese is a given. And to round things out, I picked up a couple of crullers just to be safe.

Afterward, I waddle my way to deck eighteen, to the makeshift track and force myself to walk a lap. There is so much more that I didn't get to experience here. The wave pool, the mini golf, the ice skating, the movie theater, the comedy shows, the jazz club. I could have played tennis, or gone down one of those crazy slides, or even played bingo, and I missed out on all of it.

And what about that fifties-themed diner in the atrium? Minty's? I missed out on that, too. And now it's all too late. I give a wistful tick of the head as I look at the port of Los Angeles all around me. The open waters are already a distant dream. The cruise has come to an end, and now there's nothing left but to say goodbye.

Elodie managed to scrape up a suitcase for me from the lost and found in which I packed all of my new things.

I texted Abbey and Parker and let them know I'd be boarding a plane later this evening as I take a red-eye back to Maine. Brambleberry Bay seems like an entire planet away, and not one ounce of me is ready to go back.

And what exactly am I going back to? More misery from Stanton? Not to mention the public humiliation he's yet to put me through. A part of me is wanting to shove *myself* into a suitcase.

But all good things must come to an end, and my time on the *Emerald Queen of the Seas* has certainly done that.

I roll my suitcase with me to the lounge area, where I meet

with two of my new favorite people. I marvel at the luggage they're each holding onto.

"I can't believe they're making you disembark," I tell them.

"Each and every time," Bess says. "But we'll get our old rooms back once we hop back on board in a few hours. It's protocol, per the big wigs, that the ship is cleared and cleaned before it's repopulated.

"My flight isn't until tonight, so I'll gladly hang out with you in the terminal," I tell them.

Nettie squints my way. "I've got a deck of cards and a pocket full of funny money. Who's up for trying to steal it from me?"

Bess laughs. "Nobody is better at stealing your money than me. You're on."

Before I can throw my fiscally bound hat into the ring, Neville Wagner shows up on the scene waving an envelope my way.

"Oh, is this what I think it is?" I ask as I take it from him and rip it open, only to find a shiny new credit card issued with my name on the front.

"I'd be careful with that if I were you," he says. "You haven't had the best luck with those."

"I haven't had the best luck period," I tell him. "Oh, before I forget. Would you mind reversing all the charges made to my account that ended up on the captain's credit card and ringing them up on my own?"

He shakes his head slowly. "No can do. I was given strict orders, and those charges are sticking. Consider it a gift. Welcome home, Mrs. Troublefield." He tips his hat our way before taking off.

"How do you like that?" I mutter.

A gift I can never repay. That about sums this trip up nicely.

Our disembarkation number is called and the three of us head for the gangway. A pang of sadness hits me as I spot Wes up front waving to the guests as they thank him for a wonderful trip.

Of course, Tinsley, ever the cheerleader, is by his side. She glances at me and her eyes round out before she turns away as if she never saw me. And I'm betting she wishes she never saw me—but then in less than a few minutes, I'll be a distant memory to everyone here.

"Trixie," someone calls from behind and I turn to see Elodie making her way over. "Come here, you." She gives me a warm embrace. "You take care of yourself. And keep that blog going." She wrinkles her nose. "And find your way back here, would you?"

"I wish. Thank you for being a friend. You went above and beyond the call of duty. Thank you for making my trip memorable." I sniff back tears as I give her another warm embrace before we part ways.

Bess, Nettie, and I are herded toward the exit, along with the crowd, and I can't help but scan the vicinity.

I'm not sure why I thought I'd get a chance to say goodbye to Ransom. We didn't exactly say an official goodnight after that fiasco at the Captain's Ball. But my heart wrenches at the thought of not seeing him again.

My fingers twitch for my phone, but I resist the urge to text him. He would probably find it laughable, *desperate* even.

Soon, we're next up to say goodbye to the crew lined up at the mouth of the gangway and Wes opens his arms to me.

"Trixie."

"Captain Crawford," I say as he offers me a firm embrace. "Thank you for a memorable trip."

"A little too memorable." He winces. "My apologies for everything that ensued last night. You deserved better than that."

"It's clear you and Ransom still have a few issues to work out. And you should." I shrug. "I'm a firm believer in once family always family."

Tinsley clears her throat. "And I'm a firm believer in keeping this line moving. Safe travels back to your home, Mrs. Troublefield." Her lips expand in a fiendish smile.

"Thank you for letting me teach the classes," I tell her before reverting my attention back to the captain. "Goodbye, Wes. I wish you nothing but the best. You have no idea how much I'm going to miss the *Emerald Queen*—but I'm going to miss you more." I lean over and land a kiss to his cheek. "Until we meet again."

He offers a warm smile my way, but there's a pained look in his eyes, I can't deny.

"Until then," he says.

I'm about to step away when a thought hits me. "Oh, I almost forgot! Thank you so much for covering the cost of my trip." I wince when I say it. "You didn't have to do that."

"I'm sorry." A quizzical look crosses his face. "That wasn't me, Trixie."

A crowd moves in, and soon he's engulfed with a mob of passengers eager to have one last snapshot with the captain.

"He didn't do that?" I whisper as my mind reels with the possibilities. "Ransom?" I say as I look to Nettie and Bess.

Nettie shrugs. "Most people don't know this about him, but he's got more money than the Rothschilds combined."

Bess nods. "Consider it a gift. He would want you to."

My eyes are drawn back to the ship and I suddenly find myself fighting tears.

"Thank him for me," I say as I do my best to swallow down my emotions.

Bess, Nettie, and I roll our luggage through security and back into the dome-shaped terminal where this adventure began. Families reunite with loved ones as throngs of bodies bustle toward the exits.

Ready or not, reality waits on the other side of those doors.

We stop somewhere in the middle, and a laugh gets caught in my throat.

"You know what?" I say, glancing around. "I think this is the exact spot where we met."

"You mean where Nettie knocked you over the head with a bottle and cursed you with the gift of seeing the dead," Bess points out.

"You say curse, I say blessing," Nettie counters. "Speaking of that bottle, I've got a hot date with a longshoreman out back. Either of you hussies want to see what he's got in his trunk for me this time?"

Bess scoffs. "If you're not careful, you're going to find *yourself* in his trunk."

"I've been in less exciting places," Nettie says without missing a beat, and the three of us laugh at that one.

"What's so funny?" a deep voice strums from behind and I spin on my heels, only to see a tall, dark, handsome man with eyes that rival both the sky and the sea for the sacred hue they hold. He's wearing a dark inky suit with a navy tie, and that dark scruff on his cheeks makes my fingers twitch to run through it.

"Ransom," I pant without meaning to as my entire body becomes one giant heartbeat. "I didn't think I'd see you again."

Bess and Nettie start in on a scuffle before Bess waves at us.

"I think we'll go see what that longshoreman has in his trunk for Nettie," Bess calls out as she drags her counterpart toward the exit.

"I don't want to go see what that longshoreman has in his trunk," Nettie yelps. "They were just about to get to the good part!"

"Well, it's none of your good part business if they were," Bess shouts back as she continues to yank her to toward the door.

I turn back to Ransom and drink him in urgently as if he were about to leave for war—but in truth, I'm the one with a battle on my hands, a *legal* battle.

"Thank you," I say, wrapping my arms around him without hesitation. "It was you who paid for my expenses when my credit card was shut down." I pull back as he wraps his arms around me as if he wasn't about to let me escape. "You let me believe it was the captain."

"You seemed to want to believe it." He shrugs. "Who am I to stand in the way of your happiness?"

My lips invert a moment. "I guess this is goodbye."

"I guess it is." He gives a long blink. "Stay out of trouble, would you?"

"Trouble is in my name," I tell him. "That alone should have given me a clue about my ex when I met him."

We share a small laugh on Stanton's behalf before the moment grows all too serious. Our eyes latch onto one another, and I can feel his heart drumming against my body just as erratic as my own.

He leans in a notch. "Remember when you shared that accidental kiss with the captain?"

I bite down on a smile. "And you said that when you kissed a woman, it was always on purpose."

His eyes smolder into mine. "I'm about to show you how purposeful I can be." He leans in and his lips hardly touch over mine as someone shouts my name from behind.

"Trixie?" a man bellows once again before yanking Ransom off my body and I nearly fall backward when I see an all too familiar face staring back at me.

"Stanton?"

I stiffen as I look at my soon-to-be ex-husband in a rumpled dress shirt, that wreath of blond-gray stubble shorn close to his scalp.

"What the hell do you think you're doing with this man?" He charges at me and Ransom stops him cold by simply holding out his hand.

"Don't even think about taking a step closer to her," Ransom seethes.

Stanton looks at him with a newfound curiosity as his chest

expands.

"What are you going to do about it, buddy? Do you think you mean something to her? That's my wife you were about to plant one on."

"Ex-wife in the making," I correct him. "My new attorney Fiona Dagmeyer is already drawing up the papers. Expect to be served. Oh, and she got the banks to reverse the financial curse you tried to put on me." I don't bother telling him I have a shiny new credit card on me. "Any further communication will be through her. I'm not ready to speak to you."

Before he can offer up a rebuttal, someone calls my name from afar and I turn to see Wes heading this way with Tinsley and Elodie trailing after him.

"What's happening?" Nettie calls out. "I couldn't hear a thing from where I was standing." She looks my way. "You didn't think I was going to miss the good part, did you?"

"Wait for me," Bess calls out with her suitcase rolling and bouncing behind her.

"Captain Crawford?" I say as I step his way.

"I'm glad you're still here." He gently grabs ahold of my shoulders and pants through a smile.

"Hey, buddy." Stanton smacks Wes on the arm. "Hands off, she's mine."

"Don't you dare let go, Wes. I don't belong to anyone," I tell him. "Now what's going on? Did I leave something on the ship? You didn't find another body in my room, did you?"

"No." He winces with a laugh. "I've got news. The cruise line just contacted me and let me know that one of my passenger's blog single-handedly booked the *Emerald Queen* for a year out. They've never seen anything like it. They wanted to extend an invite to have you sail with us indefinitely so long as you keep your travel blog going. You can teach your art classes, and you'll have room and board covered."

My mouth falls open as a breath gets lodged in my throat.

"Indefinitely?" I blink up at him and he nods.

Tinsley clears her throat. "You won't like the room. It's at the bottom of the ship, and it's smaller than a thimble. Hardly any space to turn around, and you'll have three roommates."

Elodie gives a sickly nod and shrugs.

"I'll take it," I say without hesitation.

"You can't take it," Stanton huffs. "You're coming home with me."

I shake my head his way. "I'm not coming home with you, not now—not ever." I look back at Wes. "And if at all possible, I'd like to upgrade my room to one with a balcony. I'll gladly pay the difference."

Bess and Nettie break out into a cheer.

"We'll find a home for you on deck fourteen," Bess says.

"I know a guy." Nettie winks as she hitches her head toward the captain.

"I'm glad you're taking the position," Wes says as he pulls me in for another embrace. "I'll go let the cruise line know, and I'll be sure to secure a room with a balcony for you." He takes my hand and kisses the back of it. "Welcome to the *Emerald Queen of the Seas*, Trixie. It will be a pleasure having you with us." He glances to Ransom. "I'll see you on board for the security briefing." He nods to Stanton before taking off, and Tinsley trails off with him.

"I'll see you on the ship," Elodie says as she blows me a kiss. "We're going to have to celebrate. Shenanigans will ensue." She winks my way before giving Stanton a dirty look. "You can suck it."

"Do you mind?" Stanton growls at Ransom. "I'd like a minute alone with my *wife*."

"I'm not going anywhere." Ransom crosses his arms, and as he does, the butt of his gun is exposed.

"Fine." Stanton steps my way. "So this is it? This is how you want to end things? Twenty-five years and you're taking off on the high seas with Captain Horny and Mr. Moody?"

I frown over at him. "I didn't end things, Stanton. If you hadn't decided that the day we left for the cruise of a lifetime was the perfect time for an orgy, we would still be together. *You* ended things. *You* made bad choices, and now you have to live with them."

"So that's it?" He tosses his hands up in exasperation. "What happened to *for better or for worse*, or did our vows mean nothing to you?"

I scoff and both Nettie and Bess scoff along with me.

"You can't be serious," I shake my head at the man I thought I'd spend forever with. "You were unfaithful three or four times in a single afternoon. I don't know, I lost count."

Bess nods his way. "And for all she knows, it wasn't the first time."

I suck in a quick breath at the thought.

Nettie nods his way. "She doesn't suffer fools or cheats. And in your case, you're a double whammy—so go on and *scrammie*."

"Ooh, that was good," Bess hisses. "That really rhymed."

"I try." Nettie winks her way.

"Look, Stanton." I sigh as I look up at him. "We had a decent run. We have two incredible children. And we've even had a few good memories along the way. But it's over. You've got your practice to get back to. I don't have much left in Brambleberry Bay. And even if I did, I'm not ready to go back. The ship is my home now. And where she goes, I go. I have purpose here, and friends."

"You've got family," Nettie says as she pops between Bess and me and pulls us in close.

"I've got family," I say as I blink away tears, but none of them are for Stanton. "Go on back to Maine and live your life. I'm going to live mine."

You can practically see the steam coming from his ears. His face turns red then purple then some unholy hue they don't even have a name for.

"I can't go back without you," he rages. "What are people going to say?"

"Hopefully, they'll say the truth," I tell him. "That he cheated on his wife and she didn't stand around to take it."

He growls my way, "You're going to regret this, Trixie. I'll make sure of it." He stalks off into the crowd, and just like that, he's out of my hair—for now.

"Ladies." Ransom offers a bow our way. "How about I get you back on the lido deck while you wait for your rooms to get ready?"

"I thought you'd never ask," Bess says as she gives our luggage to the nearest porter. "I was starting to get hungry."

"I hope they've got lava cake," Nettie says, threading her arm through mine and Bess does the same on the other side.

Ransom nods my way. "I've got a security detail to run, but I'll catch up to you ladies at dinner."

"It's a date," I tell him.

His lips twitch just shy of a smile, his eyes never leaving mine. "It's a date, indeed."

We head onto the gangway and back onto the *Emerald Queen of the Seas*.

We're heading back to paradise, and yet for me, I've already arrived.

We hit the lido deck hard, and Nettie and I eat our weight in lava cake.

Our fellow passengers begin to populate the ship, and I rattle my empty glass.

"I'd better run up and refill my iced tea," I tell Bess and Nettie.

"We're heading down to our room," Bess tells me. "We'll catch up with you in a bit."

"Glad you're on board, kiddo," Nettie says. "Maybe you can help me teach this one to loosen up and have a good time."

Bess rolls her eyes as the two of them take off.

I head over to get my refill when a man walks right into me.

"I'm so sorry," I say as I take a step back and gasp at the all-too familiar face before me. "Stanton?"

"That's right, sweetie." My smarmy ex bears a greasy grin. "You're looking at your new shipmate. I just booked a ticket for an eighteen-night cruise to Hawaii. We're not done by a long shot. And when this cruise is over, you're coming home with me." He nods as he takes off and my stomach rolls at the thought.

So much for smooth sailing.

On second thought, I'm not going to let him get to me.

I'm living my life the way I want, right in the open for all to see—and that includes my ex.

Stanton may have laid claim to my past, but he can't have my future.

If he wants to witness my fresh start up close and personal, it's at his own peril.

I'm living my best life, and I'm not letting anyone stop me.

Not Stanton.

Not a ghost.

Not a killer.

I'm determined to make the next half of my life a grand adventure filled with new experiences, maybe a ghost or two, and more than a little romance.

This is the new me.

Everything is new.

And everything is possible.

*THANK YOU FOR READING! **I hope you enjoyed CRUISING THROUGH MIDLIFE!**

Up next: Trixie's ex is on board the Emerald Queen of the Seas and so is a killer!

Be sure to grab —> Mai Tai Murder Cruise (Cruising Through Midlife 2) today!

My name is Trixie Troublefield, **and I see ghosts. It's sort of a new thing, and it's more than a problem.**

I've got good news and bad news. The good news is my travel blog *Suddenly Single! What a trip.* Has taken off like gangbusters and I've inadvertently become the queen for an entire tribe of newly divorced women.

And even better than that? Handsome Ransom Baxter, the head of vessel security, is throwing out more than a few signs that he's interested in me.

The bad news? My ex has booked a cabin on the very same ship and not only is he determined to win me back—he's determined to make me jealous with some leggy blonde.

It's going to be eighteen long nights to paradise and back before I can evict my ex out of my life once again—but a killer has different plans.

Is it bad that I'm rooting for the killer?

Midlife on the high seas is proving to be murder.

See **you on the high seas!**

BOOKS BY ADDISON MOORE

For up to the minute pre-order and new release alerts

Paranormal Women's Fiction
Hot Flash Homicides
Midlife in Glimmerspell
Wicked in Glimmerspell
Mistletoe in Glimmerspell

Cruising Through Midlife
Cruising Through Midlife
Mai Tai Murder Cruise

Cozy Mysteries

Meow for Murder
An Awful Cat-titude
A Dreadful Meow-ment
A Claw-some Affair
A Haunted Hallow-whiskers
A Candy Cane Cat-astrophe
A Purr-fect Storm
A Fur-miliar Fatality

Country Cottage Mysteries
Kittyzen's Arrest
Dog Days of Murder

Santa Claws Calamity
Bow Wow Big House
Murder Bites
Felines and Fatalities
A Killer Tail
Cat Scratch Cleaver
Just Buried
Butchered After Bark
A Frightening Fangs-giving
A Christmas to Dismember
Sealed with a Hiss
A Winter Tail of Woe
Lock, Stock, and Feral
Itching for Justice
Raining Cats and Killers
Death Takes a Holiday
Copycat Killer Thriller
Happy Howl-o-ween Horror
Twas the Night Before Murder
Smitten Kitten Corruption
Cruising for Trouble

Country Cottage Boxed Set 1

Brambleberry Bay Murder Club
Brambleberry Bay Murder Club

Murder in the Mix Mysteries

Cutie Pies and Deadly Lies

Bobbing for Bodies
Pumpkin Spice Sacrifice
Gingerbread & Deadly Dread
Seven-Layer Slayer
Red Velvet Vengeance
Bloodbaths and Banana Cake
New York Cheesecake Chaos
Lethal Lemon Bars
Macaron Massacre
Wedding Cake Carnage
Donut Disaster
Toxic Apple Turnovers
Killer Cupcakes
Pumpkin Pie Parting
Yule Log Eulogy
Pancake Panic
Sugar Cookie Slaughter
Devil's Food Cake Doom
Snickerdoodle Secrets
Strawberry Shortcake Sins
Cake Pop Casualties
Flag Cake Felonies
Peach Cobbler Confessions
Poison Apple Crisp
Spooky Spice Cake Curse
Pecan Pie Predicament
Eggnog Trifle Trouble
Waffles at the Wake

Raspberry Tart Terror
Baby Bundt Cake Confusion
Chocolate Chip Cookie Conundrum
Wicked Whoopie Pies
Key Lime Pie Perjury
Red, White, and Blueberry Muffin Murder
Honey Buns Homicide
Apple Fritter Fright
Vampire Brownie Bite Bereavement
Pumpkin Roll Reckoning
Cookie Exchange Execution
Heart-Shaped Confection Deception
Birthday Cake Bloodshed

Christmas Fudge Fatality

Murder in the Mix Boxed Sets
Murder in the Mix (Books 1-3)

Mystery
Little Girl Lost
Never Say Sorry
The First Wife's Secret

Romance
Just Add Mistletoe

3:AM Kisses
3:AM Kisses
Winter Kisses
Sugar Kisses

Whiskey Kisses
Rock Candy Kisses
Velvet Kisses
Wild Kisses
Country Kisses
Forbidden Kisses
Dirty Kisses
Stolen Kisses
Lucky Kisses
Tender Kisses
Revenge Kisses
Red Hot Kisses
Reckless Kisses
Hot Honey Kisses
Shameless Kisses

The Social Experiment
The Social Experiment
Bitter Exes
Chemical Attraction

3:AM Kisses, Hollow Brook
Feisty Kisses
Ex-Boyfriend Kisses
Secret Kisses

Naughty By Nature

Escape to Breakers Beach
Breakers Beach

Breakers Cove

Breakers Beach Nights

Escape to Lake Loveless

Beautiful Oblivion

Beautiful Illusions

Beautiful Elixir

Beautiful Deception

A Good Year for Heartbreak

Someone to Love

Someone to Love

Someone Like You

Someone For Me

A Totally '80s Romance Series

Melt With You (A Totally '80s Romance 1)

Tainted Love (A Totally '80s Romance 2)

Hold Me Now (A Totally '80s Romance 3)

Paranormal Romance

(Celestra Book World in Order)

Ethereal

Tremble

Burn

Wicked

Vex

Expel

Toxic Part One

Toxic Part Two

Elysian

Ephemeral Academy
Ephemeral
Evanescent
Entropy

Ethereal Knights (Celestra Knights)
Season of the Witch (A Celestra Companion)

Celestra Forever After
Celestra Forever After
The Dragon and the Rose
The Serpentine Butterfly
Crown of Ashes
Throne of Fire
All Hail the King
Roar of the Lion

ACKNOWLEDGMENTS

Big thanks to YOU the reader! I hope you had a wonderful time. I can't thank you enough for spending time on the high seas with Trixie and me. If you'd like to be in the know on upcoming releases, please be sure to follow me at **Bookbub** and **Amazon,** and sign up for my **newsletter.**

I am SUPER excited to share the next book **Mai Tai Murder Cruise** with you! Trixie's ex joins the fun, and a murderously good time is had by all—except the victim of course.

Thank you from the bottom of my heart for taking this wild roller coaster ride with me. I really do love you!

A very big thank you to Kaila Eileen Turingan-Ramos, and Jodie Tarleton for being awesome.

A special thank you to my sweet betas Amy Barber and Margaret Lapointe for looking after the book with their amazing beautiful eyes.

A mighty BIG thank you to Paige Maroney Smith for being so amazing.

And last, but never least, thank you to Him who sits on the throne. Worthy is the Lamb! Glory and honor and power are yours. I owe you everything, Jesus.

ABOUT THE AUTHOR

Addison Moore is a *New York Times, USA Today,* and *Wall Street Journal* bestselling author who writes contemporary and paranormal romance. Her work has been featured in *Cosmopolitan* Magazine. Previously she worked as a therapist on a locked psychiatric unit for nearly a decade. She resides on the West Coast with her husband, four wonderful children, and two dogs where she eats too much chocolate and stays up way too late. When she's not writing, she's reading. Addison's Celestra Series has been optioned for film by **20th Century Fox.**

Made in the USA
Columbia, SC
24 November 2023